MW01644792

Piercing the FOG

Cheryl Shivery Nickle

Manufactured in the United States of America

Published by Amazon KDP

Cover Design: Doris Anderson
Editing/Interior Design: Michele Chynoweth

ISBN: 9798992153606

DEDICATION

To my mother, Kathryn Shivery, for ordering me monthly *Best in Children's Books,* for my dad, Charles Shivery, for introducing me to Agatha Christie, James Clavell, David Baldacci, and Mitch Album, and my husband, John, who continues to invite me into the fantasy fiction world.

CONTENTS

ACKNOWLEDGEMENTS

I greatly appreciate the long-suffering support of my husband John throughout this years-long process. I express my gratitude to Michele Chynoweth, my friend, fellow parishioner, and editor, for guiding and leading me through the labyrinth of novel preparation. I thank Jo Savoy, my long-time friend and former colleague at North East High, for her early proofreading, editing, and cheerleading. I thank my father, Bud Shivery, for reading the first edition while the Caribbean trade winds on St. Croix enveloped us and for telling me honestly that my novel ended too quickly. I have amended that, Dad. I wholeheartedly thank my long-time friend and artist, Doris Anderson, for capturing the essence of this story with her cover design. I also recognize her husband, Ellis Anderson who, like Donkey on Shrek, called out, "Pick me! Pick me!" and designed the lettering on the front cover just as I had envisioned it. I also thank my circle of family members, friends, Cecil County residents, and fellow parishioners, whose stories embellish my written work. I am also indebted to my deceased Mount Aviat Academy English teacher, Sister Mary Paul, OSFS, for her inspiration and guidance and for telling me years later that I was one of her success stories. And thanks to my dear friend, former pastor, and spiritual director, Rev. Dan McGlynn, who went to heaven on the first day of 2024, for his constant reminder that I have a God-given talent for creativity, and I need to be open to new channels revealed to me.

PROLOGUE

WEDNESDAY: Home. Patrick and I are decompressing. Peace and quiet. It seems unnatural not to be looking out for someone following or observing us.

THURSDAY: We tune in to Baltimore news channels reporting live from Annapolis, our own Cecil County, and other counties all over Maryland. The TV stations lack enough reporters to provide adequate coverage for all areas involved. Their choppers dart from location to location. News anchors are out of their studios and broadcasting on the streets. Even unseasoned news staff are reporting live.

National networks fill the evening news with

clips of multiple press conferences, including one with Governor O'Malley. Information including mug shots and arrest footage flash across TV screens. Theodor Carlson, the hate crimes ringleader, is among those photographed, but he's not defiant or loudly proclaiming his innocence. He appears disillusioned. Did his brief Brisson Shelter experience open his eyes? Or is he unchanged?

UMCO has contacted us to offer us the three canines. We expect them to arrive on Saturday. Our dog Maggie will have three new friends.

FRIDAY. Our state's events made national news. So far, most reactions are favorable for Maryland's handling of this underground network bent on illegally and unethically ridding our communities of what they call 'undesirables.' The words FORN and UMCO have not surfaced in spoken words nor appeared in print yet. But probing questions are being asked.

A frizzy, rusty-haired on-air reporter wraps up her intriguing segment speaking breathlessly in her microphone from the steps of the state capitol in Annapolis. "How did the state accomplish this sting operation and the arrests that followed? What resources were utilized to deal with it? Were the people involved part of a well-organized entity? We wait, holding our breath, to find out which investigation details will be revealed…"

CHAPTER 1: ENROUTE

Patrick and I drove cautiously through the murky, frosty night. An aura of being in a strange place enveloped us. Not knowing where we were, we guessed we might be within the city limits of Annapolis. My lousy navigation skills had revealed themselves again. No surprise. In Ireland, many years ago during our honeymoon, I guided us down roads that became increasingly narrow till finally one reverted literally to a cow path. That had been in gray Irish daylight. This was a dark January night in Maryland. Back in Ireland we could see the folly of my directions. Now, darkness smothered all but our headlights' feeble path.

Instead of arriving on time for the annual meeting with state legislators, we would surely be late. Later than usual. The last time we attended this annual rally at the Maryland State Capitol in January, a friend was at the wheel. We, in no way, wanted to relive that experience. He had driven down a one-way street going the wrong way and had nearly caused a head-on collision. He had then turned onto a dead-end street and had to back out the length of it to get turned around. It was a miserable night with heavy rain. At least tonight there was only a chilly foggy mist.

We had gotten a late start, tending to other obligations before heading to the Maryland General Assembly. We would miss our rally group's brown bag dinner at St. Mary's High School. By now, everyone else would be arriving at the state capital building to meet with the senators and delegates for each district.

The yearly event to present Catholic issues before the state legislature was a two-diocese affair. Some people lived in the Archdiocese of Baltimore, Maryland. We residents of Cecil County and those living in other counties of the Eastern Shore of the Chesapeake Bay, were in the Diocese of Wilmington, Delaware. This was an opportunity to meet or re-connect with like-minded people to discuss issues, present viewpoints, and encourage our elected officials to agree with where we stood.

Yes, tonight, my husband Patrick and I were going to be late.

"Norah, where have you taken us?" Patrick asked a bit testily from behind the wheel. Without looking I knew graying eyebrows were arched above his glasses.

We had turned right and followed a dark street (making obvious mistakes, in hindsight) which quickly narrowed to an alley. That became the entrance to an unnamed complex with a direct route into an open factory building. We pushed slowly forward since we had no turn-around area. Our only choice was to drive into the garage-like building which hopefully afforded turn- maneuvering space.

I feared this would be like the Baltimore medical examiner's headquarters where my husband occasionally traveled for Gee Funeral Home in Elkton where he was employed. There in downtown Baltimore, you turn off Pratt Street, head down a ramp shouldered by concrete walls, and drive into a basement room which widens into a space that accommodates a couple of hearses parked side by side. But to exit, you must back up the ramp and out onto Pratt Street traffic. Fortunately, deceased passengers in the back of the hearse are beyond nervous reactions to the perils of Charm City driving conditions.

This factory entry was slightly obstructed by flimsy strips forming a glazed heavy plastic floating curtain, the kind you see at a car wash. I got out of the car and parted the strips to look beyond them. What a relief! The cave-like room was vacant and large enough to turn around. Patrick cleared the area easily. Parking the funeral coach in the funeral home's vintage garage had made him an expert at maneuvering vehicles. He turned around and headed toward the alley. Meanwhile, I paused to peek at the cavern of sagging, empty shelves, rusty bins, and ceiling hooks lit by the red glow of our taillights. Involuntarily I shuddered as it grew darker amid the decayed remains of some industry. I slid the flappy curtains back into place and turned to walk toward our car.

Immediately, I was confronted by a group of four men dressed heavily against the January chill. They blocked my exit. Their features weren't clear in the darkness. Their clothing was dark and concealing with hoods covering their heads and gloves covering their hands. They were each at least five-foot-ten (Patrick's height was my measuring stick) and though they towered over my five-foot-two height, oddly they didn't seem menacing. *Maybe that's just a description relating to wild beasts, not humans.* They crowded around me, seeming determined to keep me rooted in the same spot. Flashing a cell phone in my face, one of them announced they'd already called the cops. *Cops?!* Frantically I peered ahead into the blackness of the alley, but Patrick and our car were out of sight. There was not even a hint of red taillights emerging from the gloom.

Why was I being cornered like this?

CHAPTER 2: RESCUE?

I stared into the dark, but instead of taillights, I saw an approaching male, not Patrick. My detainers backed off, parting to make way for this new stranger, clearing a path for him to reach me. They addressed him as "Officer, Sir."

Where had he come from? Where was his vehicle? He sauntered over to me, or maybe he swaggered. This guy did seem "menacing" compared to the others. Nodding curtly to the men he grabbed me by the arm and whisked me away from them and their ongoing comments about my invading and destroying private property. Were they vagrants? How had I invaded their privacy? Their home? I guessed I should feel grateful since Officer Sir appeared to be rescuing me.

Officer Sir steered me past the alley to the street (still no sign of Patrick or our car) and into the back seat of an unremarkable, unmarked car. All of this happened without any conversation. I was beginning to feel like I had stumbled onto a silent movie set. It was surreal. I wanted to talk, to have a conversation, just to reassure myself I was safe. Why wouldn't he even glance my way, or make eye contact through the rear-view mirror? Why wouldn't he speak to me? I found my voice. I tried to find out something, anything, but he merely gestured for me to remain silent and buckle my seat belt. Resigned, I followed his instruction.

Mutely, we traveled several blocks, making numerous turns, left and right, all down poorly lit streets. In the dimness and fog, I deciphered no street signs. When we stopped, we could have been within a block or a mile of my original location and I wouldn't have been able to tell. About mid-block on a one-way street, we pulled up in front of a narrow brick three story building. It was sandwiched between other similar brick structures, townhouses fondly called "rowhouses" in Baltimore, that might have once been residences, businesses, or a combination of both. There were only the narrowest of alleyways between the structures where no car could park.

Officer Sir opened my door and gestured for me to get out of the car. He ushered me forward. We climbed steep cement steps and entered the anonymous building.

Abruptly my escort abandoned me. I had barely gotten inside the building before he brushed past me and walked down the dim hallway, his footfalls clacking on the grimy gray and green linoleum floor and disappeared through a doorway maybe ten feet ahead on the left.

Just as Officer Sir disappeared from my sight, as if synchronized, "Officer Ma'am" approached through another doorway to my immediate left. Was I the baton in their relay? Officer Ma'am, also a nonuniformed officer, announced there were serious charges being filed against me. Finally, someone spoke to me. This no longer felt like a rescue. Had there been a split-second opportunity when I might have bolted back out the door and made a run for it? But I hadn't known I was anything but a victim being rescued. Certainly, I wasn't a criminal, although I was beginning to feel like one. Stunned, I waited, holding my breath, to hear about the crime I had supposedly committed.

Officer Ma'am informed me I was accused of malicious destruction of private property. *Really? How can you damage a plastic curtain? Besides I had not damaged it.* How was merely touching something a malicious act? It wasn't an artifact in a museum or a holy relic of some saint on display in a cathedral. It was a grimy plastic curtain.

Oh, no… the complaint was about a broken window. *What window?* I couldn't recall seeing any windows let alone any glass. There was just a gaping façade where garage doors had once been installed. There were no windows.

I owed seventy-five dollars? Now that seemed odd even to me in my present situation. Nothing is that cheap anymore. Even if there had been glass in some window, it would have cost more than seventy-five dollars for replacement and installation. And who had had the time to assess any alleged damage? Where was the paperwork? Where was the window?

I had destroyed nothing, broken nothing. The building didn't even have a door. How ludicrous to propose repairing a broken window! The charges were not true. I hadn't seen or touched any glass. This officer, however, seemed unconcerned about anything I claimed. Beyond that she didn't even ask if I had the means to pay for the assessed damage. If there was an amount, shouldn't I be allowed to pay the damage, sign some receipt, and then just leave? What was going on? I needed answers!

CHAPTER 3: HOLDING CELL

Disinterestedly, Officer Sir reappeared from the area where he had exited. He directed me down the tacky linoleum floored hall to a door on the right, nearly opposite to where he had gone before.

"Where are we going now?" I inquired, nervously attempting to tuck my short dark brown wavy hair behind my ears.

He didn't reply but took me by the arm, so I had no choice but to follow.

Through the pebbly glass window set into the door, I could see there were lights on and silhouettes indicated the area was occupied. He produced a card and opened the door as one would a hotel room. From the doorway I could see it was furnished like some really cheap motel. The chairs along the perimeter were hard, molded and made of several faded shades of orange vinyl. They were placed close together, but not precisely arranged. The faux wood end tables bowed, though not from any present abundance of weight piled on them. They just looked tired. The stained carpet was made of many shades of gray. Attached to the opposite wall, near the left corner, hung a varnished wooden board. A long row of tarnished brass hooks covered its surface. Numerous outer garments of various thicknesses and conditions hung limply from some of the hooks.

The room reeked of what could only be politely identified as not-recently-washed bodies too long in the same place. It also smelled of poor ventilation and accumulated stale fast food. Several people occupied the rectangular room.

My eyes landed on one woman who especially looked like she had been there for a very long time, so long she apparently no longer cared about leaving. She sat slumped forward on her chair, holding court in the corner farthest from me, closest to the front of the building, and incidentally, farthest from the door. Her attitude distressed me. She expressed no emotion or interest at my grand entrance. A slight movement of one hand was her only acknowledgement of the door opening. Her beige sweater looked hand knit from the Aran Islands, but her jeans looked like they were from a Good Will special sale. Her brown leather walking shoes were scuffed and really worn. Her straight black hair hung well past her shoulders and curtained her facial features rendering her age a mystery.

The others just sat around or shifted in their seats, not conversing or paying attention to anyone but the person immediately beside them. They were not particularly nosy about my arrival either. I peeked and saw a balding middle-aged man in a burgundy "Fear the Turtle" sweatshirt and matching Terrapin sweatpants sitting alone along the wall to the left of the doorway where I stood. He seemed resigned to be where he was.

Two younger men, maybe Hispanic, in grease-imprinted dark jeans and holey black hoodies, were seated along the same wall but to the right of the door. Their hands appeared permanently stained with grease. Mechanics? Motorcycles? Cars?

Directly ahead, opposite my doorway location, two teen-aged girls wearing baby doll tops lounged listlessly or perhaps in boredom. One was taller than the other, and appeared somewhat anorexic, with long light brown hair pulled back in a ponytail. She wore a royal blue, black and white geometric design top with baggy jeans. I'd recently noticed a similar top on display in Wal-Mart.

The shorter, slightly heavier blonde wore a solid daffodil yellow baby doll top layered over two longer-sleeved black and white striped tops. The sleeves of the one top, with narrow stripes, went to her elbows, while the one beneath it, with wide stripes, went past her wrists. With her black spandex pants, she resembled a hibernating bumble bee.

There was an older looking male… or maybe female, slouched in the other front corner bookending the wall with the disinterested Irish sweater female. This person, who was turned away from everyone else, was dressed in mostly drab colors. The washed-out olive shirt and khaki pants looked wrinkled and stained from long, continuous wear. The once black- now gray boots seemed molded to the body. But the bright knitted wool cap in swirls of aqua and rose stood out, especially against matted chunks of gray hair. A coarse, wrinkled, chapped right hand was the only thing that moved.

Apparently, I made inmate, or guest, number eight. This left two chairs and a rickety table between me and the back of the room. The Terps fan was almost across from me. I did not remove my coat and put it on a hook. I reasoned this would acknowledge an extended visit. I did not intend to remain that long.

Their collective lack of curiosity didn't diminish mine but made me feel conspicuous if I glanced for more than a few seconds. So here I was with seven of my "peers." This gave me no comfort. From their closer seating arrangement, I surmised the guys in jeans knew one another as did the teenaged girls. The other three appeared to be loners like me. There was neither a

TV nor any canned sound system broadcasting elevator music. There wasn't even the hum emanating from some heat source. Every deep breath or shift of position was noticeable.

I knew I was out of my element, but I felt something "official" should have already occurred. Where was the desk person behind the sliding glass windows? The one you saw before you were allowed to venture farther into the police station? Where was the official sign-in place? Didn't someone want to ask my name? Inform me I was allowed one phone call? Let me call my attorney? My attorney Jay Garver's first question to his clients had always been, "Have you been arrested?" I had always responded "no," but now I couldn't be sure. Had I?

When I volunteered as an intake person for our county rotating homeless shelter, there was a strict protocol for admissions. I'd had to rummage through personal belongings to ensure no improper items were brought in. The guests signed in and their names were matched to the roster of expected guests. There was a procedure to follow, and everyone concerned knew what that was.

When I had been fingerprinted for my Alcohol Tobacco and Firearms license our local police chief, Darrell Hamilton, had escorted me to an interior room of the North East Police Station. It was organized and official. And this was in the little town of North East. Wasn't I in the Maryland state capital? Even our small Cecil County police stations were computerized and had noisy communication operations with patrol vehicles. This was so quiet. It wasn't right.

CHAPTER 4: THE DOG SITTERS

How do you judge the passing of time when nothing is happening? Officer Sir had simply left me with no explanation. Officer Ma'am arrived after maybe ten or fifteen minutes. She showed up with dogs. I felt tingly fingers of fear crawling along my spine and up the back of my neck, my personal migraine approaching signals, which got worse when she told me the dogs were there just for me. They were policing me. That is quite different from guarding someone. I didn't sense their presence was protective of me. Most of my peers took notice and exchanged looks I couldn't decipher, but they weren't reassuring. Had they too had this dog reception?

My attention became fixed on the dogs. One was a white Jack Russell terrier and, true to its nature, it energetically bounced around while managing to fix its eyes on me. The second was a nondescript shaggy gray mutt. It was neither friendly nor frightening, but completely zeroed in on me. I swear the third *(why are there always three?)* was out of a sci-fi story. With mottled darker gray fur and coal black eyes and the narrowest snout imaginable, it appeared eerily fascinated with me. I felt I was in the presence of some robotic creation. It was like facing the dreaded hound in the novel *Fahrenheit 451*.

So, was I the prey? The quarry? I wasn't on the run. Were these creatures trained or programmed to anticipate an escape attempt? Nervously, I realized that I needed to either pretend they weren't there or face them. Somewhere I'd learned that dogs can smell or sense fear. When there are three dogs threatening you, there ought to be three options for dealing with them. But I could only think of the two. Running or escaping the room would have been my first choice. But I knew that was taking a big risk, so I chose option number two. With obvious effort I tried to acknowledge the dogs. I hadn't spoken to the people, but here I was trying to communicate with dogs. *You are a dog person*, I reminded myself. My desire to win them over, or at least reassure myself they weren't as menacing as my nerves indicated, became obsessive.

To reassure myself I tried to visualize our Maggie, our hyper Golden Labradoodle/retriever named after our granddaughter Maglie. I thought back to how it had been when I first met the fluffy white runt of the litter. I tried to project the same feeling now, a welcoming I didn't feel. I stared at them. I shifted in my plastic seat while not removing my eyes from them. They all observed, but two of them did not move a muscle.

Officer Ma'am, who displayed no sign of a badge or a name tag, and made no effort to identify herself, tersely explained the dogs would remain with me. They would keep order. *Order? Suddenly, I wondered if they were there to protect me from the other humans, those I had thought of as my peers.* When had I entered a parallel universe? Where was Patrick? How had we become separated? How long had it been since we had entered that abandoned factory?

Hopefully, he was searching for me, but it was hard to envision how he would locate me. I wanted to believe he was resourceful enough to call 911 and somehow track me. But "they" hadn't even requested my name. Did he have seventy-five dollars in cash? Would they accept debit or credit cards? Hopefully, he would think to stop at an ATM to secure cash for my release. Or was it to pay for my ransom? But then he didn't know if I needed money or where I was. I didn't know where I was. And I should not have to pay anything! These and other random conflicting thoughts crisscrossed my mind.

Time crawled. There were other "police" who entered and exited, always in pairs. The dogs ignored them, keeping their stony glares on me. The two officers strictly adhered to the buddy system, like I associated with snorkeling or diving. None, besides Officer Ma'am were women. None wore uniforms. The only indication they were not one of us was their freedom to enter and exit with their annoying air of importance. That, and they all possessed plastic cards which were used for both entry and exit. I concluded there was no point in trying the handle to see if the door would open the old-fashioned way.

To escape the uncomfortable atmosphere of the room and block out the dogs, I turned my head slightly to the right and created a game of trying to match the outer garments hanging on the hooks to their owners. The University of Maryland starter jacket almost certainly belonged to the Terrapin sweatshirt guy. The waterproof yellow and black jacket seemed to coordinate with Bumble Bee girl's outfit. Those were the only easy ones. There were no denim jackets to match the guys in jeans. The hooded black ski jacket seemed not to be either of theirs since they both wore hoodies. Perhaps that belonged to the ponytail girl. The camouflage hunting jacket might belong to one of the denim guys, or to the mysterious person in olive drab and khaki. There was also a tan jacket with many pockets, like a fisherman might wear. Maybe that went to one of the hoodies guys. There was a faded, worn navy pea coat that might belong to Khaki

Person. Then again, it looked big enough to fit over Sweater Woman's bulky sweater. But her sweater would hang down way below the jacket. Would that matter to her? Maybe it was a hoodies guy jacket. The brown suede jacket with leather trim possibly matched a hoodies guy. The black wool overcoat didn't seem to match any person in the room, no matter how I designated the coats and jackets. I realized at last that there was one more outer garment than there were people present. Idly, I wondered if that meant anything.

The various pairs of officers began delivering food. I couldn't call them meals, because they seemed just a pathetic smorgasbord of leftovers from several meals. The mystery chicken or fish nuggets or the other breaded items appeared neither hot nor warm, but apparently edible as my cell mates wolfed them down. Along with slices of congealed cheese pizza, they were nevertheless consumed, as were the dry crumbly muffins and biscuits. Apparently, everything liquid was neither hot nor cold. Everything was at room temperature. How old was this food? Who had eaten the fresh portions and how long ago? Was there no refrigeration in the building? Was there no microwave? Was the food considered breakfast, lunch, or dinner? It seemed the goal was to keep us confused, guessing about the passing of the hours.

After I "boycotted" the first meal, I realized not eating was a mistake. Within minutes of each food delivery there were no crumbs left behind. Five of the listless seven became animated and devoured the food. In a way I was grateful because the thought of seeing the same stale room-temperature food age before my eyes was even worse than the idea of consuming it. The food arrived at random intervals. The second time I forced myself to join in. The dogs watched me, but did not react to my getting up, as I eased slowly off the chair. I managed to eat two donuts which, a few days before, might have been fresh. I trusted only a bottle of tepid water.

The officers seemed to randomly assess the room and depart. I didn't get the impression they were checking to figure out if we were hungry or comfortable enough. Did that mean they were watching us from some hidden camera system? They made no attempt to communicate with any of us. And no residents of the room sought to speak to them. Our only warnings they were approaching were the dogs' collective "at attention" stance, followed by the click of the card in the door slot a split second before the door swung inward.

They had an uncanny ability to silently approach and created no shadow through the pebbly window before they used their card. The heavy door masked the clacking footsteps I had heard when I first arrived. Why the stealth? Just because they could get away with it? My peers acted as if no one had intruded on our silent waiting. Had they just given up? Had they even tried talking to these alleged officers when they first arrived? Or during the first intrusion?

CHAPTER 5: THE MERWOMEN

What seemed like hours after my arrival, but may have been a much shorter interval, there arrived the two strangest women I have ever encountered. I saw kaleidoscopic images of them through the bubbly glass-paned door as they fumbled with their entry card and suddenly, I had a flashback.

I was standing in the corridor outside the principal's office at Immaculate Conception School, my elementary school. I was wide-eyed watching the latest miscreants, heads hanging low, being escorted out of the principal's office. Even being an innocent bystander had not assuaged the swelling of Catholic guilt in me.

The pebbly Flintstone window afforded a distorted view of the newcomers. They were even weirder looking when they stood inside the room just a few feet away. Their ages could have been anywhere from the early twenties to mid-forties. There was no way I could tell.

Okay. Their hair was colored in a tie-dyed pattern of blonde, brown, and purple and arranged in waves and swirls around their heads. They were in a grotesque way reminiscent of the beehive "Hons" of Baltimore fame. They were not twins but had gone to a lot of trouble to achieve that effect. They were literally 'painted' ladies- not hookers necessarily (but who knew?). The thick layer of redder-than-any-skin tone, make-up on each was just the beginning. High school girls attempting to cover up massive acne breakouts would never apply so much make-up.

Their lips were painted, but not just the lips, and not with one or two shades of color. There were actual fish designs painted on their lips and faces. On one, a painted fish tail stretched from her mouth outward and flipped upward past her cheek nearly to her ear lobe. On the other a turned down fish tail swam down the left side of her face reaching past her chin ending at the top of her neck. Their upper chests and necks were done in intricate vines, or maybe they were supposed to be seaweed or sea grasses? Their upper backs displayed the sea bottom with shells, sand, foamy green water, and a rusty anchor. They seemed peacock proud of their appearances.

Their clothing was beyond description. They probably were going for a more sexy than romantic mermaid or sea goddess look shimmering in their skin-tight outfits. Apparently, no expense had been spared when applying sequins and glitter.

No one else gasped at their arrival. From that I surmised they had previously made appearances. So, were they here now just for my benefit? That seemed to be the case.

Needing to do something, I turned from dog communication to people communication. Why not? I started by asking them about their body painting. Had they painted each other?

Of course not! I felt their disdain. They each had their own personal artist who produced new themes every few days. How could I not know this? How?

In my rural world this version of display artistry was nonexistent. My face itched at the thought of that paint staying on for days. I had once used white face paint for a geisha girl look for a Halloween party and could not wait to scratch and scrub it off.

I tried for a discreet comment on their costumes, er, outfits.

Tactful expressions failed me. I did learn a considerable amount about online shopping for handmade and exotic clothing and accessories. But who would purchase such awful items and not return them? Pea soup green and mustard yellow are not attractive sparkle/sequin shades, especially when blended. Neither do slime brown and ketchup red make a better combo. These colors were just from their waists down. Their tops, necessarily revealing to display their artful designs, were no more than spandex. Wal-Mart or K Mart could have provided them at a greatly reduced price.

I eventually learned they were "companions" of the male police officers. I translated this information several ways. Were they married to them? Were they "girlfriends?" Were they occasional company for a price? Ultimately, I wondered why they were in the room. I didn't discover those answers. They seemed accustomed to, even at home with, their surroundings--me, my fellow inmates, the dogs. They pulled up the two empty orange chairs, sat casually, and chatted with me as if that were normal.

At one point they assured me the police knew I was innocent. As reassuring as those words were, they were not accompanied by any promise of action. Other than the information about their artists and clothing connections I learned very little about them personally. Then as abruptly as they had arrived, they stood and exited using their key "card."

CHAPTER 6: INMATE COMMUNICATION

I sat glumly processing the experience. I realized I had no sense of day or night. How long had I been here? The number of "meals" and time variation lent to my confusion. No doubt a deliberate strategy. There were no undraped windows. Along the entirety of the 'front' wall hung dusty, heavy goldish drapes that traveled from the ceiling to the floor. Designer Nate Berkus would approve of the drapery length, though not of anything else in the room.

I toyed with the idea of opening the musty, gold drapes. Knowing if there was a view of the outside would help. But, if there were a boarded-up space, I'd be more depressed. However, if there was a window, no matter how grimy, I could at least have some sense of the time of day or night.

Quietly I got to my feet, the dogs ever vigilant and a few pairs of eyes surely marking my movements, and crossed the room to the drapes. I reached out to touch the thermal backed fabric, but a gasp from across the room arrested my hand in midair. I felt like a doomed horror movie character about to open the "Door." I felt the intense desire to continue. Every time I had willed foolish characters in a novel or movie to retreat, they had ignored my telepathy. Here I was with an audible signal from someone who obviously knew more of the script than I.

My big chance had arrived. I've often said you don't know what you will do in those decisive moments, until you live them. A gasp any other time might not have been a big deal, but here where silence reigned and communication was minimal, it stopped my hand in midair.

My eyes sought out the gasper.

"Well, can you tell me if there is a window or just a drape covering a blank wall?"

"No." That was the first word spoken aloud to me by another inmate.

"You don't know if there is a window, or you know there isn't a window?

"There ain't no window there."

"But why didn't you want me to even look?" In response my speaker stared directly at my canine trio.

"Will these dogs attack me if I pull back the panels?"

"Yeah."

"You seem sure about that."

"You could say I have personal experience."

The man in the Terrapin sweatshirt pulled up the right pant leg of his sweats. I saw gash marks. No bandages had been applied. The blood had congealed and dried. Ugly dark reddish black and pink skin puckered around them. Black zippers ran in crazy arcs.

Figuring this was my big chance for conversation and information, I lowered my hand but stood where I was.

"Why didn't you react when the dogs came in this time?"

"They wasn't here for me. I know what not to do. I learned."

"How long have you been here?"

"Since Saturday night 'bout seven or eight. I don't know what day it is now."

"It was Monday evening, the twenty-fifth, when I arrived. I have no idea how long I've been here. That's why I wanted to see if there was a window."

"Like I said, there ain't."

"Is there at least a bathroom we can use?"

"They're civilized enough for that. Knock on the door an' they'll take ya downstairs. It's kinda dark, an inside room with one light. And it is damp, but ya can use it."

I looked around. There was a second door I'd not paid attention to earlier. It was solid with no indication it was anything but an inner door leading to who knew where. There was no EXIT sign above this door or the glass-paned one through which I had entered. Not a comforting thought.

"What about that door?" I asked indicating the second one.

"What about it?"

"Has anybody tried to open it? Or do the dogs also attack if you do?"

"Ya don't go through there till they're ready to deal with ya."

"So, we all just wait here and do nothing?"

"Those who mind waiting an' act up learn to regret it real fast. The last two people to leave were dragged out. They couldn't walk on their own after the guards were finished with 'em."

"What do you mean?"

"They used tasers and sticks."

"Oh... I was stunned into a momentary silence. "Do we leave in the order that we came in here?"

"Nope."

"How many people were here when you arrived?"

"I'd say a dozen an' a half or so includin' that beggar over there an' those two guys over there." He pointed out those he referenced, then dropped his hand to his lap as though the gesture violated privacy or a code of conduct.

"So, some people actually left walking out on their own power?"

"Yeah, all but those last two an' one other."

"What about him?"

"Wasn't no "him". Was an old woman."

"They beat her? An old woman? Why?"

"She spoke up an' challenged 'em. Feisty she was. They 'subdued' her was what they called it. They used sticks an' tasers on her. She thrashed an' cried out."

"Didn't anybody try to help her?"

"A couple of us made a move an' they turned the damn tasers on us. We stopped soon enough."

That was not comforting. I gave up on conversation, too afraid to ask what his crime was. If mine was imaginary, that could be the case of others too. Tired of standing near the non-window, I walked to a different, available but uninviting, orange vinyl chair and plopped down heavily onto it. I'd never felt so heavy. It wasn't my physical weight, but the mental load of trying to comprehend the incomprehensible that pulled me down. I scanned the room. So many orange chairs. I'd never found orange appealing, except when dressed as a fan representing my beloved Orioles. Now it was repugnant. I feared I'd forever look at orange with disgust, assuming I'd ever get to see anything in any shade of orange beyond this chamber.

Time crawled.

Bumble Bee girl rapped on the door then resumed her seat. After a delay that seemed just long enough to be a power play, officers appeared. They didn't ask who had knocked, but glared around the room till the teen meekly raised her hand and made her potty break request. They nodded and she left, escorted from in front and behind. Her friend went next, maybe an hour later.

Time passed, dragging on. I thought of asking to use the bathroom. Envisioning the facilities didn't improve my mood. I refused to ask the females about their experiences. Glimpsing their faces when they returned showed their disgust. But necessity won over reluctance. I rose from the chair, the dogs unflinchingly staring, and crossed the room to the Flintstone door. I knocked. I felt I knocked softly, but in the general silence it sounded loud. Nothing happened. There was the wait I anticipated from watching the process. Then there were minutes after that. I knocked again, a bit louder. Finally, they showed up. One I recognized from an earlier foray into the room. His partner was new to me. Ungraciously they let me out of the room sandwiched between them.

CHAPTER 7: TOILET TALK

My first impulse was to run toward the front of the building. To my utter disappointment that door had no glass panes, nor were there windows. The time of day or night remained elusive. They steered me farther down the hall to a door on the right and immediately we descended smelly concrete stairs. The ceiling on this level seemed lower, giving me a claustrophobic feeling. The room I was let into was bare save for the toilet and sink, both heavily rust stained (I decided to believe it was rust.), cracked and chipped. The dim ceiling bulb was imprisoned inside a wire mesh cage rendering it tamper proof. I couldn't figure why anyone would prefer total dark to a lightbulb, however dim it was.

The door did not lock. Urine was the prevalent odor. I tried breathing through my mouth. I stared at the dingy gray walls, seeing many more color variations than I would have thought existed. I instantly recognized the cleaning methods employed by school janitors: scour the graffiti even if the paint fades or comes off. I looked for recent writing, for messages. There were at least a dozen spots that looked like they had been scoured off where there had been graffiti. These areas were the only clean surfaces. I decided to use the facilities before my escorts came in after me.

When I sat down, I saw it. Written in pencil. It was a short note. The graphite showed feebly in the dim bulb's path just to one side of the toilet. There was a name, a plea for someone to call a phone number. The darkness made it hard to decipher. Jade? John? Jake? Jude? Jodi? Maybe an "e" as the last letter; so, "John" or "Jodi" was out. "Flemming"? "Herring"? The number was the least difficult. I memorized what seemed to be a cell phone number. Maybe when I exited this place, I could pursue this, offer to help this person, or at least hear his or her story. Or was this person still upstairs? It would be a comfort to know this person no longer needed help but had returned home safe and sound.

As I glanced around the room, I was relieved to see the bathroom sink was no worse than my memory of our family sparkler factory's ladies' room. While growing up I had many occasions to use that restroom. At least there had been a separate bathroom for each sex. Granted no amount of scrubbing could keep it clean. A roll of industrial brown paper towels and an open can of degreaser had always been present. Today we find sanitizer everywhere. As a child, I spent most afternoons after my half-day kindergarten class in the packing room with the factory "girls." Our floor lady, who laid claim to being my third grandmother, always maintained she had taught me to count by practicing putting the correct number of sparklers in the cartons.

I shook off my reverie to focus on the room at hand. I was relieved to find they provided toilet paper. That was an improvement from our business trip to the Hunan Province in China. I still carried small packs of tissues in my pocket just in case. Fireworks factories in China have bathroom standards a far cry from ours. The drain in the floor where you squat is what you get. Even in a two-year-old very posh hotel the lobby bathroom was only slightly modified to contain a marble and porcelain enclosure around the floor drain.

Since there was rusty water here and no paper towels, I produced tissues from my pocket. I had another momentary flashback of the rusty water flowing from North East High School's faucets on Monday mornings. Before retiring, I'd been an English teacher and had been sitting in the faculty lounge grading papers when a state health inspector accompanied, Steve, our chief custodian, to perform a water safety inspection. Color didn't matter, he assured me. A little extra iron was not covered under unsafe drinking water regulations. Still, many of us continued to pay for delivery of bottled drinking water rather than consume what came out of the faucets which closely resembled what we flushed away.

Finishing up, I left the bathroom and any sense of solitude I'd experienced those few minutes alone, away from all that threatened to overcome me. My reluctant escorts were waiting. They directed me swiftly back to where I had been for only God knew how long. I kept mentally repeating the name variations and phone number I had discovered scratched on the gray wall for fear my nervousness would freeze my memory cells.

CHAPTER 8: REMOVAL

Merely for variety I sat on a different chair and almost dozed off. Occasionally someone would follow the bathroom procedure. I even heard snoring. How could anybody release enough tension to sleep? Curiosity and the need to move grew in me. My restless leg syndrome had kicked in. Had I gone a whole night without my prescription? I hadn't slept and from experience knew I wouldn't sleep without it. Though I carried a tablet in my giraffe pill case in my pocket, I balked at taking it. It would render me drowsy, vulnerable.

I glanced toward door number two. Something forbade me from stepping around the zombie-like man or woman to touch that door. I didn't want to get near him or her, or feared I would discover the door was electrified or alarmed. Or the dogs might attack. There was always that prospect. Didn't they nap like normal dogs? I guess not.

Again, I scanned the room. Why would I think I could conjure up a wall clock where none had been? For once I cursed my penchant for not wearing a watch and leaving behind my cell phone. I stretched, causing the dogs to jerk to an alert stance.

Cautiously, I got up and began to pace. I was too stiff and uncomfortable to sit any longer. Mindlessly I walked around, careful to avoid those slumbering off in their own worlds. I kept pondering, *how can they legally treat me like this?*

Now that I thought about it, no one had frisked me for weapons or electronic devices. That could have been the end of my tissues and meds. That was odd, wasn't it? Had the others been "processed" or left here like me? I looked for someone who was awake and willing to talk. As before, it was Terrapin man.

"Do we get read our rights or fingerprinted, or something official like on TV shows?"

"Haven't ya figgered out there's nothin' official 'bout bein' here? There won't be no official record. But it's sure happenin,' ain't it?"

"How can they get away with this?"

"Don't know. But they can an' they are."

"Why? I mean, why us? Why anybody? What's it all for?"

"I didn't know nothin' 'bout these people 'fore I come here, but they have power. An' there ain't no shortage of 'em either."

I sighed loudly. I moved around the room again. Time dragged on. I sat down staring at nothing. The dogs only moved to keep track of me as I shifted in the unforgivably hard chair. I requested bathroom time again. The sojourn was brief, uneventful. There were no new scribblings. I affirmed the message was as I had remembered. The guards sullenly returned me to the holding pen.

My gaze traveled around the room, and I increasingly felt like I was in the minority. I certainly wasn't guilty of any crime. What had happened to the information from the mermaids that the police knew I was wrongly being held here? Had they fed each new inmate the same line? Maybe the painted ladies had been planted to sound me out. If so, I'd been interrogated without knowing it.

I wrestled with how much information I'd divulged during our conversation. Neither woman had produced a written or electronic document. Had I been secretly recorded? Why? How was my side to be considered? My side of what? What had I told those women? My name? Yes. I'd gotten theirs too. Were they real names? Why would I consider they were? They knew I was a "foreigner" from the head of the Chesapeake Bay, the northernmost part of the Eastern Shore. My "accent" had given me away. But they claimed to be Annapolis locals.

They had sympathized with me upon learning I was expecting my husband if he could find where I'd been taken. They hadn't seemed surprised he had been separated from me. Had they believed I had a husband who would arrive and bail me out? They certainly hadn't hinted he had been apprehended while driving through the alley.

With the scarce amount of information I had let slip, they had probably accessed my whole life by now. Was this scenario followed regularly? Probably. I now refused to ask anyone else about anything.

Catholic guilt descended or ascended, or rather, engulfed me. Was there anything in my life that could be misconstrued? Time for an examination of conscience: No arrests, no points on my driver's license, retired after thirty years of teaching, married to a funeral home employee, parent, grandparent, Catholic, Democrat, master's degree in religious studies, member of three book clubs, part owner of a family-owned fireworks business, reader, gardener, scrap-booker, crafter, gym member.

There it was I belonged to Planet Fitness but hadn't set foot inside in months! I smiled at my own sarcasm. Nothing else seemed remotely suspicious to me—unless some of the books my groups discussed were too controversial? Even if we read provocative books, wasn't that the point—discussion? Seconds stretched into minutes as I formulated my examination of conscience. There was nothing intriguing about me. Nothing anyone should consider worth red flagging or investigating.

I must have dozed off.

Suddenly I was aware of two tandem teams of officers entering the room. At once everyone seemed aware of the interruption. The officers approached one of the hoodies guys. They closed in on him. I saw his momentary desire to resist fade from his face. Ultimately, in resignation, he gave them no trouble. As they passed by the hanging outerwear, he reached out and claimed the camouflage hunting jacket. Irreverently, I silently congratulated myself on my correct match of coat to owner. Then I felt shame for my petty thought and offered a quick prayer for his safety.

The entourage proceeded toward the mysterious exit door. Shockingly no key card was used. They pulled down on the handle and jerked the heavy door revealing a dimly lit dingy area.

The second hoodie guy refused to look in the direction of his departing companion. His body language conveyed his sense of powerlessness. Almost in unison, we all exhaled as the last guard exited. I hadn't realized I wasn't breathing till the collective sigh enveloped the room. The men yanked the door back into place with such finality that I felt a tremor both from the slamming and our bodies' reactions.

Then nothing.

CHAPTER 9: ESCAPE

The slight tap came from the other side of that solid, second door. I wondered why the guards were returning. Was there no other way back into the building? Why were they using the door they had so decisively shut some time ago? The door began moving in jerks, seemingly being forced as though it had not been used for many humid Maryland summers. Since only hours ago it had moved more smoothly, I was confused. Then I finally grasped that the jerks were from attempted stealth rather than difficulty. Why would anyone want to secretly enter this room?

Then, there stood Patrick, soft graying blond hair framing his face… my rescuer…my escape. I rubbed my eyes to clear away the mirage, but he was still there.

Simultaneously, from above, I became conscious of the sound of powerful engines. I looked past the door to where someone had pulled back a dusty drape in the room beyond—a window! There were gigantic aircraft flying not very far above. They were not just planes, but some huge aerial contraptions more sophisticated than anything I'd thought existed. Did Starship Enterprise have a life beyond TV/movie screens? Were they drones?

My first stupid thought was that "they" identified me as a terrorist, and "they" were about to destroy the whole area to ensure my elimination. Yes, too much time spent with James Patterson's character Alex Cross.

Patrick sprayed something in the direction of the dogs. The dogs did not make a sound or move. He grabbed me by the wrist before I could formulate any more stupid scenarios. He called out to someone else. He called her name. I thought I heard "Grace". The seemingly semi-comatose person cleared her vision, transformed into one very aware person, and moved purposefully toward, then past me.

So quickly! She was a changed person, one with a mission. She grabbed her pea coat as she rushed out. The others, realizing the door to possible "freedom" had been opened, followed. During their stampede, they all reached for their coats. I thought, how odd! Why bother? Just get out of here!

They looked at one another, then propelled themselves toward the door not even slowing down while rescuing their coats from the hooks.

There was one jacket left on the hooks, and for no identifiable reason, I pulled out of Patrick's grasp to snatch it. He gasped at me in disbelief, then regained his grip on my hand.

We moved with such speed we soon outdistanced the stampeding herd rushing down the narrow corridor and out through rusty metal double doors. I ran conscious of adrenaline rushing through me.

In fluid movements, like Michael Phelps competing in a swimming meet, everyone streaked through the final doorway. Escape. Out into the cold night air.

CHAPTER 10: TEEN FREEDOM

They snatched their jackets as they sped away block after block, slipping on the splash spatters from passing cars. They ran in synchronized movements turning left, then right. Nothing was familiar. But they only knew the area of the Best Western Motel.

How long had they been in that PLACE? The woman, the last arrival, had said it was Monday evening when she was brought in, which had creeped them out. They'd both been scared beyond imagining. What time was it now? Dawn? Dusk?

They saw lights, slowed down. Civilization.

"Mac, we need to blend in."

"I agree, Sami. We can't get caught by THEM."

"Wait, Mac! My cell phone's in my jacket. I turned it off when we left. It has GPS. Duh! It isn't dead. We can judge how far we are from the motel and decide if we can afford a cab or walk."

"We'll face a lot of questions. We went AWOL after the swim meet semi-finals. What will happen?

"Sami, it can't be worse than being hostages, and how long we've been away will make a difference."

"My cell phone says 5:48 pm. Tuesday."

"We've really been missed; it's been about forty-eight hours."

"We were to swim this afternoon. Coach's gonna lose it! But since it's semester break we haven't missed any of our school classes."

"Sami, how will we get anybody to believe us? We left the motel breaking the ban about fast food, but we didn't get a chance to do anything else," Mac added.

"I can hear coach now," Sami spoke. 'Samantha and Macey, you are suspended from this team. I am fur-ee-us with you two! How can you expect to be trusted again! We alerted your parents and police!"

"You even sound like Coach," groaned Mac.

"If cops have been looking for us, they're doing a pathetic job."

"Who do you think THEY were? THEY didn't look like terrorists, but what's a terrorist look like?"

"Beats me, Mac. But what did THEY want? They didn't get our personal information so they could collect a ransom and didn't find your cell phone. Maybe they weren't after us."

"Is your cell phone GPS helping?" Mac prompted.

"It says, 'You are here!', but I can't remember the motel address. I can't program the GPS. Now what?" Sami grumbled.

"We could call Coach and ask him to come get us after the meet. No. Let's just get a taxi, ask how much costs to go to Best Western. Then decide if we have enough money."

"But, Sami, it's Tuesday, everybody will be at the Y for finals. We won't be able to get into our motel room. Let's go to the Y."

They reached an intersection. As the light changed, they spied a cab and waved it down. The cab eased to the curb.

"Where to?"

"The YMCA, ah, please."

"Which one?"

"There's more than one?"

"Yeah. Bay Area and Backtown."

"Which one's running swim meets?" asked Mac.

"I don't know. If you kids don't know where you're going, I can't take you there. You're costing me money."

They both broke down sobbing uncontrollably.

"I can ask around." He got on his radio requesting assistance. Three minutes later he was transporting them to Backtown Y. They pooled their money watching the meter amount climb.

"How much farther?" Sam asked, her voice cracking.

"Just a couple of blocks."

"We only have $16.75. Let us out now and point us in the right direction. We'll walk the rest of the way," offered Sam.

"No. I don't know what's wrong, but I won't just drop you off. You're too scared. What were you thinking? Did you just take off?"

Mac spoke up, eyes down, "We went out for fast food. Just a little way from the motel. Then, the..." her voice trailed off.

"Then?" he asked softly glancing through the rear-view mirror.

"We were sort of kidnapped. It was Sunday evening after we swam. THEY picked us up- we thought they were cops. It was just getting dark. They gave us crap about hanging out like delinquents," said Sami, her voice quavering at the memory

"Let me get this straight. They weren't cops."

"No, some guy busted in, and everybody started running out. We didn't know where we were, so we just ran till we found lights and people," added Mac.

"Are you girls for real? Did this really happen, or have you been out and need a real good made-up story to cover your asses?" he challenged, pointedly staring into their eyes from the mirror.

"No!" cried Sam.

"Yes!" cried Mac.

"I mean, NO we weren't messing around," explained Sam.

"And YES, it's true. But THEY didn't want money. THEY never got any information about our families," Mac added.

"Okay, here we are at Backtown YMCA. You two check if your team is here before I leave. Go! I ain't about to leave you stranded here. I've got kids at home- at least they'd better be at home! Go and report back to me."

Sami and Mac streaked toward the Y. They disappeared inside and returned a minute later, crying and smiling through their tears.

"We're okay now!" Mac insisted.

"Here's all our money and thank you for everything! We can get more money from our coach if you need it," Sam offered.

"No, I'm relieved you are safe. No more wandering. Got it?"

"Yes, sir!" they chorused.

"One more thing. I believe you but need to talk to an adult before I leave."

"Yes! Thank you! But what's your name?" Sam inquired.

"Yes, sir, what is your name?" inquired Coach Jansen as he approached the cab.

"I'm Greg. Greg Benkoski. And you are?"

"Sir, I am Coach Jansen. These two are Samantha and Macie. It's time you were properly introduced. They will remember you. So will I! Please take this extra payment for rescuing them." He handed over an amount of money the girls couldn't see. "We established a reward for information leading to their safe return."

Greg reluctantly accepted the cash. He nodded his gratitude, promised to use the money for his kids, waved, and pulled away. The girls turned and ran toward the Y where three chaperones, their parents, and two uniformed police officers stood watching to assure they didn't disappear again.

Immediately Mac and Sam were escorted to a private office

within the Y where the officers began to patiently, sympathetically unravel the girls' story. Within minutes the officers contacted their superiors who alerted UMCO. Then the girls were again debriefed by an undercover agent. For secrecy UMCO representatives introduced themselves as representing the state social services. Information elicited from the girls was immediately shared with headquarters.

CHAPTER 11: FINDING SHELTER

Bernard T. Olah lost no time escaping the prison he'd endured for days. He knew his number to be interrogated was soon to come up, and he had no back-up plan to avoid long-term lock up. He also knew if he hadn't spent two consecutive days casing that High's convenience store reflecting back *it hadn't been so convenient* he wouldn't have been spotted. If he hadn't made off with two hundred and fifty-three dollars from WaWa last month, he'd be less nervous now. If he hadn't taken off his gloves to get the bills from the drawer, leaving his prints on the cash register, he'd be better off. But the money had been hard to grasp. If he hadn't been arrested for robbery at the 7-11 last November, his fingerprints wouldn't be on file.

If…if…if…

If he moved swiftly… He slipped on his jacket covering his Terps sweatshirt. He pulled out gloves and a dark knit cap, to alter his appearance. He turned behind the building adjacent to the one he had just vacated and negotiated the narrow alley, an obstacle course of overflowing garbage cans, torn open trash bags, and discarded furniture. He took the first intersecting street and kept going till he was beyond the echoes of other running feet. He heard distant vehicular traffic. He stopped to assess the night sounds. Was it night? A distant metallic clang startled him till he heard the accompanying piercing meow. A feline trash picker. There were intermittent whispers he gradually recognized as discarded paper items being blown between two houses. He sighed and attempted to breathe normally. He realized he had miraculously been sprung from a no-win situation. Was this Divine Intervention? No, God wouldn't be doing him any favors. He wouldn't do favors for the likes of himself if he were God.

He leaned against the concrete side wall of a gray building. They hadn't identified him because they hadn't checked his fingerprints. But they were on file and could connect him to the second robbery even if he hadn't gone to trial. What game were these guys playing? He knew they were not 'for real' cops, but who were they? Where could he go to safely chill till he got himself together? In olden times, he could have run into a church and claimed 'sanctuary'. Now the damned churches were locked so people like him couldn't steal from the poor boxes or remove any valuables. He'd have to break into a church to ask for sanctuary- not smart. He needed to blend in. God he was hungry. Was that thought a prayer? If so, it was his first in a long time. Was there anywhere he could get a meal and a bed for one night without getting arrested? Maybe a shelter? A mission place? He'd seen one last week. Which store had he been checking out then? It was one he had deemed too risky. Where was that?

He moved cautiously, trying not to disrupt the evening quiet. It was evening! He realized he was glimpsing the setting sun. Darkness would be on him soon. He felt the temperature dropping. He travelled west keeping as much light as possible ahead of him.

Finally, he approached a few businesses and pedestrians. Alleys appeared to be his only welcoming hospitality. He continued for blocks and encountered two people bedded down for the night. He did not want to be them. They'd surrounded themselves with an arsenal of shopping carts with blankets and newspapers for insulation. He passed another person just beginning to make up his bed.

"Hey, Buddy. Why don't you go to a shelter?" he asked quietly, hoping not to startle the guy.

"Because, I can't get in," was her reply.

"You mean they're filled up?"

"No, ya fool. They won' take drunks." She displayed her bottle taking a gulp. "What's yer escuse fer bein' out here?"

"I don't know about any shelters. I'd go if I knew where one was," Bernie hinted.

"Keep goin' three blocks, then make a lef' an' go fer one more an' ya'll see the sign fer Mercy Mission. Don' tell 'em Elly sent ya."

"Thanks, ah Elly was it?"

"Yeah, Elly. Go get warm an' eat their leftovers."

He nodded his gratitude and picked up his pace. Hope stirred.

Three blocks, turn, one block. Where was the shelter? Had that old hag lied? Was she back there cackling? Then he glimpsed a sign swinging in the breeze just around the corner. Bernie walked toward the M and S, the other letters too blurred to decipher. Still, it beckoned him.

He pushed the buzzer and was admitted into an anteroom furnished with a counter and posted admission requirements. He scrubbed up and joined other late-comers like himself. He sank his teeth into the cornbread and slurped up the warm chili.

In a while he'd talk to the others. Now he just wanted to feel the warmth and flavor of decent grub. Tomorrow, he might even try to put some things right…or not.

Before he settled into his assigned bed there was someone interrogating him about his need for shelter. He ended up remaining awake most of the night relating his experience to one person after another. He watched them communicating with their headquarters. They didn't seem concerned about his past wrongdoings but zeroed in on his recent captivity. He knew in time they might want to speak to him again.

CHAPTER 12: GOOD NEWS, BAD NEWS, HOPE

Carlos moved, hesitated. Where was Jorge? How could he explain Jorge was missing? He looked left and right, rattled two doors. Both opened without protest. Empty. He saw a desk and a chair in each and a lamp that could be swung around to temporarily blind someone. He smelled fear. One room smelled of Jorge's Axe cologne. He knew it was pointless to remain. Jorge was gone. He followed the others outside.

He appraised their flight patterns, then chose another route. Better to leave many trails. He congratulated himself on his clear thinking under pressure. He took another dozen strides and almost collided with an "officer" scanning the area. He executed a silent about-face, sprinting to his left, sweat forming on his face despite the cold. He felt no confidence in eluding the adversary.

He kept going till his leg muscles begged for mercy. He doubled over his head scraping the wall of a building. He considered stopping for temporary shelter, but the instinct to create distance between himself and them was greater. He slowed his pace, realizing they would be alert for someone running. He pulled up both of his hoods tugging them as far over his head as possible. He dug his hands in his pockets, trying to appear casual. He had a sense of the neighborhood, but it wasn't his territory. Still, he wasn't totally lost. Several blocks away was a mom-and-pop store that sold lottery tickets. He headed there. What he'd do after that, he hadn't worked out. His imagination, usually vivid, had absconded. He felt he was facing an insurmountable obstacle. The store was his temporary haven.

On he walked, nodding to those appearing friendly, avoiding eye contact with others. He saw lights up ahead: "Dirty Man Store" spelled out in dingy brown against a yellow background. Why would anybody name a food store that? Who'd want to shop here? But, despite the name, the shop had a steady business of repeat customers. He pushed open the door to the accompaniment of a jangling leather strip. Heat embraced him. He stepped forward and stood still. It was so normal.

Two customers were waiting to pay, one with a six-pack of Bud Light and a carton of a dozen eggs, the other with a whole display of Tasty Kake Butterscotch Krimpets and a slip of paper with lottery number requests. Carlos walked to the coffee dispenser, poured a large cup of very strong black coffee, and grabbed a Tasty Kake Honey Bun. He thought it was evening, but the coffee and Honey Bun were morning fresh. How long? He looked at the depleted stack of *Baltimore Sun* papers and read the date. Tuesday, January 26. The interviews for him and Jorge had been set for Saturday evening. He'd known he'd missed it, but seeing the date made it real. No chance to reschedule. Even if he told the truth. He felt bad for his friend who had set up the interview for them. He had even been their transportation.

He paid and sat at one of two tables squeezed into an alcove left of the door. He fought the impulse to move on. He observed other customers, a few coming in to get warm. The old man at the register didn't mind. He greeted most by name, and they called out "Evenin' Dirty Man." He smiled and offered free coffee.

A petite lady with gray-white hair braided up and fixed around her head chided them.

"You should not call him 'Dirty Man'. He is very clean and so is his store. And his name is Deartese- D E A R T E S E."

"Oh, Miss Emma, they mean no harm. Besides, I even put that name on the sign outside. I advertise it."

"But you are clean, Norman."

"My customers know it. It's our little joke."

"I know. You are very clean, and so is this fine establishment."

"Thanks, Miss Emma. Your usual order this fine evening?"

"Oh, of course." With that, he washed his hands and busied himself at the next counter slicing white American cheese and baloney, a quarter pound of each. He wrapped them separately, scooped a dill pickle from a barrel, wrapped it, and retrieved a kaiser roll from a bin. He slathered the insides with Kraft mayonnaise and Grey Poupon mustard. He packed everything in a paper bag, added napkins and a bag of Herrs' Old Bay chips. Meanwhile, Miss Emma made herself a large coffee with extra cream and three sugars. Norman handed her the bag.

"Eat hearty, Miss Emma."

She murmured her thanks and left. Only as the door swung closed did Carlos realize no money had changed hands. What was this place? He refilled his cup and approached the counter to pay. Mr. Deartese waved him off.

"Refills are on the house tonight."

"How can you afford this? The coffees, the old lady's dinner?"

"Easy, Friend. What do they call you?"

"Carlos."

"Well, Carlos, I make my profit with a busy lunch trade. The customers know their tips pay it forward for those short on cash. It just works! People care about one another. Here's the proof."

Carlos thanked him and resumed his seat. As he finished, he mentioned to the old man, for no apparent reason, that he was an out-of-work auto mechanic, but when he got a new job, he'd be back to 'pay it forward'. Mr. Deartese nodded. Then paused.

"Wait. I have a friend, who has a cousin, who runs an auto repair shop. His main mechanic, his brother, went out west on vacation where his wife's from- New Mexico, or Arizona. Anyway, he called the other day and told his brother he was staying out there. His in-laws got him a job and a place to stay. It seems his wife and her family had it planned beforehand. I just heard about it today. Are you good at this mechanic stuff? Are you reliable? Do you have your own tools? Would you be able to relocate to another county?"

Carlos grinned, "Yes, sir-to all four things."

Let me find Raffy's card. He can hook you up if the job's still there. In fact, you can call from here." He shuffled through piles of cards in a drawer under the counter. Then he straightened up and went to a bulletin board by the front door. "Here it is. I remember now I told him to post it on the neighborhood board." He handed Carlos the card.

"Chesapeake Service Car Repair. What have I got to lose?" Mr. Deartese beckoned Carlos toward the phone. Suddenly nervous, Carlos dialed the number and held his breath.

The voice on the other end sounded so smooth and professional he thought he was listening to a canned message and waited for the 'beep' to leave his information.

"Hello? Anybody there?"

"Oh, yes! I thought you were an answering machine. Sorry."

"Get that all the time. What can I do for you?"

"Hi. I'm Carlos Cruz. I'm at the Dirty Man Store in Annapolis. Mr. Deartese told me about a job. Are you hiring?"

"Yes, we are. Where have you worked before?"

"Al Mason's Car Repair, for a year and a half…till last week."

"Were you fired?"

"No, sir. Mason's brother graduated from tech school, and he had promised to make room for him. Plus, business has been slow lately. Two of us lost our jobs."

"Are you certified?"

"Yes, sir."

"Well, if Mr. D told you to call, you must be okay. If he vouches for you, you must be solid."

"No. Hold up. He gave me your information. We just met tonight. I've been by the store before, but he doesn't know me."

"And honest, too. If Mr. D handed you the phone, he's vetted you. He's quick in his assessments. I've never known him to misjudge anyone. I am Sean, the owner, and you're hired on a temporary basis. You start tomorrow morning. Let me give you directions. If business increases as I am expecting, I may have a second opening soon. Didn't you say two of you lost jobs?"

"Yes, I did." Carlos felt positive. He had to get home, find out if Jorge had returned. Maybe there'd be good news. He listened to the address and the time of arrival in the morning. He thanked Sean and hung up. He thanked Mr. Deartese who extended a hearty handshake and said no appreciation was necessary. Carlos left, walking purposefully toward his neighborhood.

CHAPTER 13: TO SAFETY

Alvinia Gloria Maloney, bewildered, shook her head. She picked herself up and shuffled along, then accelerated at an amazingly fast pace. She grabbed her coat from the rack and disappeared from the sight of the others. She was not like the lot of them. She was not some criminal who belonged locked up in that jail.

She exited that prison building, and then turned and strode directly around to the front. She first stopped and peered back at that door through which she had been forcibly brought hours ago. She paused and squinted as if memorizing the sight of her humiliating nightmare. Then, like a soldier, she marched toward it and stomped up to the second step. She stood still, then spat decisively at that door. In her mind she also spat at those evil people who had detained her.

Satisfied, Alvinia abruptly turned on her heel and determinedly marched back down the steps. She was done with this place!

Once on the street she moved determinedly, walking faster and faster. Soon she had three, then four blocks between her and that disgusting building. But she had no idea where she was.

She slowed her pace. Where in heaven's name was she?

She just wanted to go home, put on her favorite bright orange knitted sweater and black corduroy slacks- her comfortable Baltimore Orioles patterned clothes. She wanted to prop up her feet, settle into her favorite chair, turn on the TV, and enjoy a cup of tea.

But first, she needed to find out where she was. She walked less purposefully and began studying her surroundings. Surely, she would soon locate a familiar office building, or street name, or business sign, or church. She had thought she knew Annapolis well.

Now she was free, but she admitted she was hopelessly lost.

It was getting dark and not a soul was about.

"Excuse me, Ma'am. I think I may have been sent here to rescue you."

She whirled around ready to strike out at the owner of that voice, to defend herself against another attack from Them. Her right arm was poised in mid-air.

A gentle, but firm hand restrained her. She frowned in confusion. She looked up to see who held her in such a respectful, yet decisive way. He was young, but everyone was young to her these days. He was dressed respectably in dark wool blend trousers and wore a light gray overcoat that almost, but not quite hid his gray and white striped shirt. About his shoulders hung a soft gray flecked woolen scarf. His gray eyes reflected concern, honesty and sincerity. His black, unruly hair made him appear almost cherubic to her mind. He moved slightly and a distant streetlamp cast a halo-like aura over his head. Her angelic rescuer!

"Ma'am, truly, I am here to rescue you. That is, if you are someone who has just escaped from that illegal fake-police prison. Honest. I am not with them. I would like to escort you to the hospital to be checked out. Is that acceptable, Ma'am?"

"Why, yes young man, I suppose that would be quite acceptable, replied a hoarse-voiced Alvinia Maloney who had not spoken aloud in some time. She offered a slight smile to her rescuer.

CHAPTER 14: TAKING FLIGHT

We followed an uneven crumbled sidewalk, turned a corner, and ran for blocks. I realized after a few minutes the others weren't behind us. In the dim light, I saw our car, tucked in among several others. I don't know how I comprehended it was dusk, not dawn. I'd been confined for around twenty-four hours, if it was Tuesday. Patrick, Grace, and I sprinted to the car.

When we were safely locked inside the car and moving away, I sat with my mouth hanging open in shock as I watched my husband use his cell phone to contact a place he called "Headquarters." He spoke to a Sergeant Williams and announced, "Mission Sacramental Grace accomplished." Then we drove a circuitous route through the city of Annapolis. I wondered. *Were we maneuvering like this to make sure no one was following us?*

What the heck?

And who was Grace?

My mind went back to my navigation "error." Perhaps I hadn't made a mistake? Why would we have been meant to enter a strange building and become separated? Had those men really been threatening me? Were they "staged?" And if so, why? Did I know this man seated beside me, my husband? Had he deliberately left me to be "arrested?" Frustration, confusion, and anger all battled inside me. What was going on? What had I become mixed up in? Who had Patrick just been communicating with? And…who was Grace?

"I need answers NOW! Let's start with Grace here!" I demanded of Patrick in a shrill voice, glaring at him.

The young Asian woman with long black hair worked into a ponytail popped up from the back seat, leaning forward offering her hand to me. "I'm Grace. I just helped in your rescue from false imprisonment."

Still furious, I hesitated before extending mine. "That tells me little, except for the 'false' part. It's good to confirm I wasn't there legally. How did you assist in my rescue?"

"For your own good, your own safety, you were kept in the dark. If you'd known about the operation, and they found out, they'd have harmed you. I was observing you from your first moment in that despicable room," she smiled.

"Who are THEY?"

"First, they are not the real, legitimate police. They are vigilantes who have begun to take control of certain areas of our state. They fake evidence, force confessions, and then turn people over to the real authorities who are then obliged to follow up. With a supposed confession in hand, cases are often open-and-shut- easy police work. Some officers don't ask probing questions of their sources. They accept the gift of a practically solved case. Their innocent victim, who usually has something to feel guilty about, doesn't put up much resistance. The vigilantes are satisfied with getting what they deem 'undesirables' off the streets. Once caught by these people, very few come into their clutches again. This makes them smug about the success of their tactics."

"You're saying people are detained for bogus crimes, but since they feel guilty of doing something else, they don't bother to protest and just accept their false 'arrest' and don't fight the ultimate consequences?"

Grace responded, "If they're fortunate, they're turned over to the real police. If they protest, we believe they often don't get that far. I contrived to be one of the arrested and was awaiting my fate. However, the longer I waited and the more snippets of conversation I overheard, the more I suspected my cover was compromised. I had to act. My escape can now be attributed to the general breakout. Since they lost all their detainees, they have multiple trails to follow. God willing, ours isn't one they pick."

"And I fixed the door to seem it had been jammed, not entirely closed properly, so the escape can be interpreted as a breakout, not a rescue," Patrick added. "They can waste time arguing over who was careless."

My husband did that?

I turned my attention back to Grace.

"So, you intentionally got into their custody, but then later needed a way out before they could confirm who you are? Who *are* you? Who do you work for?"

"Undercover Maryland Covert Operations. For short we call it "UMCO."

"Patrick? You are a part of this too. That isn't a question. But it demands a lot of answers from you." I frowned hard in his direction, my thick eyebrows probably touching.

"Yes. And before you unravel, I know we've never kept secrets from each other. But this was necessary for your safety."

"And what was the incarceration? Was it for my safety too?"

"I, we, knew you could handle the situation. I was never far away. I had you tracked and had audio of everything happening."

"How? I left my purse, cell phone, everything, in the car."

"Yeah, you usually do forget your phone. We're going to get

an around-your-neck phone holder. But, you rarely take off your glasses except when you're squinting to do that knit/purl thing. So I bugged them."

"For the record, it's counted cross-stitch or needlepoint. You don't thread needles for knitting…So you bugged my glasses? This must have been done at night. It's the only time I take them off. What would you have done if I'd already had the cataract surgery that Doc says is in my future? Or if I'd gone back to wearing contact lenses? "

"You haven't yet. And you don't wear contacts."

"Did you also bug my sunglasses, or would you have backed off if this hadn't been a night or rainy-day operation?"

"Yeah." Since he always answers a 'this or that' question this way, I knew his 'yeah' referred to bugging my sunglasses as well.

I took a deep steadying breath. "Are you certain we are safe?"

"Absolutely not."

"What the?!"

CHAPTER 15: TO BLUE HERON COTTAGE

"We'll be safe once we're out of Maryland and enroute to the cottage in Onancock."

"Okay," Now I knew exactly where we were headed. "How do you know the cottage is safe?"

"It's in your parents' names, and I remember Jake and Liz next door are in New York awaiting the birth of their grandchild. Practically everyone else on the street has headed south for the winter. The neighbors are accustomed to seeing various vehicles at the house at random times. They're aware we occasionally use it as a stopover enroute to other places. I also brought our key."

"So, you were prepared." I glowered at my husband. He'd been so devious. Why? Patrick had never kept secrets before in all of our forty years of marriage. *This is so unfair!* "You knew to bring the key. How long did you know about all of this? I assume we were not planning to attend any meet and greet sessions tonight? No… wait, was the Maryland General Assembly rally even last night? Or the night before? What day is it?"

"Tuesday evening, the twenty-sixth."

"I was in there for almost twenty-four hours?!" Disbelief rose in me. He, my own husband, had deceived me, deliberately put me in danger! I needed answers. I needed them now!

"Just about." Patrick responded cryptically. I wanted to lean over and smack him on the back of his neck like Jethro used to do to Tony Dinozzo on *N.C.I.S.*

"Where were you while I was held hostage in that dreadful place?" I testily challenged him.

"I was plotting your escape route."

"What does that mean?"

"It means we had to collect equipment needed for the mission."

"What equipment?"

"Tools to break into the building where you were kept. Also I needed to wait for headquarters to launch the drones which monitored the movements of the escapees and their detainers.

"Oh…And you know how to use these tools?"

"I've been trained."

"Oh…And will we be expecting to meet people at the cottage?"

"Yes, by morning."

"Okay, we left home Monday evening and should've been in Annapolis by six-thirty. If I was there for all those hours, it must be around five o'clock Tuesday evening?" He nodded. "What about our pets?"

"Rose and Scott are pet-sitting. Remember we're blessed to have adult children and spouses living nearby."

"Patrick, why have you kept all of this from me? How long have you been associated with this UMCO?"

"I was recruited back when we attended the American Pyrotechnics Association conference in Toronto last summer. I got involved because they needed a so-called tourist to gather information about possible sabotage plots in and near our hotel and at certain restaurants and bars. They found out from the conference registration who was in attendance and staying at that specific hotel. Remember when the intercom in our hotel room told you to evacuate because of a fire? I was the one who triggered that event as a ruse to help search certain areas. We even had firefighters respond to the scene."

"I remember feeling it was surreal. I feel that way now! Plus, I am angry!"

Then I turned my attention to the thin young woman in the back seat. She braced herself for my torrent of questions but seemed generally unruffled by my outburst.

"Okay, Grace, I am almost as furious with you! How did you know we were coming to Annapolis to rescue you? How did you know I'd be there in time? How did you contact anyone? How did you know the situation had become dangerous?"

"You were the two closest available operatives," she replied maintaining steady eye contact and amazing composure.

"Wait. I'm an operative now? When was I recruited? I don't recall signing any official contract. Never mind. I won't like the answer."

"I was taken into custody Monday morning, Grace continued. There were two dozen others there. One by one they were processed out. There were incidents your friend, the Maryland Terps fan, mentioned. People left the room, came back shaking like frightened animals, gathered their belongings, and exited with one of the fishwives. The dogs unnerved us at first. They'd bring them in. Then the "wives" gathered data to ensure they had the "right" people. Later officers took people away and they didn't return. I witnessed one person escorted out with an apology.

I knew my turn was coming up. More people had entered, but almost all of those there before me were gone. Then they skipped over me, so I alerted headquarters. Before you ask, my bracelet gives off signals if activated. That was about three-o'clock Monday afternoon. For your safety I didn't acknowledge you or the two who arrived just before you. I used my dazed attitude to be invisible, to concentrate on conversations and movements. I wasn't positive you were my savior."

"I didn't know I was even supposed to be a savior. How did you eventually know?"

"You weren't like the others. You exhibited curiosity and outrage in your body language."

"So much for my being an enigma." I thought for a moment. "Why was only one hostage removed while I was there? Who are these monsters who are imprisoning innocent people? What reason do they have for jailing us?"

"I'm not sure why fewer people were removed. There seemed to be fewer personnel than earlier. That was troubling me. These people are vigilantes, operating outside the law, taking the law into their own hands."

"So, let me get this straight. Have you learned enough about these vigilantes?" I pondered the whole situation anew. "These vigilantes are really the criminals? What are they after? What is their end game? How do they pick people? Randomly?"

"Yes, they are the bad guys…but…we…UMCO…is still investigating their operation. We chose you because Patrick was already involved. But we had to keep you in the dark so you could literally play the part we needed you to play."

"Basically, I was fish bait?"

"That's one way to describe it."

"And if those dogs had attacked me was there a contingency plan?!"

"We figured you'd keep a calm head in the end."

"Thank you very much!" I replied sarcastically.

"After our debriefings, we'll all have a clearer picture of

everything."

"Our debriefings?"

"Of course. You may have valuable insights I didn't have, especially of your ride to the holding pen. We're just asking you to hold on and be patient." Grace looked directly into my eyes with her piercing dark brown ones, which were like lasers now. Her voiced lowered, "And Norah, thank you for saving me…and saving the others."

"You're welcome." I sat silently for a few minutes as we drove on digesting all of this. I had even more questions now. I turned back around in my seat to address my husband.

"Back to my being taken into custody—Patrick, how did you arrange my capture? When I got out of the car, where did you go? Who were those men who accosted me outside the abandoned factory building?"

"I was never far out of sight of you. UMCO, like every organization, uses subcontractors. Those guys are locals who pick up extra tax-free money for doing small jobs. By day they are ordinary blue-collar workers. A few are from the electric motor plant that used to operate there. Others have gas station or convenience store or fast-food jobs."

"So, there is a network available to do a variety of things for different organizations. Do they know who they work for?"

"No. They recognize it's safer that way."

"So, I was safer as I stood there with that gang, than I was when the "police" arrived. That seems backwards. Everything about this last day seems wrong. Was there a broken window? Did my having no purse or any identification raise their suspicions?"

"No and no."

As we drove south toward Virginia. I ran out of questions settling into a brooding silence listening to Patrick and Grace exchange brief comments. They weren't cryptic, but they weren't wasting sentences if a word or two sufficed. We turned onto Route 50 and headed down to Virginia's Eastern Shore of the Chesapeake Bay. This felt safe, and I could breathe normally once more with relief. We were on our own, away from the group for which I'd evidently been recruited to work, and from my captors. I couldn't judge how much longer it would take to get to the cottage near Onancock. We'd not traveled by this route before.

A sign showing mileage to Salisbury was the first recognizable road marker. Once in Salisbury we could get on Route 13 and be at Blue Heron Cottage in an hour.

"What were you detained for, Grace? Is that even your real name?"

"Vagrancy. They have a penchant for the homeless, street people, those unable to get into shelters. No, I'm not Grace, but my name, for your safety, won't be disclosed unless needed."

"Why single out the homeless? What do they think they're doing? Because they can't put their lives on a success track doesn't mean they're a threat to humanity. I've helped with our county's rotating homeless shelter. Most are decent people, temporarily overwhelmed with problems. They're less likely to be a danger than many of my high school students were. How do we get such slanted views of people? Who nurtures such suspicion? I guess the homeless also have few resources to contend with these people, especially if they think they're the law. I'd like to corral some of Cecil County's homeless to challenge these people. I met people with spunk, kindness, and determination."

"Before you ask," Patrick cut in, "they're called among other things, 'The Free State Liberators.' They see themselves as freedom fighters for 'real' Marylanders. Immigrants are a target—legal or illegal—they don't differentiate. These people possess a certain level of paranoia not present in recent decades."

"I just can't believe they get away with this stuff! This is America...Maryland...Annapolis, our state capital. We were supposed to meet with our local delegates to discuss the immigration issue. Do they know what is happening? Are they condoning this? Do they know about Undercover…UMCO?"

"Some do, and secretly applaud our efforts. Others don't and we must keep it that way to protect the missions. We're aware that some privately support vigilante behavior considering it ridding society of problems, saving taxpayer money."

I lapsed into silence, shaking my head in disgust. I still couldn't believe my own husband put me in a hazardous position. I felt like he was some stranger.

I gazed at Patrick, and he shot me a look, his blue eyes filled with tears. "I am truly sorry for all of this, my love. He sighed and turned his attention back to the road and continued, "For what it's worth, I am really Patrick, your husband." He grinned, which made me smile in return. This solid man always had a way to calm me down, to lighten the mood when I was super stressed. I glanced at my emerald and diamond engagement ring and the wedding band engraved with "I am my Beloved's and he is mine" from "The Song of Songs" in the Bible. I knew he had always been passionate about social causes as had I, and this was one of his personality traits that had endeared him to me in the first place. After all, we had met while serving on our parish council when our social concerns committee was officially launched.

It was starting to appear that this wasn't merely a social issue. It was real and ugly, beyond what I experienced in my world of family gatherings, high school classes, Sunday Mass, book club discussions, fireworks company meetings, and time with Patrick. My experience of confrontation was sibling debate over how our fireworks company should evolve to challenges in the economy, how to implement new mandates from the Cecil County Board of Education, or mediating teen drama disputes—this was serious, malicious targeting of the less fortunate.

We approached Salisbury and got on Route 13 to Virginia with light traffic. As we passed Pocomoke City, I became more alert anticipating the Virginia state line. Crossing it was a nonevent. Passing Parksley brought memories of the railroad museum and the Club Car Café. Familiar sights. We turned off Route 13 heading to Onancock, turning left at the gas station onto West Street, which became Hill Street. Even in stress, Patrick and I couldn't refrain from our corny comment about the Hill Street Blues blue houses across the street from each other. One day we'd ask if they had painted their homes to honor the old TV show or were oblivious to the connection. We passed the first of two cemeteries and found our road. At the elementary school we turned onto Heron Road, then Clapper Rail Road and our drive near the entrance to Cove Lane. Blue Heron Cottage welcomed us, our safe haven.

CHAPTER 16: MORE ANSWERS

There were no lights on in the adjoining homes or across the lane. We felt alone, even safe for the moment. The creek backed up to the backyard and beyond our neighbor Jake's house, and to the left was the tee to the Eastern Shore golf club's fourth hole. To the right was one house, then a walking trail leading through the woods to another narrow path.

Patrick used the remote to open the garage door and drove in, closing the door behind us. We entered the cottage through the family room door. We carried very little in the way of supplies, unlike our usual trek lugging food, clothes, and assorted books, movies, and magazines.

My parents purchased Blue Heron Cottage about six years ago. Their trailer in Ocean View, Delaware—in fact the entire trailer park—was sold despite 99-year leases. Now there are condos where our trailer and dock on the Delaware Bay once were. My grandmother's trailer had been the summer spot for four generations. The Atlantic Ocean with free beach access at Bethany Beach was a ten-minute drive. Our fishing and crabbing boat was tied up at our dock just steps from the door. Outlet shops, amusement rides, and favorite restaurants were minutes away. It was a comfortable place to crash, even in winter. We shed many tears when we learned all legal appeals had failed to save the park. My father and his friend Stew searched for the kind of retreat we had lost and found it in Virginia.

The Eastern Shore of Virginia was reminiscent of what our family had known back in the early 1960s in Oak Orchard, Delaware. The traffic was less, the neighbors fewer, the pace slower than 21st century Delaware beach resorts. While most of us lamented the loss of the nearby beach, Dad didn't miss it at all. He bragged he hadn't set foot on the beach in years. Here, in Virginia, he still had fishing, crabbing, golfing, and neighbors to join him. Instead of finding a new spot for the trailer, he'd bought a house, with Mother's approval, of course. Thus, Blue Heron Cottage.

After bathroom breaks, raising the thermostat, and turning on lights only visible from the water, Patrick, Grace and I explored food options. Thank God for Joe Corby fundraisers! Pizza from the freezer, popcorn, and Pepsi made our meal. Over dinner we devised our plan. We'd sleep in shifts with one on watch observing street traffic.

We expected our visitors to arrive early and be disguised as laborers for a contracting firm arriving in a commercial company van. Grace would leave with them. One of them would take our car to the abandoned house Patrick and I had discovered while kayaking last summer. Finally, Patrick and I were to kayak to the abandoned house and drive our car back home. We would take our two-seat kayak from the back garage doorway, put it over at the end of our dock, and paddle two inlets past our cove. Patrick assured me that someone would later return our kayak to the garage.

I had misgivings about kayaking in winter, even for this short distance. I questioned the need for such extreme evasion. Why not just leave in our car as soon as Grace left? Or wait a short while and drive home? Patrick insisted "Headquarters" demanded this diversion. We would leave no trace of our stay at the cottage. All food remnants and paper would be removed by the crew. Dirty towels, sheets, and clothes would be stored in our car.

Grace had her pick of any of four upstairs bedrooms, while we had our Swan Room, the first-floor bedroom. We had claimed it the day my parents went to settlement. We had furnished it with our old bedroom suite, decorated it with my ceramic swan, a framed copy of my only published photograph—a swan floating on the Northeast River, taken from the town park—and a handmade grapevine swan basket. Luckily, our meager supply of clothes in the dresser and twin closets provided a change of clothes. The upstairs bedrooms held clothing and personal items of other family members, so Grace was free to rummage for anything she needed.

All the bedrooms had a "bird" theme. Dad had early on remarked that each bedroom should be decorated with a different bird, the only interior decorating suggestion he had ever made. Upstairs, the master bedroom with dressing room and bathroom, was named the Blue Heron Room. There were also the Egret Room, Pelican Room, and Canada Goose Room. The Blue Heron Room had inspired many gifts for Mother and the name given the house.

There was no point in turning on the great room gas fireplace, or going into the family room where the fire could also be enjoyed. That double fireplace would have been a selling point for me—that and the quiet creek leading to the Bay. The fewer rooms we disturbed this trip, the better.

We glanced into the comfortable family room but resisted the appeal, remaining in the sitting/reading area of the great room. Grace went to bed, and we retired to our bedroom. Patrick had the first watch. Once we were finally alone, we clung to each other. All my questions, including curiosity about the helicopter-like noise, were unimportant. His touch was all that mattered. Our reality, husband and wife, the familiarity of being together, was paramount. I needed to re-connect, to re-anchor myself to what was normal.

Clinging to normal sadly only lasted a few moments. Then Patrick focused out the window of the darkened room, and volunteered answers.

"As I said, UMCO first approached me during the Toronto episode last fall during the APA convention. Before that I had no idea any state level group existed. They saw my funeral home job as a clever cover for covert operations, since I travel at a moment's notice. I'm always 'on call' now, since my traveling to locations around the state doesn't raise suspicion. After all, I travel in a hearse. People look away from me, as if seeing a marked funeral home vehicle might affect their own mortality.

"Anyway, they met me at the funeral home one Monday and proposed the partnership. I thought it was a joke and tried to come up with somebody we know with that much imagination or resources to set up such a hoax. But it was real. The more they talked of events behind the news we hear, the more I was convinced this was something I should discuss with you. But they absolutely forbade me to tell you. They said they only recruit one person at a time, they were interested in you, but not until I was established and they could see a way for your activities to blend into covert work.

"They seek out people who have no schedule or have erratic ones. Your teaching kept you on a predictable schedule, and any absence would be noticed. Your substituting since retirement, and occasional work at the plant, have given you more flexibility and appeal to UMCO. It was just a matter of time before you would be approached. Our plan to be at Lobby Night accelerated the process. You will be debriefed. Then they will ask you to join de facto fashion."

"Since I already know of their existence, do I have a choice?"

"Definitely."

I took my restless legs prescription and pondered all Patrick had disclosed while he kept watch. I fell asleep. He didn't wake me when he turned over the watch to Grace. The next thing I knew Patrick was shaking me, saying to get up. He and Grace had thankfully covered my shift since I had been sleep deprived the night before.

Our contacts were ten minutes away. I had time to use the bathroom, throw cold water on my face, pull on clothes and brush my teeth before a woman and man approached the creekside entrance.

Another woman from a van came to the front door. She was dressed in a quasi-uniform with a company name embroidered on her jacket. She carried a small case and clipboard.

All three were brisk, business-like, and didn't introduce themselves but seemed concerned for our welfare. In less time than I expected they outlined plans, removed all remnants of our overnight sojourn, and said Grace would depart with them. The uniformed woman went out to the van, pretended to write a proposal, returned to the front door and handed it to me.

Grace and the other man and woman got in our car. I understood the clever plan. For any observers they would seem to be the three of us who had arrived the night before.

They would drive a circuitous route ensuring they weren't being followed, leaving our car at the abandoned house where they had alternate transportation. We awaited high tide to paddle away.

CHAPTER 17: ABANDONED HOUSE

It was still not seven when Patrick and I lowered the kayak from its harness and grabbed the paddles and a tote containing emergency items. We headed out through the back garage door to the creek, dragging the kayak across the yard, then lifting it up as we went down the dock. We lowered it in record time, simultaneously hearing the front garage door open and our car engine start. The diversion of "our" driving away in our car was covering up our actual departure by water. Clever. Once more I was impressed while at the same time just a bit freaked out that I was living this, not reading about it in a novel or viewing it on the big screen.

While we are not novice kayakers…yes, we are. No wonder I was so nervous. We had bought the kayak three years before, then brought it to Virginia thinking we would use it often in the summer and fall months. Then Patrick developed carpal tunnel syndrome for which he had had surgery. No kayaking then. Then he took a fall with (not off) a ladder from a roof and spent nine months recovering, first in a wheelchair, then a walker. We lost two summers that way.

Just last summer we had finally gotten back in the kayak. Our expertise had gotten us out of the cove, around the next point, past the golf course and yacht club. We had ventured across the channel to "far" parts of the opposite shore and nearly into the Chesapeake Bay. It was during one of those trips that we discovered the abandoned house. It was beyond the point of the strip of land across from the house, around the shoreline, down past another cove, perched on a bank. It looked so full of possibilities. It begged to be reclaimed and attended to. One day, by car, I traced the route to that house while Patrick and Dad were out flounder fishing.

Now we would hopefully get a closer look than I had had from the dead-end road leading to the dirt path driveway. And I prayed fervently that we'd be dry when we got there. The water was cold, and I did not want to dwell on being in it. Just a few minutes would be dangerous, if not deadly. Life jackets might keep us afloat, but not protect us from the temperature.

It took a few minutes to get into anything like a pattern with our rowing. Patrick, behind me, tried patiently to follow the rhythm of the woman driver. I'm sure he swallowed many comments before we managed to move in sync. Like so many aspects of our journey, our departure time had depended on outside influences. In this case, the tide. Only during high tide could we maneuver in the creek. Only then were the sandbars a bit underwater. For this kayaking trip, unlike our previous ones, we had a definite destination in mind. We would not be returning to the dock, and we were in a serious frame of mind. The solitude and proximity to nature were not our focus. Every sound we made seemed loud. In the middle of summer, we'd had a few observers as we paddled along. Now we wanted none. The dim morning light made everything eerier than I'd ever imagined. It was desolate, but that was what our mission required.

We gradually eased along the creek and out past the end of

the closest sandbar, leaving a wide berth. This was not the day to run aground. We set our sights for the buoy and tried to maintain a constant speed. I did my best not to alter the pattern or rhythm. We made decent progress, especially for us. The angling into the second cove became tricky. We'd forgotten there were several private docks along the shoreline and one sandy expanse that stretched far into the creek. As a result, we had a narrow channel to paddle through. The challenge was just one more in a long series of physical and mental ones in recent memory.

Thirty-five silent, tense minutes after our launch, we neared the beach. The abandoned Victorian house loomed just beyond. To our relief there was a cement ramp near the house. Because of the angle it was visible from only a short distance away. Even in winter the overgrowth was so dense it was hardly noticeable. We landed and lifted the kayak across the cement. Just past the ramp was the dead-end road. The side road branching off it was the deeply rutted driveway to the house.

We saw it was definitely abandoned. There were several outbuildings behind it, and one was unlocked. That was where we were to store the kayak. They had guaranteed it would find its way back to Blue Heron Cottage.

Since we had not been here before, it was a moment of exploration. We found a path that led around to the front of the house. It must have once been something grand. Through the trees beyond we could see our car. We looked longingly at the house, just peeked, then turned and left it behind. Our curiosity must be satisfied later.

Though we had not capsized, we had wet feet from the trek dragging the kayak to shore. It was a relief to get into our car with heated seats. We drove down the road, not completely confident we knew the way. At the first intersection we turned onto a wider road. We met no traffic for miles but eventually came upon a familiar road.

Our first introduction to civilization was a lone gas station and restaurant. There were a few cars there for breakfast. Imagining the smells of scrapple and bacon made me dive into our emergency stash for Herr's crackers and bottled water. It wasn't what we craved, but stopping wasn't on our itinerary.

Finally, a road sign pointed us toward Denton, Maryland. Our many previous fireworks deliveries to a Denton storage unit enabled us to navigate from there. Having delivered fireworks to retailers over the years now felt like preparation for this task. This trip was the longest I could ever remember taking. The road signage requiring driving with headlights on seemed more reasonable and sensible than ever. *All we need is a close encounter with a deer.*

CHAPTER 18: THE FARM

I'd assumed our home in Cecil County was getting closer mile by mile till we turned onto Route 313 and took another unexpected left turn onto a familiar country lane. Patrick got out and entered the code on the gate across the driveway. I fleetingly wondered how he knew the code to my family's goose-hunting farm in Kent County. Patrick was not interested in hunting, so I assumed he had never been there. *But why ask? Could this be our debriefing location?*

The long, flat lane was like a narrow furrow between fields of crop stubble. The farmhouse resembled the one in the movie version of Truman Capote's grisly thriller *In Cold Blood.* I had thought this many years ago in my late teens, when I first drove down the lane. I could not shake the foreboding feeling as we approached. The house had fallen into greater disrepair than I had imagined. Years of emptiness had not enhanced its appearance. Neglect was written on it in heavy, erratic script.

Patrick seemed familiar with the place. When had he been introduced to "The Farm?" In all our years of marriage, we'd never visited it. He knew about it since we paid taxes on it each year, but it wasn't on the way to any destination we'd had. Visiting had been far down on the list.

Now we crept down a dirt and gravel path that had been a lane. We went to inspect the farmhouse more closely. By this time, it had dawned on me that my debriefing was definitely taking place there. I asked Patrick and he confirmed it. I kept my ears alert, awaiting an approaching vehicle.

We crossed the dirt yard to the sagging porch door and gingerly climbed the half dozen protesting paint-deprived wooden steps. The porch floor had worn in places with rotten boards, although there were a few solid patches. A swing hung lopsidedly from rusty chains, and for a moment I could see Scout and Atticus Finch from *To Kill a Mockingbird* looking out on their world and noting how we need to walk in others' shoes to understand them.

I turned around and took in the view from the porch: pond, neglected barn and other outbuildings, house trailer, woods, and that long lane. Meanwhile Patrick tried to unlock the front door. Inserting the key in the lock was easy. Getting it to turn was not. After he worked at it a few times it grudgingly cooperated.

Inside the dust triggered repeated sneezes. I had no real memory of the interior of the house. I knew I had previously been inside, but it had been well over forty years ago. For many years the house had been rented out, so during our trips there to cut standing pine for Christmas wreaths or to watch the Canada geese, we'd had no need to go inside.

The first room we stepped into was an entry hall wallpapered in faded stripes. In its center, uneven stairs drunkenly led to upper floors. Walking toward the back on the left, we passed the living room seeing only a tired, beaten-down couch angled by the gray-painted brick fireplace and dusty wide-board hardwood floor. On the opposite side was what had been a dining room. The only clue to its function was a precariously hanging ceiling light. "Chandelier" would have been too generous a description. The uneven plaster walls had been painted cream but were overlayed by shades of caramel. At the back we scraped open a protesting solid swinging door which led to the kitchen which was anything but empty.

Why I hadn't been given a heads-up, I still don't know.

If this had been a TV movie and I were a detective, or spy, or agent, I'd have reached for my weapon and shot everyone before they had a chance to identify themselves. Since it was reality, and I had none of those professions in my resume, I just stood there in shock, not a great reaction to a possible life-threatening situation.

Prepared or not, I faced my inquisitors. No, I was not a criminal, but sensed the three of them considered me untrustworthy, or had little faith in the value of my observations. I had put my life in danger, albeit unwittingly, so some respect was surely due me. My grilling team was comprised of those already familiar to me from the brief Virginia encounter just hours before. There was one point in their favor. I recognized them. They were the same man and women who had posed as Patrick and me driving away in our car and the woman who had posed as the repair person in the van. They were different now. They were verbal and a bit intimidating in their new role of questioning me.

Gradually they lightened up, spoke, even smiled. I relaxed a little. Some of my spine-tingling abated, but the tightness in the back of my neck persisted. My migraine symptoms returned. What a surprise. My debriefing team obviously had had time to arrive and set up. Since their vehicles had been nowhere in sight, I'd assumed a team was on its way…wrong again.

I looked around. The room had a few knotty pine cabinets, an old, stained porcelain sink, a cracked faded blue-and-gray-geometric-patterned linoleum floor (which really clashed with the knotty pine cupboards), and empty places where appliances had been. The walls, probably once a milky shade, had curdled to cream. The overhead light resembled ones I'd seen in houses years ago. If I pulled the lamp, it would readjust closer to the floor. Its coppery finish was not diminished to a green patina, but a cruddy, rusty brown. On second thought, the lamp might crash to the floor because the suspension cord was dry rotted.

Our hosts provided gray plastic folding chairs, a portable blue plastic table, and battery-operated lighting. At least there weren't candles or kerosene lamps. Their high-tech recording equipment made me uneasy. I was going to be "taped." What if I answered incorrectly? Were there "wrong" answers? My responses would be saved in some computer. What if my inaccurate information caused confusion or put someone in jeopardy? I was second guessing myself. Tension mounted again within me. Icy fingers resumed their movement up and down the back of my neck.

Despite their encouraging me to get up and walk around, I felt enormous pressure. They elicited from me every iota of information I could retrieve; more than I'd been aware I knew. I acknowledged they were good at their jobs, were accustomed to dealing with untrained observers and knew how to cross check my memory. I was impressed with them and my ability to produce so many details.

"Describe separately each person in the room with you."

"There were two teen-aged girls who seemed to be friends—they stayed close to each other. They dressed in low-end department store clothes, obviously trying to look in style. Both wore jeans and baby doll tops over multiple layers of other tops. One was tall, almost too skinny to be healthy, with light brown hair in a ponytail. The other had blond curls and seemed more average in weight next to her friend. She was the one who looked like a bumble bee in her yellow and black." I continued describing the others, visualizing them, struggling for accuracy.

"There were two young guys, maybe in their early twenties, possibly Hispanic, in jeans and hoodies. I saw grease stains on their hands. I guessed they were auto or bike mechanics. They knew each other. One was taken away by force not long before Patrick arrived.

"There was someone in bland khaki and olive clothes, who never turned around, just faced the wall. I can't say if it was a man or woman. The clothes were really wrinkled. I had the impression it was an older person. I'm trying to recall why I thought that." I paused, thinking back. "The gray hair just poked out of the knitted cap and kind of stuck out in matted clumps. The hand was wrinkly, rough, maybe chapped from being out in the weather." Other than Grace, there was only one person left to describe.

"The last fellow inmate is the one I spoke to. He was middle-aged, maybe fifty or so, and going bald. He wore University of Maryland Terps sweats and kept me from being attacked and subdued for looking behind the drapes. He warned me against it, then explained and showed what the dogs had done to him when he tried. His wounds were nasty, not even covered with a bandage or cleaned with antiseptic. He didn't seem educated—at least his grammar wasn't perfect. He also told me about the bathroom and how to get to use it. He said he'd been in the room since Saturday evening. He claimed there had been a dozen or so people in the room when he got there. Most of them had been sent out.

"The two guys and the person in the corner were the only ones left of those who arrived before him. He also told me there was no apparent order to when you were dealt with. Obviously, he thought that was true since he was still there. From what he said, I assumed the teens and Grace arrived after him. No one besides the one hoodie-and-jeans guy left while I was there. The Terps guy said that the last two guys to leave were dragged out.

He said they were beaten and tazed so badly they couldn't stand up. He also said one old woman tried to protest and they had hit her with their sticks and turned tasers on her and on anybody in the room who made a move to help her.

"They" documented my impressions of every person I'd encountered. They noted my descriptions of physical appearances and mannerisms. They prodded me for details of the building's layout, the order of events, any spoken word or gesture. I gave my impressions of the "merladies," the officers' "friends." I felt relieved Grace could corroborate my information, because as I described them and their behavior I thought if I were listening to this, I'd have doubts about the accuracy of my descriptions, much less my sanity.

It was then I remembered the scrawled message on the bathroom wall. Should I speculate and give them this information? Had it been there for months? Was it in any way connected to their mission? Part of me wanted to blurt out the information. Part of me wanted to keep just this to myself, at least for a while. I decided to divulge the message contents. I knew if I were a heroine in a novel, I'd have made a different decision.

"I can't say for sure that this is even connected, but when I was in the bathroom the first time, I read a message, just a name and phone number really. It was smudged and in pencil and could only be seen while sitting on the toilet."

One of my inquisitors, the taller of the two females, and seated directly across from me, looking fatigued and trying to suppress a yawn, said, "It's remotely possible. It could be connected. Tell us what you remember." I thought I detected a repressed sigh coming from the lone male of the team. He was probably no older than thirty but exuded a sense of self-satisfaction that I found disquieting. I turned my focus toward him sitting to my left and continued with my recollections.

"Okay, but you give me the impression you don't really value my information or see its importance."

"Not at all." This time it was the other, shorter woman to my right who seemed more neutral in her posture and tone. I swiveled in my seat to make eye contact with her and continued with my possibly unimportant, irrelevant information.

"The first name started with a "J". It was short, maybe four letters. The second letter was probably an 'a' or an 'o', possibly a 'u'. It ended with maybe an 'e' or 'i'. It looked like 'Jade' or 'Jake' or 'Jude' or maybe 'Judi' or 'Jodi'. The last name seemed to end in 'ing'. It was something like 'Fleming' or maybe 'Herring'. The lighting was bad. The phone was a Maryland number. I recognized the first three digits as the same as mine." I gave them the phone number. *There!* I had kept nothing back. All was recorded. Perhaps I wasn't as poor an observer as I'd thought. But then I'd never have considered the importance or implication of so many details. Did my impressions really match Grace's? If they already had this from Grace, a trained observer, why did they need mine?

How long was the debriefing going to continue? How many hours had we been doing this? The back of the house faced west and was bordered by forest just beyond the small back yard. Although there was a kind of makeshift burlap curtain over the window, the outside was semi-visible. The changing sky led me to believe that noon had probably come and gone.

Finally, there was a short food break. They served nothing hot, but at least the sandwiches and chips and sodas were a few steps up from our crackers and water breakfast. Had we paused for a late lunch break? Was it mid-afternoon? Even later?

CHAPTER 19: MY TURN

Eventually, I perceived they were ready for me to ask questions. I had forgotten this might happen. My being put on the spot so abruptly produced faltering questions.

"Are my recollections really useful?" I blurted this out of my frustration.

"Yes." The cryptic male acknowledged.

"Did anyone try to follow our car when you left this morning?"

"No." This time it was the taller woman in the chair facing me.

"Am I helping your goal?"

"We can't tell you at this time." She quickly inserted.

"What is your goal?"

"Sorry. Not for you to know." The snide male answered with his air of superiority. That answer came straight from a page in my father's 'book of rules to live by.' It eliminates a lot of explanations later. But being on the other side and the one 'not needing to know' but wanting to was irritating, downright frustrating! I wanted to be the judge of my being useful or not.

But without information, how could I even guess? *Not fair.*

They were dismissive about things from my perspective.

"Do I have future roles to play?" I asked. That could only be answered in the future as issues presented themselves.

"Are there any questions you had anticipated I might ask for which you could give me a concrete answer?"

They responded, "Probably not."

"Where do we go from here?"

"You go home."

How can I possibly do that after everything that has happened?

"I just go home? I just forget about all that has occurred?"

"Yes."

"How will I know if you have more questions, if you need me again?"

"Oh, you'll know." Talk about enigmatic.

"Don't I get a secret code name or a number? Isn't there a password I should commit to memory? Come on."

"No, and No, and No."

"Okay, how long have you been using our farm?"

"For quite some time now."

"What does that mean? Months? Years?"

"Months."

"How did you know the code or where the key was, or did you break in?"

"No, we did not break in. Your sibling provided the information."

"My sibling? Who else knows you're using the farm?"

"Obviously your brother, Christian." Suddenly, I had many more questions.

"That's not obvious to me. So, Christian's involved?"

"Yes."

"No way. This is not anything like him."

"Nevertheless, he is involved."

"How long has he been involved?"

"A while."

How accurate! I thought sarcastically. It reminded me of an eye care product commercial. The doctor asks a patient how long she's been using over-the-counter eye drops. She answers, "For a while now." How helpful is that? The doctor doesn't ask her for clarification. She just writes a prescription. I, however, wanted clarification.

"Longer than Patrick?"

"No."

"Because of Patrick?"

"You could say that, and the location is conveniently remote."

"Yes, and seldom used, but farmed, so some traffic in and out is not unreasonable. Is that what you mean?"

"That and deer and duck hunting seasons are no longer the very hectic times they were some years ago."

Christian, the youngest of my siblings, the only one with light brown curly hair, was the one who checked on things, supervised, or did repairs, so he had a *need to know*. I had wondered why we hadn't tried to rent out the farmhouse in recent years. So, the prohibitive cost for drilling a new well, and possibility of lead paint in the house were bogus excuses? I wondered if we were getting "rent" or compensation from UMCO. Doubtful. But not impossible.

Before I could question them further, we were interrupted by a message. One of their cell phones vibrated, then another. It didn't seem a casual interruption. Patrick and I exchanged glances, but his shrug told me he had no insights, or none he cared to share. What we heard from the kitchen side of the conversation was terse and unhelpful.

When they put away their phones, they suggested a break. Other developments required their attention. They left us alone. Nothing would take our minds off recent events. Pacing the perimeter of the room was boring. There were no extra food supplies, and no electronic diversions available. It was useless to conjecture about what they were doing.

"Patrick, do you think they've arrested some of the vigilantes? Is it too soon to go after them? Maybe they have picked up some of the other escapees. How will they keep them safe?"

"We probably won't know anything till it's on Baltimore news stations and everyone else knows about it. You can see they're as stingy as a three-year-old with a new toy when it comes to sharing."

We lapsed into a bored, agitated silence.

When they returned, it was probably less than twenty minutes later but felt like hours. To our surprise, they filled us in. One of the detainees had been found, given emergency medical attention, taken to a safe house for questioning and follow-up medical attention. They had an update on the individual's information and status. I wanted to know which person they had found.

"Who was it? Who did they get to safety?"

"We can't divulge names for security and safety reasons, but she was the person you didn't know the sex of, the one who barely moved while you were confined."

"Will she be okay?"

"We think so. Medical personnel are continuing to evaluate her and will recommend additional treatment if needed. Nourishment and safety are probably her main needs."

"How was she found?"

"When we swept the area from the air, we spotted her. She was moving awkwardly and seemed disoriented. We picked her up immediately but weren't positive she was from the detention cell. We questioned her briefly and waited for Grace's information. Your information affirmed what we had learned. Having three sources is always better than one, or even two.

Again, we can't divulge her name, nor disclose where she is. For security reasons, she has not been informed about you or Grace."

"Someday I want to meet her. We share a common bond, whether we ever spoke or not. In fact, I would like to meet all of them again, not just to know they made it out, but to know their stories. We were kind of like Chaucer's *Canterbury Tales* pilgrims, a group of strangers ending up together, but we didn't get to share our stories. I want time to know them from their stories. This could be the inspiration for my great American novel."

They were not interested or amused.

I'd already been forming a plot in my mind. Now I just needed to sharpen my writing skills. But that could wait.

Patrick interrupted my reverie. "Back to the present, and facts. Did you capture any of the fake police?"

"No. That's not our current intention. We want them to think they're free to conduct their operations. When we've built a solid case and clearly understand those operations, we'll move to shut them down. Patience is needed to eradicate the whole system."

"I realize that, but they have to suspect something with that sci-fi helicopter flying overhead," Patrick observed.

"They are not stupid. We put out a cover story for the helicopter and drones. You'll read all about it in the newspapers."

I couldn't resist, "Are you calling this some kind of Homeland security issue?"

"That about sums it up."

"Will you at least let us know how the woman progresses?"

"You might receive a post card from a friend visiting D.C."

"Thanks."

"If you recall anything additional, even if it seems a minute detail, or just an impression, we'd like to hear from you."

"And I contact you—how?"

"Patrick can send us a message." He nodded ever so slightly and once more I felt out of the loop.

And with that, we were dismissed.

CHAPTER 20: HOME

The hour-long drive home in the Wednesday twilight lasted forever and at the same time flew by. A few snow flurries half-heartedly drifted down, but nothing stuck to road surfaces. My thoughts were whirling all over the place. I felt elated and let down by the experience. I wanted to know how things would play out, to know the later chapters of the book. I was grudgingly glad I'd shared the phone number information. If I had kept it to myself, I would have been too much like some fool would-be heroine in a thriller making a fatal miscalculation. The information was with those who knew how to process it. I reluctantly resigned myself to the wisdom of that.

Once we were home, I settled on the couch in our living room and read the Tuesday and Wednesday issues of the *Baltimore Sun* online. The Annapolis incident coverage wasn't as big a deal as I'd expected. When you *are* the news, does it seem more earth-shaking than it really is? Was the matter deliberately played down? I tried to be happy about this instead of disappointed. Too much coverage could lead to increased interest, premature attention. That might drive the vigilantes underground or slow up their operations. I went online for WJZ, the Baltimore CBS station, and scanned their coverage. I checked the other networks but came away with little new information. I marveled how so little can be said in so many words when the intention is to be obscure.

The news sources all referred to an alleged person or persons of interest who had been reported in the Annapolis area. Police forces had detained several unidentified persons of interest for questioning. So far, no arrests had been made. It was unclear if all of those questioned had been released. Supposedly, rumors, hints from credible sources, claimed that some anti-Catholic group had planned to disrupt the lobby night with the Maryland state senators and delegates. The plot was foiled, but the instigators were being sought throughout Monday evening and all day Tuesday. The investigation was ongoing.

The mention of threatened harm on a certain group qualified as a possible hate crime and an attack on loyal citizens. Finally, Governor O'Malley issued a statement deploring hate crimes of any kind and praising Maryland State and Annapolis police forces for thwarting a possible serious crime. He maintained his support for bringing any perpetrators to justice. He reasoned that planning the crime was nearly as serious as committing it, since the individuals had not abandoned their plan on their own. That was oblique also.

"Were any people in custody?" the young blonde reporter asked.

I found little concrete truth in the coverage. How did reporters check facts? The government or some police agency issues a statement, therefore the public believes the story because the press reports? I felt uneasy about what was left out. I hoped that eventually more of the truth could be revealed and actual hate crimes being committed would be exposed along with the identities of those who put themselves above the law while pretending to enforce it. What a twisted path they traveled.

For days I looked over my shoulder as I drove around completing errands in Cecil County and nearby New Castle County, Delaware. Household needs seemed so mundane. On Thursday I went grocery shopping at Elkton Acme. I remembered Patrick's McCormick peppercorn medley and a tin of Old Bay for a new crab recipe. There was more than a hint of snow in the long-range forecast, so checkout lines were exceptionally long. But the lady behind me who suggested she give me her cart if I needed more room for my bagged items, and even offered to empty the light-weight items from my cart, was especially kind. Why did I suspect her of being devious? I said 'thank you, but, no' to the offer of the cart. and fished coupons from my pocket, my debit card from my credit card case, and my canvas totes from under my groceries.

On Friday morning the bright blue sky promised an exceptionally beautiful day. By eleven o'clock Patrick and I both knew how we'd spend the afternoon. We packed a picnic lunch and headed for the North East Town Park. Leaving our lunch in the car, we began walking the track that circled the park.

It was brisk, but sunny. A fairly strong wind blew off the Northeast River, but the glint of sun on the waves was invigorating. It was a respite from winter, a teasing that spring would follow. We entered the walking track passing the Upper Bay Decoy Museum. It had been many years since I had been inside. We passed the first single picnic table pavilion and smiled at one another. Our first walk in the park together was the day Patrick proposed. There on that unassuming wooden bench connected to that unremarkable picnic table, under that slanted wooden roof, I had agreed to a new life.

We looked out over the North East Creek as we walked along. Patrick reminded me we weren't in a race. Translated, it meant I should remember my tendency to walk fast needed to be tempered to his slower pace, if this was to be a couple's thing. We nodded to an older man very slowly walking his collie in the opposite direction. We checked for the blue heron we've often spied along the shore of the peninsula jutting out from the north across the creek. The usual population of Canada geese and mallards were out in force, swimming and waddling around on the banks and sparse winter grassy areas. The park belonged to them too.

We passed our favorite photographic spot, an ancient, gnarled tree. Facing the crook in the tree with the river beyond often produced choice photographic opportunities. I loved framing photos looking through a "frame" provided by nature. Working around the tree from different angles had led me to discover the hole in the tree. My first thought had been of Boo Radley in *To Kill a Mockingbird*, though I'd never seen a hint of the kinds of treasures he had left for Jem and Scout. Only dried seaweed seemed to collect in this hole. We veered off the track momentarily to inspect the beach along the canoe and kayak launch area. Involuntarily I shuddered remembering our recent kayak trip.

As we approached the parking lot we saw a town police car. Out stepped a tall dark-haired officer donning his patrol hat, our good friend and my former student, Officer Tom Daniels. We called out our hellos. He paused and squinted in the bright light to see who had spoken, then he sauntered over.

"So, you are the only nature photographers out here today."

"Yes. You never know when something you've seen hundreds of times will appear interesting because of a change of light or the way branches bend differently. One day years ago I took several photos of a swan just offshore here. We ended up using it for the Water Festival Booklet cover the following summer," I said.

"The North East Water Festival…now that was a few years

ago. I remember that swan photo but didn't realize you'd taken it. So, you have a skill other than teaching English. You could have given me photography lessons when I was your student. I just noticed you down near the point. What inspired you today?"

"Just that old tree with the hole in it. It's begging for a secret message between lovers to be hidden there. You know, like 'meet me at the stroke of midnight the night of the next full moon down at the end of the pier,' something romantic like that. Maybe next time I'll stage a shot with an open envelope complete with a sheet of stationery sticking out of it. In case there's no breeze coming off the river, I might even bring a battery-operated fan to make it seem like it's blowing in the wind," I laughed.

"When I see a lot of equipment set up down there, I'll know what's happening," Tom joked as he walked on toward his car.

We resumed our walk moving on toward the children's playground where kids were climbing, swinging, and sliding. Their adults were nearby on benches or at the bottom of the equipment. One mother, in the process of gathering up her daughter, called out to me as we passed by. I recognized her as another former student and introduced her to Patrick. She introduced us to her daughter as 'Mommy's old teacher and her husband.' After a few moments' conversation, we continued our walk. Patrick insisted on repeating that I was an old teacher. We passed the bathrooms and began our second lap.

During the third lap Patrick spotted Kathryn, our locally famous Blue Heron. We took turns with the binoculars, searching for other wild fowl. A lone white swan swam along the creek toward town. The only other thing of interest was the old man with the collie, who also had binoculars, but seemed to be watching us. Casually turning, I mentioned this to Patrick. We pointedly ignored the man pretending not to notice him observing us.

After our next lap we retrieved our lunch, making our way to our picnic table. Here we could observe without seeming to do so. We ate and watched the others in the park. The old man and the collie had retired to the main picnic pavilion beyond the playground. The couple with the stroller had stopped walking to let their children play on the equipment. Another man with a pronounced limp walked the track. He was overtaken and passed closely by two young bicyclists. His jerky reaction and outburst were out of proportion to the near collision. That riveted our attention to him. Patrick was quick to observe that the man lost his limp after the near encounter.

It seemed that the man had briefly forgotten his physical impediment. We watched as he continued to talk, and realized he was wearing a headset, partially concealed by his scarf and hat. Then miraculously, he regained his limp. He looked around to see if anyone had noticed. We stared directly at him. I wanted to wave but resisted the urge. Whether he was someone faking an injury for insurance purposes or keeping tabs on us wasn't clear until he abruptly spoke into his earpiece and limped away and simultaneously the man with the collie stood up and resumed walking.

I wished then we'd brought our dog Maggie. She could have encountered the collie, providing an excellent opportunity to see the man up close. It had started out as a perfect preview of a spring day. Now all we wanted was to be done with suspicious encounters. We hastily finished our food and retraced our steps to the car, not bothering to complete a final lap.

There were several vehicles in the parking lot. I surreptitiously photographed each license plate before getting in our car. Later we contacted Tom Daniels to request he check who owned them.

Saturday and Sunday arrived and departed. No word from UMCO. No new newspaper coverage. No suspicious vehicles following us.

We now possessed a list of names and addresses provided by Tom, who urged us to be careful and cautious if we thought someone was targeting us. We'd only told him about the men in the park and intimated they had made us uneasy. He had descriptions of both men and was working to match them to the cars, but we all knew that drivers don't always use vehicles registered to them.

CHAPTER 21: NORMAL LIFE

February arrived quietly. My Monday dentist appointment was in North East. The drive was uneventful, but I constantly checked the rear-view mirror and glanced back and forth at roadside residences. No one suspicious followed me. I had a routine cleaning. But, by the time I left the dentist's office and headed back toward Elkton, snow was falling, just light, fluffy stuff. Again, I scanned all areas around and behind me. There was a quickly traveling dark blue Camaro that swerved wildly around me into the oncoming lane occupied by three teens showing off their driving skill in winter weather. Idly, I wondered from which ditch a tow truck would extract them.

Next, was a trip to the vet. Getting the three cats, my old orange tabby Wilbur, Patrick's calico Susie, and our gray shaggy long-haired WC (Warehouse Cat) into the car was challenging, but once each was in its travel case, things were okay. Wilbur burrowed into the thick, green towel in his case, while Susie rearranged her giraffe towel. WC paced pointedly ignoring his Sponge Bob towel.

I drove back toward North East. As I passed the Spoken

Word Assembly Church I slowed down to avoid a familiar tow truck helping the teens I had seen earlier from a roadside tree collision. I shook my head and waved to our friend Sean and an employee, a youngish Hispanic guy I did not recognize, in his Chesapeake Service truck.

I traveled on Cemetery Road then headed out of town on Turkey Point Road to the vet. The snow had picked up in intensity but that wasn't what concerned me. I noticed an approaching gray car with one functioning headlight and damaged front fender suddenly nearing my rear bumper. I stared curiously to see if the driver was familiar but couldn't see well enough to determine if he was the collie-dog owner. I did see there was a dog bouncing around in the front seat. I was relieved when he drove past me as I turned into the vet's parking lot. It took three trips in and three out to accomplish the vet visits. Fortunately, for once, there was no dramatic behavior displayed by our felines.

I tuned in to WXCY on the radio for a weather update. The prediction was now amended to ten to twelve inches contradicting the earlier forecast which had been dismissive of any accumulation. We hadn't seen that much snow in a decade.

Driving home was more challenging weatherwise. Traffic was almost nonexistent, something I appreciated. As I approached North East town limits, I knew better than to turn onto winding Cemetery Road. Mauldin Avenue, the direct route through town, was blanketed, but not slippery. The county trucks had recently treated the area. Lugging the three cats to the house was still a chore.

It was another two days before the roads were clear enough to run out for incidentals. I consistently checked out the sparse traffic passing our house but saw nothing suspicious.

Early Wednesday morning, armed with various items, I headed to Home Depot in nearby Glasgow, Delaware to pick new paint colors for our bedroom. Even in that large store with so many staff members and customers moving about, I felt uncomfortable, suspicious of others. I found myself reading sinister intentions in the most innocent comments or glances. One man stooped to tie his shoe and looked around. I swore his penetrating eyes zeroed in on me. I was borderline paranoid. I left with several unpromising paint samples, an outlet cover for the living room, and a heavy-duty flashlight to replace the one I'd misplaced in our attic. I felt less guilty about wasting time, but technically, my mission was unaccomplished.

Enroute to Elkton I suspiciously regarded vehicles I concluded were driving erratically, too slowly, too fast—just about every car, truck or van I encountered. I was spooked, wasn't I?

Back at home I continued to scan the news for updates on the Annapolis incident but saw nothing. National and world news services focused on a female suicide bomber who had killed forty-one people in Baghdad and injured over one hundred others. Even I found myself focused less on the Annapolis victims and our possibly being under surveillance. It wasn't until Saturday afternoon when I went to switch our canvas folding chairs from Patrick's car trunk to mine in preparation for our granddaughter Maglie's indoor soccer game, that I discovered the jacket in the trunk.

CHAPTER 22: DISCOVERY

There it was. I felt an involuntary shudder pass through me. I had stowed it there when we had parked in the garage at Blue Heron Cottage. How had I forgotten it? It might mean something. Perhaps there was valuable information in the pockets?

I felt like a criminal whisking the jacket into the house. Even though I had quickly tucked it into a shopping tote, I felt conspicuous. In the dead of winter there aren't any neighbors abroad, but I had to check my impulse to look over my shoulder to see if anyone was passing on foot at the end of our lane. Often trying to act casually leads to acting suspiciously. I know I looked like someone hauling in stolen goods, but I had to get the jacket to a secure location. I was ultra-conscious of our neighbor Boyd's penchant for being at his computer at the window facing our drive. Was he there now?

Once in the house, I had no idea where to store the jacket. Maybe the car trunk had been a great place. Patrick was working a funeral and wouldn't be home for hours. His cell phone would be turned off. I had no way to contact UMCO personnel. I had nothing to tell them anyway.

I had time to search the jacket myself. This tan jacket with all these pockets must hold something of interest.

I locked the living room, flower room and bedroom doors cutting off access from outside. I went to the library and drew the drapes. I was sure no one could see in. After turning on the floor lamps, flooding the room with light, I settled on the loveseat to examine the jacket. Should I wear gloves for this? It sounded ridiculous to think that. But maybe I should, especially since I had handled it twice already. I grabbed a pair from under the kitchen sink and got on with my search. I found lots of lint. I reasoned I should be exact about my findings, so I returned to the kitchen for sandwich, quart, and gallon storage bags; while there I grabbed pen, pencil, paper and scotch tape from the cubby holes in the miniature secretary desk crafted by my grandfather. I'd label each bag by pocket and record the contents. I felt professional…and ridiculous.

From the label size information, it seemed to be a man's jacket. The tan was very stained, several shades darker than when new, judging by the color just under the collar and inside the front opening. The four flap pockets on the front with brass buttons were Velcroed shut. The upper two were slightly smaller than the bottom two. On the left sleeve was a zip pocket extending down the arm. Inside the jacket was a fleece lining and a slit opening to a deep pocket. No wonder men didn't need purses. There were enough pockets here to carry everything one might need.

Two bulging pockets obviously held items. I checked them first. The drab off-white knitted gloves with tan leather palms had become unsewn in places and seemed small for the jacket wearer. I found a lady's size medium tag on them. Both were in the same bottom left pocket. Who puts both gloves in one pocket? Did this mean the wearer was a woman and maybe left-handed? I halted that line of reasoning.

I'm left-handed and I put each glove where it can be pulled out by the hand that wears it. I know we left-handed people are different, but why both gloves in one pocket? I held the gloves to my face. It was more impulse than anything else. I felt ridiculously like Patrick Jane, the main character in the TV series *The Mentalist*, or Sherlock Homes trying to divine every scrap of information.

What I experienced was an unexpected fragrance as I breathed in. Spicy, warm. Familiar, but elusive. I set the gloves on the coffee table, and I examined the rest of the pocket's contents. Besides the gloves was a crumpled K Mart receipt for a diet Pepsi, M&M's, gum, and a prescription. It was dated exactly one week before I arrived in the cell. That would make it a Monday. The receipt told the time of day, cashier's name, store address, phone number, and that items were paid for in cash. I could follow up on this information. More perplexing was insurance co-pay data. The jacket didn't belong to a vagrant. This person had health insurance.

Inside the upper right pocket were a peanut butter M&M wrapper and an opened pack of Trident sugar-free Apple and Golden Pineapple gum. Of the 14 sticks noted on the package, there were three left. I unwrapped one finding a yellow gum with a green center with a tangy, sour/sweet smell. I've never liked gum. I get rid of it as soon as the taste fades, but this gum was appealing. No, I couldn't chew the evidence. I rewrapped the stick and slid it back in the pack. The last item in the pocket was a diet Pepsi bottle cap. Conflicted person. Junk food, sugary candy and diet soda. I could identify with that, but I'd have had caffeine-free diet Pepsi, and white chocolate candy. Before going to the third pocket, I catalogued the items found in this one, bagged them, and returned them to the pocket. I felt almost professional.

The right-side bottom pocket contained only multicolored lint, a few generic paper clips and several loose staples. Perhaps the bottom pocket had held the purchases before they were consumed? Dutifully I listed the un-useful items, put them in a sandwich bag, and returned them to their pocket.

The upper left pocket was empty. One more indication the person was left-handed? Maybe.

The sleeve pocket was zipped shut and took a little persuasion to work open. Once I felt inside, I wasn't sure what I had grasped. The light of day revealed several orange Swedish fish congealed into a mass. They were no longer pliant, yet still somehow sticky. I removed a fair amount of lint from them. If they had been saved for later, later had come and gone. I probed deeper to ensure nothing was left in the bottom of the pocket. I came out with a wad of tissue. It didn't appear to have been used, but was balled tightly, yet not entirely soft.

Inside I found one earring. Since it was a zip pocket, I could see why one would store an earring in it instead of the Velcro fastened others. The earring post was minus the back piece. That might explain why it wasn't on the person's ear. But wouldn't you take off both earrings if one came apart? I guess you might if you had only one piercing in each ear. My daughters and granddaughters each had multiples. I went through the ear-piercing process once. That was enough. I still remember being goaded into it. When your child wants to get her grandmother's ears pierced as a Mother's Day gift, how can Mom say "no"? But suddenly Mom was the first one to get her ears pierced. The next time, on a weekend Ocean City beach trip with a much-loved colleague, when she invited me to join her in getting a second piercing, I politely declined. I found resisting a friend's request easier than disappointing a ten-year-old daughter.

This earring looked and felt like good jewelry. Once I found the 14k marking I knew it was gold. It also had letters stamped on it. I couldn't read them, so I rummaged in my sewing basket for my grandmother's old magnifying glass. It was buried and tangled in several strands of unwound thread. Using it, I could better decipher the letters. They appeared to be JFM. Of course, the knowledge meant nothing. The earring jacket was a flat, almost square piece with crimped edges. The detachable post held a trinity of blue sapphires. I grabbed a twelve-inch ruler from one of my craft bins. The whole earring measured about ¾ of an inch across. I noted the information, bagged, and returned the items.

The inside-lining pocket I checked last. It held nothing but a laminated fishing license from years past, so faded it was indecipherable. Was the jacket a thrift store purchase? Did the license belong to a previous owner? Did it belong to the female I had surmised was wearing it last? Women do fish. Both males and females fish from the bank of North East Town Park; granted men outnumber the women, but there are women out there fishing.

My dad's rule for me and my siblings had been, "If you fish, you bait your own hook." Worm, minnow, whatever. I mentally added this conflicting piece of information to the puzzle of who had been wearing the jacket. Like an oddly shaped jigsaw puzzle piece, I couldn't quite twist this to fit in the picture I had formed. Maybe later, it would make sense. I bagged the license.

I wrote down my findings and conclusions. I considered transferring them to my computer but hesitated. For now, a hand-written list sufficed. My conclusions were just my own: the person was female; it was vaguely possible she was left-handed; she had small hands, and maybe multiple piercings in her ears. She had good taste in jewelry and cared about not losing the item. The condition of her gloves led me to surmise they weren't her best pair, or maybe her hands weren't a priority, or that was all she had and couldn't afford to replace them. The jacket was no fashion statement. It could be the jewelry was from a long time ago, in better financial days. Or, it could have been found. Not stolen. No, not the way it was tucked away in the pocket. It meant something to her.

I examined the jacket for more hints about the owner. What I discovered was the identity of her scent. It was the familiar spicy, vanilla odor of Bath and Body Works Vanilla Noir shower gel. Well, this was a confirmation of sorts. This person had access to bathing facilities. How this furthered my investigation, I didn't know. Investigation? Was I thinking I was investigating something? Embarrassed, I shoved that idea aside.

I concluded that if I ever did do investigations, I would have all materials assembled beforehand. For now, I returned ruler and magnifying glass to the craft room, bags to their kitchen drawer, pen to its home in the crock atop the desk, and paper and tape to their pigeonholes inside it. I tossed the gloves in the trash can.

Now, I was faced with the dilemma of where to hide the jacket. I walked around the house. There was my cedar hope chest behind the living room sofa, with our collection of Irish literature and memorabilia arranged on top. There was the heart-shaped wicker hamper where I stored future birthday gifts. There was the linen closet where anything could disappear among sheets, quilts, and towels, and the library coat closet containing my blazers, winter coats, Patrick's outerwear back to his karate days, and even a high school jacket. Why not take Edgar Allan Poe's advice, and hide it in plain sight? I camouflaged it with the other garments and chose a woolen scarf to wind around the collar of the jacket.

It was then I discovered the other pocket.

CHAPTER 23: IN PLAIN SIGHT

On the underside of the collar was a zipper which concealed a small space. I brought the jacket back out. The pocket held the stub of a pencil and a twice-folded lime green sticky note. Excitedly, I unfolded the paper. I no longer had on gloves. That was probably a mistake. My fingers shook. The paper was blank. Frustration! I wanted to ball it up and toss it out. But, I walked back to the kitchen, got out another sandwich bag, and filled it.

When I tried to stuff the bag back in the secret pocket, my fingers felt something else. In my excitement and disappointment at finding the sticky note, I had not continued to probe the pocket. I discovered a velvety maroon pouch.

Inside was a silver and gold, badly tarnished locket. Why was it concealed? The round locket had scroll designs and letters in the center. The script was ornate, but there appeared to be an "I" or "J" on the left. The middle letter, larger than the others, was an "F" or "T", followed by a "B" on the right. Now my hands really shook. This jacket just HAD to belong to the bathroom scribbler. No message on the paper could have been more reassuring. Like many monograms, the initial representing the last name would be etched in the center and would be larger than the other initials.

Using my fingers, I attempted to pry open the locket but couldn't. I went back to the bathroom for my green diamond-patterned needlepoint box that held tweezers, nail clippers, and a variety of manicure and pointy-edged scissors. Something in the menagerie had to work. I was conscious of not destroying the locket, so I put off my usual bullheaded 'I will get this open right now' attitude and considered carefully which implement to use. I settled on a miniature pair of pointy scissors and succeeded in getting them into the locket seam. I gently worked them back and forth. Nothing happened. I tried twisting them ever so slightly. This threatened to bend the metal of the locket. I removed the scissors and studied my arsenal of tools. There was the dental pick I had bartered for, eventually trading fireworks to my dentist for it. It had worked wonders for between teeth till the novelty wore off. It was my next choice. It worked so easily; I made a mental note to sterilize it before putting it back in my mouth.

In the left side pocket of the locket was nestled a black and white wedding photo of a smiling young couple. The bride wore a modest, yet attractive gown. It reminded me of the style of the gowns in my parents' wedding photos which would date the picture to the late forties or early fifties. A colored photo of a single female in a high school or college graduation pose faced them from the right. The resemblance between the women was remarkable: they both had the same wavy, curly hair, though the older woman in the black and white photo had hers cut shorter. The rich auburn hair of the young woman could be imagined on the other female. Both had the same round face and penetrating eyes. They were related. Mother and daughter? Grandmother and granddaughter? I knew they were related and were important to one another.

My wall scribbler had a family who cared for her. I had to find out what had happened to her. I needed to know if she was all right. Did she make it back home? Was she still missing? How had she been caught up in that despicable net cast for undesirables? I sat at the library table turning the locket over and over. I didn't want to let go of it. I wanted to clean it up, polish it, but I felt I didn't have the right to do that. Its tarnish had been earned. I got out the magnifying glass again to see if there were any marks or details that might be clearer under the lens. After bright light and studious examination, I concluded the last name began with "F." That was good. There were fewer last names beginning with "F" than "T."

On inspiration, I carefully worked the black and white photo from its slot. On the back, in faded script, was: "Barbette and Michael, married May 15, 1963. My estimate was about a decade off. On the other was "Joy, graduation, Niagara U., 2008." I couldn't wait to search for my missing person. I had so many pieces of the puzzle. I felt a strong sense of connection with her. We had never met, but I knew we would. I only hoped I would not meet her in a prison cell or even worse, a cemetery.

Returning to reality, I was disconcerted to see how much time had passed. I reverently placed the locket back in its pouch, then in a sandwich bag, and nudged it into the pocket. Once again, I hung the jacket with its precious contents in the library closet. I checked my jeans pocket for my cell phone. It wasn't there. Where had I left it? I hadn't made any calls today.

I searched the usual spots- my side of the navy leather double recliner in the living room, the loveseat in the library, and my giraffe-patterned pocketbook Patrick called a suitcase. It wasn't in the usual places. I ran out to the car. Then I ran back in the house for keys to unlock the car. It wasn't there. Finally, I gave up, picked up the land line, and called my cell phone. Back on my dresser, from under a pile of folded laundry, came a muffled ring. I quickly checked for messages. There was one from hours ago, while I was out running errands.

After the funeral Patrick had to drive to the Medical Examiner's office in Baltimore for work. He wouldn't be home for the start of Maglie's game, so I should leave without him. I should also carry my phone with me. When was I going to learn this lesson? Today? I would try to keep it with me. Starting now, I must consciously put it within reach.

Almost simultaneously with that thought, my phone buzzed. Maglie was calling, her regular habit, to remind me when and where her game would be played. I checked my watch and realized in only an hour-and-a-half I needed to leave. I promised her I'd be there before the game began and put my phone in my pocket.

Searching for my mystery woman must wait. Surely, in fiction, people didn't just put this stuff on hold. It was important. But I reminded myself I wasn't an investigator or really connected to UMCO. Yet I was officially a grandmother. I grabbed my bulky hunter green winter jacket and wrapped my most recently knitted scarf comfortably around my neck and collected my purse from its resting place on the kitchen chair. I scooped up Patrick's two suits and a pair of charcoal dress pants I'd promised to drop off at the dry cleaners. I said a quick prayer the store was open. Instead of heading west I'd first detour a mile to the east. I pulled out my hunter green knitted gloves and started out the front door but turned around before my fingers turned the lock on the doorknob.

In the instant I looked down at my green gloves, I re-interpreted my idea of hiding the tan jacket in plain sight. I went back to the library closet, took off my scarf and jacket, retrieved the hidden jacket and scarf and put it on, then hung up my own jacket and scarf. The fit wasn't perfect, but the jacket was not too small. The scarf I had wrapped around it would suffice. This was the ultimate in-your-face deception. I was smugly proud of my inspiration. I would know exactly where the jacket was at all times and be able to keep my eyes on it.

CHAPTER 24: CLOSE ENCOUNTER

I got into the car and soon pulled into the Hung Dry Cleaners parking lot. I noted the neon "OPEN" sign. My brief conversation with the Korean seamstress led her to offer me a quick repair solution for the trousers while I waited. There was enough time.

I found myself conscious of other customers while I awaited the zipper repair. As I filed the receipt in my wallet, a slender man with graying streaks in his sunburn-colored hair entered. He seemed pleasant at first, so I paid him little attention. Then he balked at the price the clerk quoted for cleaning his coat. It was the same price displayed in red block letters on the sign suspended from the ceiling. He rudely scooped up his coat as the lady reached for it. He turned around mumbling something about foreigners ripping off decent hard-working people. He stomped out the door which, fortunately, opened and closed automatically. I could tell he was disappointed he had been robbed of the satisfaction of slamming the door. He got in a dusty red Chevy pickup with Maryland farm tags and threw gravel as he whipped out of his parking place, but got nowhere because traffic was backed up beyond the parking lot. I felt bad for the clerk and was unsettled myself.

My hackles were up. Had he wanted the coat cleaned, or was he checking on me? He hadn't been wearing any outerwear. Had he just removed the coat as a pretext or decided on a whim to get his coat cleaned? I was wearing *the jacket.* Had he looked closely at me? I squinted to read the Maryland farm tag on the back of his truck, still stuck in standstill traffic. I reached into my purse for my red mini notebook. Without removing it from my purse, I manage to grasp a pen and scribble the tag number as he squeezed into moving traffic. What had he told the clerk his name was? It was a common local name. Hamilton? Hammer? I recorded that. My neck was tight with paranoia. Before I could continue to brood, the seamstress handed me the repaired pants. I paid the small fee and left.

During the brief drive to the game, I made mental notes about follow-up avenues to pursue with my new information. I repeatedly checked my rearview mirror for the pickup or another suspicious vehicle. Would I recognize one if it passed slowly by me? The traffic on Route 40 was light on the way to the sports complex. Arriving a little early, I pulled out another of my mini notebooks. One was in the car console, the red one in my purse, one at my bedside table, and another in the kitchen secretary desk. I always tried hard to capture stray thoughts before they passed from my consciousness. I knew how fleeting my memory could be.

I jotted down ideas I wanted to pursue. I needed to review the names on the list of license plates owners. Would there be a match to the name the man had given at the dry cleaners? Maybe check the jeweler, the photographer of one of the photos, the K Mart surveillance tapes- as if I had authority to request them. I'd watched too many NCIS marathons. I closed the notebook, put it in my jeans pocket, and set the "case" aside. I gathered two chairs from the trunk, shoved my giraffe purse into my snack tote, and joined familiar faces walking across the parking lot. There were other grandparents I knew, and former students whose children were my grandkids' ages. It was satisfying seeing them become the adults I worried they'd never be. Not that all of them were models of success, but many of them tried.

Upon entering the arena, I became Grandmother Fan. Years ago, our older daughter Evie, Rose's sister, had spent her sophomore, junior, and senior years doing stats for the North East High varsity soccer team. As her mother and a teacher at the school, I had attended all home games, but I had had only limited experience with indoor soccer when her boyfriend had played in a winter league at Cecil Community College. Now her daughter, Maglie, was a sports fanatic. In spring and summer, she played softball, in the fall, volleyball, and now, she had joined an indoor soccer team.

I sat with my family and caught up on gossip. My daughter Evie, short for Eve-Lyn, named for her great, great aunt, on whose birthday she was born, raised her eyebrows giving her patented, quizzical look as she appraised my outer apparel. With her wavy dark brown hair and dark brown eyes, she was a flashback image of me at her age. I asked if she wasn't impressed with my Goodwill find. She shook her head as only a daughter can when faced with familiar quirks of an otherwise sane mother. I whispered I'd explain later but knew it wouldn't be soon.

I heard the latest teenage drama tales from her, the mother of the teen. We shared snacks and family news while her husband Gerry moved off to set up the video camera to capture the action. By game time, we'd shared our news, including Patrick's being detained by his trip to Baltimore. We speculated about the identity of the body he had to pick up. We knew most of the people in the North East community. In ways it remained the small town of my childhood. It was comforting when others knew you by name. At this thought, I felt a moment's pain for the jacket's owner. Was she missed as much as my daughters might be?

Then the action on the floor diverted our attention. Soccer.

Tonight, I cringed as Maglie dove to keep the ball out of the goal area, barely escaping full-body contact with an opposing team member. I felt her frustration as a side movement almost failed to keep the ball from scoring a goal. As ever, she wore her intensity on her facial features and showed it through her body language. I'm usually mild-mannered but metamorphose into a loud cheering fan at my three grandchildren's events.

During the second half of the game, Patrick arrived and informed us snow was falling again. The updated forecast was for several more inches. He helped himself to Evie's offered snacks and mine. We closely followed the play on the floor. I was so absorbed that I didn't think to inform him of my discovery. The fast pace kept us focused. The occasional roughness caught us up in the moment. Our girls were ahead by a goal. Victory was made sweet by Maglie's thwarting a tying score attempt in the last thirty seconds.

We said our good-byes to Evie and Gerry and waited till after the obligatory team meeting to congratulate our girls. Maglie was radiant. Victory is such a spirit-lifter. As we emerged from the complex, we were greeted by a gentle snowfall. Patrick walked me to my car, carrying our chairs, and suggested we meet at Pier 1 for a late dinner. He had read my mind.

The ten minutes to the restaurant would have sped by, if only I hadn't remembered my jacket discovery. How could I share the news with him in a public place? How could I keep it to myself?

We sat at our favorite table for two in the stained-glass window niche, and since the prime rib special was still available, we ordered it. Cathy served Patrick his coffee and me tea in my personal tea pot, an embarrassment to our younger daughter Rose, named for Patrick's mom.

Our conversation focused on the soccer game and the weather. Cathy delivered my steaming cup of crab bisque, of local legendary reputation, and Patrick's cup of pasta fagiolo, a house specialty. Then came the main course. What a meal! I needed a small take-home container.

By the time we paid our bill and were back in our vehicles, it was nearly ten pm. And seriously snowing. The usual eight-minute drive home included a strong wind kicking up and blowing snow horizontally extending it to a fifteen-minute trek. It was comforting seeing our outside lights glowing. I was glad I had turned them on.

As I opened the car door and stepped onto the slippery surface, I knew I had to reveal my secret findings to Patrick as soon as we set foot in our home.

CHAPTER 25: SHOW AND TELL

As soon as we settled in the living room I began.

"Patrick, there's something I've got to tell you…"

"What did you drop and break this time?" My husband winked and I knew he was joking. But this was serious.

"Oh, nothing. That's not it."

"Okay? You over-used a credit card?"

"No. I couldn't decide on paint colors for our bedroom, or I might have been tempted to spend a lot on paint."

"Last guess- you used your debit card and didn't record the transaction."

"No, you always find that out before I do. No. This has to do with this jacket I'm wearing."

"It looks like something Evie found at a thrift store and thought you'd wear it walking Maggie in the park when nobody is around."

"Close."

"Close?"

"Well, not really. Remember when I ran back into the prison room and grabbed that last jacket?"

"That's it?"

"I found it in the trunk today when I got out our sports chairs."

"So, you had to wear it?"

"I figured evidence should be kept safe. Hiding it in plain sight is better than putting it in a secret place that might be discovered. Besides, I'm liable to forget where I hid it."

"Agreed. But, what's so valuable about this jacket?"

"Well, there's the K Mart receipt, and the earring, and the necklace, and perhaps the fact that both gloves were stored in the same pocket, and the pencil, and the faded-out fishing license."

"Pick something and explain."

By now we were in the living room, where I had laid the jacket between us on the couch. I glanced up at our drawn curtains for reassurance. Patrick caught my glance and frowned.

"All right. The K Mart receipt has date, time, and store location on it. It also shows she bought a prescription and has insurance. There may be surveillance tapes."

"She? Aren't you jumping to conclusions? Even though there is jewelry, it doesn't mean the person holding it was a woman. And there is a fishing license that, odds are, belongs to a male."

"It's a man's jacket, but the gloves are a lady's medium." I produced the bagged gloves, raising an eyebrow at his comment.

"Okay." Patrick laughed at my bagging the evidence.

"I put everything back where I found it. Isn't that important?"

"Probably," he conceded. "Continue."

"The earring is gold, maybe hand-made, a one-of-a-kind piece from a jeweler, not a chain store. The locket is engraved. There are photos in the locket- an old black and white wedding shot, and a college graduation photo. The two women really resemble each other- the bride and college grad. The dates for both are written on the backs. The locket was hidden in a collar/zip pocket. I almost didn't find it. And it was in a jewelry pouch."

"Does the pouch have a name stamped on it like Dianne has on her Goldworker pouches?"

I paused. In my excitement to open it, I couldn't even recall if the pouch was black like our St. Croix friend Dianne used for her creations, or some other color. I reached in and removed the baggie. The maroon pouch showed through the plastic. Tarnished gold lettering peeked out. I opened the bag with trembling fingers. We stared at the faded, but decipherable name—Cameron's Fine Jewelry. How had I missed that information?

More clues! More information!

I was nearly giddy. "Patrick, certainly, we can Google this place and get all the information we need from the people at the store."

"Norah, they won't agree to talk to a stranger over the phone. And this information should be passed along channels to UMCO."

"But I need to know she's all right. I must meet her. Look at her face." I cried as I pulled open the pouch and let it drop on the jacket. Patrick reached for it but couldn't open it.

"Hold on. I'll get it." I ran to get my tools of the trade. When I returned with my needlepoint manicure case, I saw his eyes roll. Amusement? Tolerance? I opened the locket and presented it for inspection. Then he rewarded me with a look showing I had impressed him.

"Even if you have this need to know her, I'm still not sure we should pursue this on our own." Ominous words. Words I did not want to hear. Words to which I wanted to be deaf. Some force within me was stronger than reason, than simple logic. I desperately wanted to follow my inner urgings. We had come to that moment I had dreaded and hoped would be postponed forever. Grasping at intangible straws, I tried another angle.

"She wasn't one of the people in the room with me. This was the *extra* jacket. She was there *before*. She wrote the bathroom message. We have a phone number for her. I gave it to the team, but I still remember it. They haven't reported anything back." My pleading look earned a sigh from Patrick.

"We don't have to do anything this late at night. It isn't information that needs to be rushed to anyone."

I let out my breath. As usual, I hadn't realized I was holding it till I resumed breathing. I took out the earring and shared my suppositions with my husband. He nodded thoughtfully. He gradually warmed to this investigation. I showed him the receipt and explained I wanted to check out the K Mart and now the jewelry store and Niagara University. Sometime before midnight we came to an unspoken agreement to pursue the clues together. I hung the jacket and its treasures in the library closet and collapsed in bed.

We turned on the weather channel on our bedroom TV which gave us the latest snow accumulation. Sunday morning Mass at St. Jude's looked doubtful. We fell asleep to "Ice Road Truckers." Patrick heard maybe fifty seconds of the broadcast. I was asleep before the fifteen-minute timer turned it off.

CHAPTER 26: CHAOS

The alarm sounded at 7:16 am. Patrick didn't believe in on-the-hour time designations for waking. He was already up and had checked our parish website for the possible cancellation of Mass. St. Jude's, just south of North East, sits atop a steep hill with a right-angle curve at the top making snow-covered ascent difficult. The direct access to Route 272 makes descent even more perilous. Outside snow was swirling, having accumulated at least eight inches. Visibility was poor. Mass at St. Jude's was canceled, and Patrick had already called our younger daughter, Rose, to inform her and Scott, who live less than a mile from church but hadn't considered checking the website. They had probably not gotten out of bed yet. Now, they were going back to sleep.

Our more accessible main parish church, Immaculate Conception in Elkton, was open only for Masses at 10:15 and noon. Patrick arrived in the bedroom with my Irish Breakfast tea in hand, steaming from the ceramic mug that proclaimed. 'I'm a grandmother. Ask me how to raise your children,' something he'd given me on the birth of our first grandchild. I lingered over my tea, then pulled on sweats and slipper socks and padded down the hall to the kitchen. Maggie eagerly greeted me. I let her out the back door. She wallowed in delight, sending snow in every direction. Ten minutes became twenty before she returned for breakfast. I toweled her dry, fed her, and she settled onto her fluffy bed in the flower room. The view from there included male and female cardinals, two tiny chickadees, my special favorite titmice, and brazen, noisy blue jays returning to Patrick's feeders since our abominable snow dog was back inside.

We settled comfortably in our double recliner, cats on both armrests and one on Patrick's footrest, and opened the drapes to view nature's awesome display. The fireplace added cozy warmth. I had a pot of tea, and he had his largest mug full of Irish Cream coffee. Neither of us volunteered to venture out for the Sunday *News Journal.* Chances were excellent it hadn't been delivered.

I took out the jacket. I held it. The fabric was familiar to my touch. I really wanted to know its owner. Although I knew intellectually, I couldn't know her by touching the cloth, I felt it draw our spirits closer together. Perhaps it was the added dimension of her scent. Scent! It was not an odor. There was no unwashed, human body reek on this jacket. Certainly, that told me more about her. But what? I had gotten this far before. She probably wasn't homeless, didn't live in a shelter. My trail of thought dwindled down a vague avenue to nowhere.

By nine-thirty we were showered and ready for Mass at Immaculate Conception. Sensibly we took Patrick's four-wheel-drive truck with cement blocks in the bed for added weight. Our downhill driveway was packed with snow, its right edge blurred with the lawn, the left even with the bank of shrubbery. We eased out onto Route 7 and headed to town. Despite the snow continuing to fall, traffic was moving at a moderate pace.

Our main parish church and St. Jude's mission church are only seven miles apart, but few parishioners move as easily between them as we do. At St. Jude's in North East, I'd come to know most of the people for years. In Elkton, Patrick had done the same. Between us, we usually recognized half of either congregation. It's good worshipping with those you know.

We pulled into a parking space on Bow St. and we crossed the drive, entered through the side door to the gathering space and headed down the right aisle, slipping into the fourth pew from the front. As we knelt in prayer, Fr. Joe, our pastor, entered from the sacristy door, spotted Patrick, and with a "Come, follow me," recruited him as the proclaimer. Patrick slipped into the sacristy to go over the readings.

Attendance was sparse for the ten o'clock children's Mass. Many families with young children had prudently kept them at home. The congregation was predominantly adults.

Early on I occasionally glanced out the windows flanking the left side of the church to check the snowfall. During one of these brief glances, I caught a man intently staring at me. He was at least five pews behind and close to the center aisle, on the other side of the church. There was no reason to be staring in my direction. All the windows were to the left where I had just looked. No one had moved about toward the bathrooms beyond the doorway to the right. And no one had entered for a while. It seemed the snow had discouraged the usual late arrivals, or they had added extra time and gotten here early. Thinking of that, I remembered my grandmother Irene, a member of St. Mary Anne's Episcopal Church in North East, who used to boast that she and her fellow altar guild members who laundered the altar cloths and arranged the flowers arrived early so they could sit in the last pew. I said a quick prayer for her, and other loved ones gone from this life.

When the liturgy began, Patrick processed in with the Book of the Gospels and placed it on the altar. He and Fr. Joe bowed to the altar and Patrick rejoined me in the pew.

Soon Patrick rose to proclaim the readings. He joined Judy, the cantor, at the foot of the sanctuary. Both bowed toward the altar and continued to the sanctuary. Patrick proclaimed the reading from the Book of Jeremiah. When he finished, he stepped back and Judy led the congregation in the psalm responses. Patrick then proclaimed from 1 Corinthians. Throughout both readings, his tone reflected one who felt the power of the words from Scripture. He and Judy left the sanctuary together.

When Fr. Joe stood for the Gospel procession from the altar to the ambo, a slight disturbance caused many congregants to turn. It was the man who had been staring at me. For some reason, he had started to leave his pew, then changed his mind, and tripped on the kneeler. Did he not know that the rest of us were just rising to stand for Gospel proclamation? I turned around, as did almost everyone else in the eight pews ahead of him.

I nudged Patrick, "He's been staring at me."

"I know. When I looked out over the people to begin reading from Jeremiah, everyone else was pretty much looking forward, but he was zeroed in on you." I shivered.

Fr. Joe recalled us to the liturgy as he began, "The Gospel of the Lord according to Luke," We listened as he recounted Jesus in the synagogue talking of how a prophet is never accepted in his native place. Then Jesus himself was rejected, but when they went to drive him out, he slipped from their midst. Fr. Joe concluded with, "The Gospel of the Lord."

I shifted to the left finding I was again under surveillance. I mouthed to Patrick, "He's staring at me again." Patrick hesitated, then looked in one direction, then gradually in the man's direction. He WAS staring at me. Patrick smiled pretending to nod to someone sitting just beyond the man. It confused him.

By the time he looked to see who was nodding back, everyone else was seated for Fr. Joe's homily. The man hastily sat down.

Father's homily was abbreviated because of the continuing heavy snowfall, but he touched on the readings of the day and how they applied to our lives in modern America.

"We are called to serve, but maybe not as dramatically as a prophet like Jeremiah. We all experience doubt, as did Jeremiah. We sometimes even try to get away with saying, 'Not me, Lord. Try somebody else,' as Jeremiah did. As Christians, we are called to put love above all other virtues, as St. Paul declared in 1 Corinthians: 'Love is patient, love is kind…' And so, just like Jeremiah, Paul, and Jesus, we can plan on being disrespected in our own homes, our own communities. But we are never alone. And remember, we are always called to love."

As we stood for the creed, I watched out of the corner of my eye. The man was slow to get up. He was obviously unfamiliar with the flow of the Mass. He wasn't there to support a friend or offer an acquaintance transportation because there was a marked gap between him and the nearest person.

When we sat for the preparation of the gifts, I reached in my purse for our envelope. As the usher walked down the aisle, the stranger seemed unprepared for the collection and noisily dug in his pockets depositing coins that jangled against one another, heard by everyone even above the organ. No one would have noticed if the noise had not initiated from the same spot as the earlier incidents.

We went forward for communion, our side progressing more slowly since there were more people seated there. The stranger's row, though several pews back, went up before us. Consequently, I reached Fr. Joe just after the stranger approached Mary Ann, the Eucharistic minister, with the other ciborium. I heard her say, "The Body of Christ." I heard him reply, "Thanks." My eyes made contact with Fr. Joe's. We shared a fleeting confused look before he raised the Body of Christ to me and I responded, "Amen."

As we stood for the final blessing, our pastor's parting remarks startled me, reinforcing our welcoming of visitors but reminding them that we regard reception of the Eucharist open only to those who truly believe that what they receive is the body and blood of Jesus Christ, and the proper response is "Amen." He glanced toward the man, as did we who had heard his "Thanks." I had to bite my lip to keep from laughing.

The stranger seemed uncomfortable. He held himself rigidly.

After the final blessing the closing hymn began. Our pastor and altar servers recessed down the main aisle. Before they reached him, the stranger made a break for the exit. He avoided the main double doors crossing to his right. I smiled inwardly anticipating his discovering the side door was locked. It had not been used in my memory, since it didn't lead to a parking area. He'd have to push through people and pass Fr. Joe's outstretched hand or go through more people to cross over to the left side exit.

No one lingered afterward, and greetings contained short weather-related comments. We briefly spoke to Fr. Joe, left through the main doors, and headed down the snow-packed sidewalk. As we walked to our truck, I mentioned my unease to Patrick. I wanted to get home and check on the jacket.

"Am I paranoid?"

"Maybe. Maybe not." As those three words escaped his mouth I tuned toward our truck along the street. As we crossed the driveway to the church parking lot, I checked for approaching vehicles. From the parking area behind the school a truck with Maryland farm tags pulled out. Despite being snow-dusted, it was recognizably red. It registered in my mind that this looked like the truck at the dry cleaners. In the passenger seat was the man who had been staring at me during Mass…and in the driver's seat was the same the rude customer from the dry cleaners. I squinted intently. Yes, the license tag was the same. It was the same truck. Now I was unnerved.

CHAPTER 27: PURSUING LEADS

We watched him turn onto Bow St. and right onto Park Way. Then he was out of sight.

I urged Patrick to follow. Without questioning me, he unlocked the truck, got in, and started the engine. Before I fastened my seatbelt, he was backing onto the street. As we turned to follow the red truck's path, I recounted the dry cleaners incident. Patrick now shared my concern. He sped up as much as possible, considering weather conditions. At the corner of Park Way and North Street we stopped. There were recent tire tracks going in both directions. Sighing visibly, we turned left heading for home. We had a fifty/fifty chance the truck had gone this way. At the end of North Street, our luck ran out. No red truck was heading east toward Newark, nor west toward home.

By the time we reached our drive, the marks from our departure ninety minutes before were completely erased and there were no recent vehicle tracks. The path to the front door was also undisturbed. Still, I quickly went through the house to the back door.

Footprints were visible on the deck. Maggie had been jumping at the door from the inside, depositing her snowy pawprints and puppy slobber in great abundance on the glass. Patrick went out the front door to establish the source of the prints. He tracked them east across the back yard, down our neighbor's lane onto Route 7. They had probably left their vehicle in the Wawa parking lot across the street. There were no tire marks in our neighbor's lane. The weather reflected my mood—chilled and gray. I opened the library closet door. The jacket was there.

We finally shed our outerwear. Patrick lit the fireplace. The flames should have brightened the room but failed. I turned to the novel I had chosen for our next book club meeting, John Irvings's *A Prayer for Owen Meanie.* I had enjoyed it years before and was anticipating a re-reading and subsequent discussion this winter. I had started it before our Annapolis sojourn but hadn't picked it up since. Patrick had his Kindle open to his latest escapist fantasy-world novel of mythical supernatural creatures. We sat together on the sofa, quietly reading. The snow continued falling heavily. Gusts sent swirls dancing outside our windows.

Then Patrick broached the obvious subject. "We contact UMCO today, not tomorrow."

"How do these people know where we live? I'm assuming it was 'them'."

"Nobody from next door has stirred. Both of their vehicles are parked, and snow covered. There are no tire tracks in their lane or footprints coming from their house, either the front or back doors. But there are footprints both coming and going across our back yard, past our garden shed, and down their driveway."

"What do we say? Report?"

"How about 'we found some evidence' for starters. We need

to report what we've discovered."

"But what have we really found?"

"A jacket, a necklace. Footprints, the man in church, a strange truck, same man, the men in the park…"

"Yes, but…it's all speculation. I don't want them to think I am jumping to conclusions and dismiss me before I am recruited."

Patrick was silent for a full minute. I waited impatiently for him to speak. When he finally did, I was surprised by his tone.

"I'll give you till tomorrow. No one would pursue this anyway till then in this weather. You're right. What we've put together may be more imagination than reality."

We dropped the subject pretending to think of other things like the Sunday *News Journal* which hadn't been delivered. The snow blew against the windows. The three cats curled around the raised hearth fidgeted for a warmer spot occupied by one of the others.

We turned on our laptops and absorbed ourselves in the game of Farmville. There were crops to harvest, barns, sheep pens, chicken coops to tend, orchards to harvest. Neighbors to visit. Recipes to make…

Virtual farming and our cozy living room with the fireplace wafting out heat in contradiction to the falling snow combined as a patient force keeping me from immediately following up on the leads. I needed to talk to the jewelry store personnel, to the K-Mart pharmacy employees, but I knew they were bound by HIPAA rules. The weather discouraged driving. Local forecasts showed no break expected in the next forty-eight hours. I could do one thing, though. I could use the telephone, call the 'Number' written on the bathroom wall.

Mentally I rehearsed what to say. I realized I needed different avenues of dialogue depending on who answered. How could I keep someone on the line long enough to convince the woman I wasn't someone from the group that had imprisoned her? I couldn't identify myself as an UMCO agent. I wasn't one…yet. Maybe this mental rehearsing was unnecessary. I had been imprisoned. She had been imprisoned. I had read her message and needed to know if she was all right. Pure Divine Inspiration. Simple truth was the best option. Patrick concurred.

With my fingers shaking nearly as strongly as my heart beating in my chest, and with Patrick nearby, I made the call. The ringing startled me. At last, I was acting. I was doing something.

"Please enjoy the music while your party is reached."

Both of our granddaughters have similar messages followed by whatever music they have adopted as their current favorite. This selection surprised me. Enya sang plaintively, hauntingly, across the airwaves. I relaxed a fraction.

"Hi, it's a joy to hear from you. Please leave a message. I'll get back to you as soon as possible." Clever. She left her name without saying it. I had a split second to compose a coherent message.

"Hi, Joy. My name is Norah. Recently, I was kept somewhere I'd rather not mention in a phone message. I read your penciled note. I need to know you also made it back from that place. I'm calling from my cell phone. If you would rather contact me at home, I'm leaving that number too." I recited both numbers. As I hung up, I prayed I sounded as sincere as I intended to be. *There, it was finished.* I had acted. Relief. Then, unexpectedly, Patrick swooped me up in an embrace communicating how much he approved! With relief also came confidence.

We would find her.

Inaction after action. The day dragged on. Every time either phone rang, I felt anticipation mingled with anxiety, then acute disappointment with each interrupting call. Our daily life was an intrusion: Evie called with an update on a friend's health. She didn't understand my unusual abruptness. I didn't explain.

I Googled the jewelry store finding a promising listing. I recorded the phone number, email address, physical address, and hours of operation. Using Patrick's cell phone, I called Cameron's but got a recording. The snowy weather had probably kept the owner from opening the business, or it was closed on Sundays.

I went to the K-Mart website and got updated information about the store number on the receipt.

I spent time looking at the Niagara University website. After acquiring a lot of extraneous information, I was able to view past yearbooks. I found her! Her name was Barbara Joyanna Flemming. Her degree was in social work. It listed her home simply as Stevensville, Maryland. From the phone directory, I copied the names and numbers of all seventeen Flemmings in Stevensville (a familiar place from past fireworks deliveries), and Annapolis, just across the bridge. Some had addresses. Others were vague. But it was information.

By early evening I was restless, had made so many mental and paper notes I was confusing myself. A simple plan of action was always a good choice. I would make breaded pork chops with mushrooms for dinner.

After supper, Patrick surfed the TV for something, gave up, and picked up a copy of *Smithsonian Magazine* and became absorbed in an article. It was more diversion than I could find…I attempted reading *A Prayer for Owen Meanie* but couldn't concentrate for long on the threads of events. I confused the characters and began daydreaming about our own real-life events. I put the novel aside.

That night I slept restlessly, dreaming of dark events, always trying to get somewhere without knowing my destination. People I recognized, but couldn't name, kept giving me tips, but each took me in a wrong direction. I awoke drenched yet chilled. My stubborn nature didn't allow me to get out of bed and wander from room to room. I turned over and tried to sleep. I shifted and twisted to find a sleep-inducing position. I reached across the bed for Patrick's comforting warmth, and even in sleep, he instinctively drew me closer to him. Eventually I drifted off, secure in his embrace. If I dreamed after that, I couldn't recall it when I awoke.

CHAPTER 28: SNOWY ROAD TRIP

Monday morning arrived gray and dismal, but without more snow. After debating about road conditions, we got in our truck and headed for Annapolis. We armed ourselves with maps, a programmed GPS route, snacks, drinks, extra clothes, blankets, and a bit of cash. My mind had raced over many scenarios, so we prepared for them all.

I wore the Jacket, but also took my own. Our drive was uneventful, but long. Twice I suspected we were being followed, but the vehicles turned off the road each time. We arrived in Annapolis past noon and located Cameron's. It was then that I thought, 'What the heck am I doing? How can I just walk in there and get information?' My stomach revolted. I was glad I'd had no lunch. We conferred and decided if we both went into the store, we would seem like respectable people, which we were, so… I took a few calming breaths, struck a victory pose, and headed for the entrance with Patrick by my side holding my hand.

An elderly salesperson glanced up as the door chimed, announcing us. He seemed pleasant enough with thin, longish graying hair and kind hazel eyes hidden behind the thick lenses of gold-rimmed glasses. He was slightly stooped as if from years bent over his work. I hoped he'd been there long enough to recall the purchase we wanted to learn about. I glanced around the interior and assumed it was a business that had long occupied the premises.

The exposed stained wooden rafters were dotted here and there with framed decades-old newspaper sales ads and photos of smiling customers showing off wedding and engagement ring purchases. The glass topped, marble-based jewelry counters were polished to perfection, despite their age. And the cozy cushioned seating welcomed prospective customers. I wanted to purchase something from this inviting environment but forced myself to focus on the errand at hand.

Without disclosing the circumstances, I explained I'd found a locket in a pouch with the Cameron's store name on it, and wondered if he would look at it to see if he recognized it.

"I've been here since my uncle Tom apprenticed me before I finished high school. I've been the owner for thirty-five years. I may well remember any item from the last fifty plus years. My uncle was Thomas Cameron, my mother's brother. I'm Thomas Cameron Fadley, his namesake. And the two of you might be?"

"I'm Patrick and this is my wife, Lenorah Parish."

"Please call me Norah," I spoke up smiling.

"Because there are photos in the locket, I can't believe the owner meant to discard it," I offered.

Mr. Fadley explained most of their work was custom jewelry made on the premises. I took the pouch from my purse and handed it over to him. Gingerly, he removed the locket and turned it over. He nodded in a reminiscent way, then frowned.

"This was made over forty years ago. How did you get it?" A harshness crept into his voice making me nervous.

"We were in town two weeks ago for the lobbyist night for Catholics. I found it then."

"So why did you take so long to come here?"

"I didn't realize I had it at first."

"You found it, but didn't know you had found it? Perhaps you should explain, because I do not follow you." His voice was still tense.

"I'm not sure I can completely. I found it in a jacket that had been left behind. I grabbed it as I ran out the door, but I didn't look in the pockets till more than a week later, two days ago, last Saturday."

With misgivings still on his face, the store owner decided to be a bit forthcoming.

"There were five of these lockets made for a bride who kept one for herself and gave the others to her four bridesmaids."

"This could belong to any of five people?" I stared at the wide wooden floorboards beneath my feet. I was disappointed.

"No, only the bride had these initials. The others were left blank till the girls married, then we engraved their married initials on them. That was a long time ago."

"How will I know where to return it if it was that long ago?"

He produced a velvety tray and gently laid the locket there before opening it. He stared tearfully at the photos. "That's the bride there in the black and white picture. She was a beautiful bride."

"You sound as if you knew her."

"Oh, I did. Indeed. I did." He hesitated for a moment, sighed, and said in almost a whisper, "Who are you? What are you after?"

"I want to return the locket."

"I could arrange for it to be sent to the owner."

"But I need to know she is all right."

"Who are you asking about? The bride?"

"No, I think I'm looking for the girl in the color photo."

He hesitated again. He took a deep breath and looked straight at me and then Patrick. His gaze was so penetrating I felt fear. Then the chime of an exquisite gold and glass clock in a shadowy corner startled me. When its magical music had faded into the atmosphere he spoke again.

"I'm going to trust you… She married my brother, Matthew, you know. I was the best man."

"Not the girl?"

"No, Barbette, the older lady."

"This is fantastic! Is she still living? Who is the younger girl? Do you think Barbette gave her locket to her?"

"So many questions! I don't know how much information a stranger has the right to request. Yes, Barbette is still living…in a way. She has Alzheimer's and rarely recognizes any of us."

"I'm so sorry. That must be so painful to live with," I replied.

"But she has occasional good days."

I hardly knew how to pick up the thread of our conversation. I stood there awkwardly. Perhaps that helped him decide to trust us.

"The other photo is her granddaughter, Joy, her pride and joy she always said. Joy just finished her degree in social work and has been living away from home on some kind of internship or service year. I forget what it's called. It's through the Catholic Church. The Oblates of St. Francis de Sales. Have you heard of them?"

"Yes, they have a place for their retired priests in Childs, just a few miles from where we live in Cecil County. At one time it was their novitiate. All the new seminarians spent their first year there. They also had a summer camp for boys, Camp Brisson, in Elk Neck near where I grew up." He nodded as if acknowledging the accuracy of my information.

"Joy is helping street people live in a community. She's serving the local homeless. I worry about her safety, but she made a one-year commitment."

"Where is she doing her service? Is it local? I've heard of a program that the Oblates sponsor in Philadelphia."

"This is a new branch with two locations in Maryland. One is in Baltimore, and one here in Annapolis."

"So, she is here in Annapolis?" Patrick asked.

"Yes, but she's immersed in the program and doesn't come home except for special occasions."

"I really need to speak to her. Is there any way you could arrange for me to return this to her personally?" I asked.

He grew quiet. He was very thoughtful for long moments. He looked at Patrick and at me.

"How do I know you're the nice people you seem to be?"

"What? Excuse me? I thought you trusted us. Wait. Is she okay? Was she harmed or in danger recently?"

He looked intently at me before he responded. "There was a problem…several weeks back."

CHAPTER 29: MY SIDE OF THE STORY

Before he could continue, I blurted out, "I was there too. They held me prisoner too. Patrick rescued me. That's where I found the jacket. I snatched it just before I ran out of the place!"

"You don't understand all of it. It wasn't just Joy. First, it was Barbette who wandered out of the house while my niece, Joy's mother, was on the phone. We searched, called neighbors, the police."

"But you got her back?" I asked breathlessly.

"Yes, after a while."

"Joy rescued her?"

"Not quite."

"What then?"

"Joy should tell you herself. It's rather complicated."

"Can you contact her? Would you contact her? Wait, is this her cell phone number?"

He looked at the paper I held out with the Number written on it. He paled. "What have I done? I've brought more harm to her!"

"No! I memorized the number from a message penciled on

the bathroom wall in that awful place. I've been trying to find out who she is and if she made it out safely too. I called this number yesterday and left a message, but she hasn't called me back. I guess I'm beginning to see why she would be reluctant to answer."

"I know better than to trust just anyone. I've lived a long life, seen a lot. Joy has recently learned a painful lesson about human nature, at such a young age."

He sighed, then agreed to call Joy and leave a message that he had met us and felt she might want to return my call. He didn't suggest she meet us. I wondered if Joy was in hiding or keeping a low profile. In any event, he was shielding her while trying to accommodate us. What had happened? We turned to leave after thanking him. On impulse I handed him the jewelry pouch.

"Whether we meet her or not, this is safe with you. I know you'll put it in her hands." Moisture glistened in his eyes. He nodded slightly. Then he stared directly at Patrick.

"You don't talk much, do you?"

"When I'm the chauffeur I just drive and escort my lady here. She's on a mission and I sometimes know enough to follow her lead and to always have her back."

"Smart man. You make a good couple."

I smirked and Patrick just grinned with a glint in his blue eyes. When we were on the street, I looked at him quizzically, but he pretended not to notice. I let it go and asked my "chauffeur" if he could locate a restaurant for lunch, and since I employed him, I'd pay the bill and deign to let him eat at my table.

We found Dock Street Bar & Grill not far away. There was even available parking. A hostess greeted us pleasantly, told us the lunch specials were still available, and invited us to sit in a booth by one of the front widows. The place generated a warm, cozy atmosphere smelling pleasantly of fried foods, beer, and sweet desserts. We referred to the specials board and ordered a cup of the soup of the day, crab bisque. While I added a crab salad platter, Patrick chose the broiled crab cake with Old Bay fries. Obviously, crab was out of season, but we gambled that what we ordered would be pleasing. With hot tea for me and coffee for him we were set. We tried to talk about other things during lunch. It was pointless to speculate. It was also pointless to think we could spend time on other subjects. We were too caught up in the drama.

I willed my phone to ring but had no success. We finished lunch and agreed it had been a good meal, but the soup didn't quite measure up to what Pier 1 served. With nothing better to do, we walked back to the truck. We discussed possibly remaining in Annapolis. Should we return to Cameron's and talk to Mr. Fadley again? Would we be intruding or pushing our luck? We drove as we debated and ended up in the lot of a sparsely occupied public park. We got out and wandered. After only a few minutes the chill had thoroughly penetrated our layers of clothing. As we walked to the truck, we resolved to head home and patiently wait for Joy to initiate further contact. My cell phone vibrated in my pocket. Without looking at the number I answered with my professional voice. I totally knew it was Joy.

Wrong.

"Do you want to know the latest about your brother Christian's daughter, Fern? And know what your daughter did now?"

"What? What?" I asked my granddaughter Maglie who had a penchant for sharing all her news with me as if I were one of her teenaged peers.

"First, she could have been kidnapped! At the Annapolis swim meet last week. We just found out today that two of the other girl swimmers from a different team were taken off the street and held captive in some creepy old building. Fern wasn't supposed to say anything, but she couldn't stand keeping it from me. The girls escaped, or rather they were sort of rescued by some guy that sounded like he looked a lot like Pop-Pop Patrick. The girls were really scared. They ran away from the building with a whole bunch of other people, all grownups. They were finally picked up by a cab driver and driven to the YMCA. Fern said they were hysterical once they realized they were safe again. After that no one was allowed to be alone for the rest of the meet."

I swallowed hard, took a deep breath, and innocently asked if Fern had said anything else. Maglie told me that was all she had shared. I said I was thankful the swimmers had safely returned to their families.

"And what about your mother?" I asked hesitantly.

"She lost my job application!"

"How could she manage to do that? Evie would never lose anything important."

"Well, she did!"

"Why would your mother even have your job application? What job application are we talking about anyway?"

"I'm applying to work at Pro Physical Therapy next summer. Mom was checking what I wrote. It must have got mixed in with her price lists for fireworks and her order sheets for the Outlet."

"Oh, well, perhaps she can find it tomorrow when she goes to the office. Pro Physical Therapy's a great place for you to apply. It suits you. I guess if you don't find your application, you'll have to get another one and re-do all your information."

"Yeah. And that is your daughter's fault." I could envision this five-foot two teenaged version of myself standing with her brown eyes throwing sparks with her long dark ponytail swishing in agitation.

"I'm sure she didn't do it on purpose. Now, why did you really call me?"

"I was going to stop in to see you on my way to Planet Fitness.

I was just checking to make sure you were home."

"Sorry, we're out."

"Where are you?"

"Well, we are in Annapolis."

"Annapolis? No! What are you doing there? It's a dangerous place!"

"It's a long story. I'll explain the next time you stop by."

"Okay. See you soon. Please tell me you are coming home this evening."

"That's the plan right now. We may be on our way shortly. But, since we have you on the phone, could you take care of Maggie, your namesake—let her out, set out her evening food in case we run late?"

"No problem. I have my leopard key. Bye. Love you."

Only Maglie would have her keys covered in patterns to easily tell them apart. It was a good idea. Maybe I should do that. It would save time repeatedly sorting out keys.

As I hung up, my phone vibrated again. I spoke a bit testily to Maglie needing to update Patrick and keep the line open for the expected call from Joy.

CHAPTER 30: JOY SPEAKS

"Excuse me?" It clearly wasn't Maglie. "Maybe I have the wrong number."

"No! Don't hang up! Oh! Sorry. I thought you were my granddaughter calling me back."

"Is this Norah?"

My heart beat rapidly. "I'm Norah, yes. Is this Joy?"

"Yes. My uncle suggested I contact you. I hope I've gotten you before you started for home."

"Oh, my! I'm thankful to hear from you. Let me put you on speaker phone so my husband can hear you too, if that's all right?"

"Fine. Sure. Speaker phone's fine," answered the remarkably smooth confident voice.

"Hello, Joy, this is Patrick. It's such a relief to hear your voice."

"Thank you. I got your first message but hesitated to call. I'm very suspicious of people these days. But this afternoon Uncle Cam assured me he'd met you and I should sit down with you."

"We certainly want that too."

"He offered his work lounge for us in the back of his store, if you feel comfortable there."

"Well, we know the location."

"Can you meet just after four-thirty? I'm working and can't arrange coverage till then."

"Are you at the shelter?"

"Yes."

"Would anyone mind if we met right there?"

"Hmm, that would be more convenient for me than the jewelry store. If you don't mind occasional interruptions, we could talk as soon as you arrive."

"Perfect!" I exclaimed.

"Excellent!" Patrick echoed.

"It's called Brisson Shelter. Let me give you the address. Do you have GPS?"

"We do," we said in unison.

Joy gave us the street address and after hearing where we currently were, told us we could be there in under ten minutes. She offered to have someone watch out for our truck and show us where we could safely park, so we described our vehicle.

At last. Tension invaded my stomach. Anticipation?

In eight minutes, we were in a depressing part of town. My adult eyes noted the disrepair of building fronts, neglect of sidewalks. We passed what looked like an inner-city project and I flashed back to my many childhood visits to my cousins living in Baltimore. They lived in the projects, but I didn't know that then. I just knew it was crowded and there were kids everywhere. My country life, with only three friends living within a mile or two, had sparked envy at their closeness to so many other kids. I didn't think of how cramped and crowded their little place was for a family of eight. I didn't consider the lack of privacy in a row home where some rooms were only separated by curtains, not doors. I didn't realize how much I took for granted our acres of yard and the woods of Elk Neck beyond.

Dismissing the reverie, I scrutinized buildings, people, and their conditions. The people mirrored their surroundings. Maybe the reverse was also true. There must be something to urban renewal, community gardens, green spaces. If my living space is nurturing, I'm nurtured despite wrongs in my life. My classroom had been inviting, reflecting my vision of the students who spent their time in it. Maybe that had been a far better thing than I'd realized.

I concentrated on what slowly rolled by me. People were not hurrying. Were their destinations places they cared to reach? Many wore clothing too light or of too few layers for the weather.

Eventually we spotted the street.

As we strained to find the address, we were accosted by a young man, not out of his teens, vigorously waving his Orioles baseball cap directing us toward a narrow alley running alongside a rambling, four-story brown brick building. Above the stoop of what must be the main entrance, was a professionally painted sign with the name "Brisson Shelter" and beneath it in distinctive script: "Live Jesus." The familiar Oblate mantra. This alley did not lead to an eerie, gaping, unused warehouse with flapping strips across the opening. Instead, it led to a small gravel parking area surrounded by wire and wood fencing. Through the crisscross of the wire, we glimpsed a cleared patch that had evidently been a garden. Six-foot tall wire cages for tomato plants were stacked horizontally three high along one edge, and stakes were laid in another pile.

The young man, Jay, caught up with us, introduced himself, and ushered us to the back entry of the building. The steps were sturdy concrete, clean and plain. They led to a shallow covered landing that led to a mud room adorned with boots, umbrellas, a few snow shovels, bags of sand, and a huge, galvanized trash can artistically labeled "bird seed." We followed Jay's example and carefully wiped our feet on the huge mat.

CHAPTER 31: ENCOUNTERING JOY

Though I'd seen Joy's photo, I was unprepared for meeting her. She was taller than I expected, maybe five-eight or so. Her subtly dyed curly blondish-brown hair was swept back casually behind her ears. She had a distinctive presence, an aura about her. She was calm, yet agitated, forthcoming, but secretive. I wondered what vibes Patrick and I sent out. Obviously, she was assessing us. She should be. How did we measure up to what she had pictured? Did we seem sincere? Would she trust us?

She spoke, offering a brief tour of the facility. That seemed smart. As we walked, she demonstrated how many people were there and how integral she was to the goings-on, subtly communicating she wasn't alone, people were there, and she'd be missed if something occurred.

Soon we began to find some comfortability with one another while concentrating on our surroundings. We learned a lot in a few minutes. There was a large community, a jumble of ages, ethnicities, and attitudes living there. They were probably no more dysfunctional than any group, related or not, living in the same place and following rules set by others. Joy was an enforcer of rules, but she seemed to do it with quiet authority. Apparently, it worked. The one attitude exhibited toward her was respect. Some seemed to genuinely like her, while others maybe not so much, but respect was shown regardless.

We saw three community rooms, one with a TV, lumpy, plaid, mismatched cushioned sofas, upholstered chairs, several metal folding chairs, and a collection of retro floor lamps, basically an immense family room; the second had a tired upright piano, cushions on the floor, comfy-looking upholstered chairs scattered about, and card tables along one wall. Another wall contained shelving from ceiling to floor with a ragtag collection of board games, a vast selection of jigsaw puzzles that would have appealed to both our daughters, two shelves of movies, classics and fairly new releases and a bookcase filled with sections of books fancifully and artfully labeled as non-fiction, biography, history, faith, novels, romance, mystery, sci-fi/fantasy, cooking and crafts.

I examined the books and felt a kinship with the place. The books were categorized and alphabetized containing coloring and activity books, board books, stories, and young adult novels. A sign-up sheet was attached to a clip board, along with a notice about places around the city that swapped or loaned books.

Another wall boasted five computer terminals, each with a minimum of privacy afforded by carrels. There was nothing state-of-the-art about them. I figured even I could operate them.

In the third room were Disney movies, children's toys from squeezable squeaky animals for toddlers to dolls, blocks and vehicles for older ones. There were four shelves devoted entirely to blocks.

The immense communal dining hall had large refectory tables accompanied by assorted benches and chairs. Pinned on the walls were drawings of a great range of subjects and abilities. It made the place homey, like refrigerator art so often does for an otherwise sterile kitchen. There were, it seemed, artist sections, an area for an individual artist to add to a collection or switch out drawings. It was obvious, because preferences from artist to artist were distinct—the choice of predominant colors, a particular way of shading, a subtlety or brazenness of shapes. I felt I'd been invited to a public showing at an art gallery with multiple featured artists. One artist's penchant for depicting wildflowers and herbs caught my attention. Some details were so exact they nostalgically transported me to late spring, the feeling of dirt between my fingers, the scents of basil and heliotrope, the lingering honeysuckle odor, heavy on warm early evening air.

"I'd like to meet this artist," I told Joy, pointing to a delightful scene of wild ragged robins that seemed to reach freely for the sun. "We appear to have much in common."

"It's odd you should zero in on that artist," she responded, but did not offer an explanation. She turned immediately to lead us into the kitchen. It was much larger than the one we had for our county rotating shelter, but obviously, served a larger, more permanent community. It was all business, certainly the result of strict adherence to health department requirements.

Joy ushered us up to the second and third floors, and we entered a few people's rooms after obtaining their permission. I appreciated that. These people had so little, a bit of privacy and control over their lives must mean a lot to them. It afforded them a small amount of dignity and respect. The rooms were monastic in their simplicity, but made individual, despite their similarities and the obviously low decorating budgets of the residents. No matter how temporary a home is, there is a certain nesting instinct in many of us.

The designated male and female showers reminded me of being on retreat years ago. I wondered about water pressure and availability of hot water but didn't inquire. The accommodations far exceeded America's Best Value motel in Ohio, where Evie and I and three friends had almost stayed last spring. I shuddered remembering the drained indoor pool cluttered with spare bed headboards, refrigerators, and air conditioners haphazardly dumped where lounge chairs and side tables should have been. In our rooms, the extra corroded opening in the tub, the eaten away skid strips in the tub floor, and the hole in the wall below the sink convinced us it wasn't for us. We five had had reservations, but the rooms were not as advertised on the internet. We had cancelled our reservations after finding accommodation in a Best Western about three hundred feet away. We had slept with both eyes shut, which we wouldn't have done in the other motel.

Joy raised her eyebrows at my obvious reaction of approval. Hastily, I explained about the motel that had been so far below the standard of what I was seeing now. She nodded her appreciation.

We ended our tour in her first-floor office, a larger room than I anticipated. It was comfortable, but spare. She offered us seats. There were several choices. She explained the room doubled as a small group sharing space. We sat, silence enveloping us. Once we were on the brink of discovery, none of us knew how to begin.

Patrick had the presence of mind to offer some information about his involvement. I was relieved. If I had started, I might have said something that UMCO might disapprove of. For once, I remained quiet and was glad of it.

"I got into this, this Maryland protection service. We experienced an event involving missing documents and a possible bomb threat in Toronto some time ago, and I was approached…recruited to help without Norah's knowledge. My wife has just recently become involved. Until she was imprisoned in the building where these vigilantes would take what they consider "undesirables," illegally removing them from the street to put them in basically a holding cell until they could get them arrested and charged for bogus crimes, she knew nothing about my involvement or the existence of any group working to fight crime on a different level in Maryland. Now we're both committed to helping those who fall victim to these vigilantes. We'd like to hear what you know to add to what we've experienced. We want to help and would appreciate your help."

Joy gazed at each of us, sadness and shock on her face, and shook her head.

"So, you've been there too?" she asked me, through the tears threatening to run down her face."

"That's how I found you," I said softly.

CHAPTER 32: FIRST REVELATION

Joy began her story.

"I'll start with an incident from last fall. An older woman named Sarah moved in here at Brisson on November eighteenth after she experienced a problem with where she was living. Her sister Emily had given her a bedroom in her apartment, but they'd never been close. They tried to get along, sharing cooking and cleaning. Sarah bought the groceries, since charging her rent would have violated her sister's lease. Her sister is seven years younger than Sarah, has a son who's in and out of employment, and off and on living with his mother. The situation was tense with him around. Sarah had spoken her mind about her nephew. Frequently. And, on the evening before we met her.

"That morning Sarah got ready for work at Dunkin Donuts. She was on her way out the door when the phone rang. Emily answered it. Sarah poked her head in the kitchen to be sure it wasn't for her. Emily waved her on. Sarah assumed it was her nephew, had no desire to hear his latest woes, and went to work.

"When Sarah returned home from Dunkin Donuts around mid-afternoon, her key wouldn't fit in the lock. She rang the doorbell but got no answer. Her sister should have been home. They had regular schedules and rarely deviated from them. Sarah worked weekdays from ten to two, just to be busy and get out among people. Emily volunteered at a local public library branch on Mondays and Thursdays. The eighteenth was a Wednesday. For over half an hour Sarah stood on the landing pondering the situation. Then she noticed how shiny the lock was and realized her sister had had the lock replaced! She was so put out she didn't know what to do.

"She stomped off and went back to Dunkin Donuts where she stewed and commiserated with her fellow employees and regular customers. She refused to go home or call her sister. Finally, a customer suggested she go to a shelter for the night. She didn't even know where one was. A customer guided her here.

"She only had what she'd taken to work—her uniform and a change of clothes in a tote. We took her in. We fed her breakfast the next morning, and she headed to work in a cab. We expected her to go home after work. But she was on our doorstep again that evening. She'd gone to work and turned in her resignation at the end of her shift, intending to come right back to the shelter. She had had to take a taxi to work. She knew she couldn't afford to keep doing that, so she planned to quit and begin looking for something closer to the shelter. Before she quit, her manager called another Dunkin Donuts a few blocks from here and set her up with a job beginning the next week. Sarah made one stipulation. No one at her former job was to reveal her whereabouts to her sister. She was adamant about that.

"That night she rejoined us, and we 'enrolled' her giving her a more permanent space and supplying her with basic necessities—toiletries, towels, night gowns, things like that. She had some cash, so we placed her on a program to contribute toward her expenses here.

"She became a community asset. She helped with aftercare for children whose parents worked late. She read to them, played games and helped with homework. Parents taking evening classes asked her to babysit or help with their course work. She became a recipient and a giver.

"We learned that Sarah had been an art teacher for twenty years, so we took advantage of her talent. Hence our dining room art gallery where your new favorite painting hangs, Norah. She had one requirement. She did not wish to reunite with her sister. Her sister had no legal responsibility toward her, so we had no obligation to inform her of Sarah's whereabouts. Sarah settled in, and we soon forgot she'd arrived under those circumstances.

"On Tuesday, December twenty-third, Sarah didn't show up for babysitting at four. By five-thirty I'd called Dunkin Donuts, but learned she'd left on schedule at two. After that I contacted Vintage Value thrift store. It's in our neighborhood on her way home. She was a frequent customer. The store manager told us she had been in around two-thirty. I worried, but I had no right to question her behavior. By six-thirty, she had missed dinner. At ten o'clock I contacted the police. I explained about Sarah. They were sympathetic enough to take her information, probably because she's eighty-four—not that she shows her age. She only looks seventy.

"The next morning around six, a police cruiser delivered Sarah. They had found her wandering the streets, confused, and shaken. She was very cold. They'd taken her to State Street Clinic. Aside from the chill from being outside, she was declared fit to go home.

"After the police departed, she told us what had happened. In the afternoon, after making purchases at Vintage Value, she had wandered to a local park and sat on a bench. She had her tote bulging from her uniform and items she'd purchased for friends at the shelter. The afternoon was unseasonably warm, so she sat enjoying the sunshine. She kind of dozed off. She was jolted awake by someone standing over her blocking the sunshine. He shook her roughly. She was confused, then realized where she was and tried to get up. Two men bent over her, shouting, accusing her of vagrancy and said she had to go with them. She tried to explain she had a job and a room at our shelter. They hushed her up and hauled her to their car. It was still broad daylight.

"They took her to a building and held her there. She wasn't told where she was, nor charged with a crime, but was locked in a room with several other people. Some scared her. She said people were removed one at a time. She described two strange women dressed like sexy cheerleaders who asked questions of each person soon after they arrived. I assumed the women were hookers but wondered if Sarah was just confused.

"She said she was abruptly escorted out by two men through a second door, taken directly outside, and driven to an unfamiliar park. They stopped the car and dragged her out. They told her to forget what had happened and to tell no one or they'd find her again and not let her go free.

"She was stunned, wasn't sure which direction to go. She began walking. After a time, she still didn't recognize landmarks, so she tried retracing her steps to where she'd started. Before she got that far, a police car pulled up beside her. The officer called her by name. She freaked. She assumed they were after her again.

"Since she reacted strangely, the officer calmed her down. He didn't shout or manhandle her. He showed respect. He convinced her to get in the patrol car, then drove her to the clinic. They were gentle with her there. Bravely, she told them her disjointed tale. They thought of keeping her for observation, but she convinced them she was coherent. They had her file a police report while she was there. She had few concrete details but no names, no addresses, except for the park where she had been apprehended.

"Upon being rescued, she had told the officer to drive her to the shelter. Once he was reassured, she wasn't a medical emergency, he delivered her to us. By then, as I said, it was six in the morning.

"We were so relieved Sarah was safe, we hardly questioned her for further details then. We got her a hot breakfast and insisted she go to bed. We phoned her work and explained her absence as best as we could. At noon, she woke up and insisted on telling her story. She was precise in her details, except for the location where she'd been held. Her account seemed bizarre, almost dream-like, but she insisted it was accurate. We believed her. At least, we believed she honestly recounted what she remembered, but it seemed unreal. We didn't exactly doubt her, but we couldn't reconcile her ordeal with anything we'd experienced or heard about before.

"We recorded her account and passed it on to the officer who had brought her home. Gradually, things got back to normal—our normal."

Joy paused, took a deep breath, and stared at us. I thought she had ended her narrative, so I nodded, then Patrick spoke.

"So, you learned of this place from Sarah. But your message was on the wall. How did you end up there?"

CHAPTER 33: SECOND REVELATION

After a brief pause and a deep sigh, Joy continued. "The week after Christmas was hectic. I spent extra time with my family, relatives visiting from Delaware and New Jersey. Lots of visitors were in and out of my parents' house. It was chaotic. We let down our guard watching out for Grandma Barb, my mom's mother. She has Alzheimer's. There were so many people around, there wasn't an opportunity for her to be alone on her own.

"Somehow, on December twenty-eighth, there was a lull in the amount of company. Mom was on the phone with a friend. She didn't hear Grandma slip out the side door. By the time she hung up from a mini therapy session with Bessie (she's a recent widow and lives over in Centreville), Grandma was gone. Mom panicked, calling everyone she could think of from her cell as she searched on foot. Then she got in her car, and frantically drove block after block. But not in any order. She was frazzled, blamed herself.

"By the time my dad caught up with her, the police were on alert because of Grandma's Alzheimer's. Grandma made the noon news on Channel 13, the CBS station in Baltimore.

"We provided a description of Grandma and hazarded a guess as to what she was wearing. Since her winter coat was still in the closet, we worried even more. Her favorite white ugly Christmas sweater with crocheted rose-colored poinsettias, evergreen branches and jingle bells was missing, so that was a start. The white sweater was distinctive. She had been wearing a dark green turtleneck and gray corduroy pants when Mom had helped her dress. We gave her description, and it was on all the major TV and radio stations by the earliest evening news broadcasts at four. We also found she had taken her knitting bag and purse. What she thought she was doing or where she meant to go, we couldn't figure out.

"We tried our parish center at St. Mary's hoping she might have thought she was supposed to go there for the Leisure Club she used to attend on Mondays, before she became so confused. But, with it being the week between Christmas and the New Year, the parish center was closed. We contacted the Senior Center where she occasionally attended the Adult Day Care program. Another dead end. I got emergency coverage here at the shelter to help coordinate our search efforts. My mother was exhausted and blaming herself. We kept reiterating she should not feel guilty. She had done nothing wrong. Still, she felt horrible.

"By evening, all our visiting relatives had returned from errands and stops at friends' houses. They joined the search. Neighbors dropped off sandwiches and salads for dinner. By dark, we were really alarmed. The police told us to stay home. They would inform us of any leads or tips. They did call twice to verify information from callers, but the information didn't lead anywhere. But at least people were aware and trying to help.

"Grandma Barb made the eleven o'clock news in a big way. Reporters interviewed both my dad and Uncle Cam. Not what either wanted for their fifteen minutes of fame. The weather had turned cold, and snow had been forecast, but the snow held off. I kept checking shelters around the city, but no one had any information. The police were in constant communication with hospitals and emergency clinics. We kept vigil in my parents' kitchen, the coffee and tea pots in continual service.

"At three in the morning the police phoned. They had responded to a call—the description of the sweater closely matched and the caller, an employee at an all-night convenience store, had kept the woman there until officers arrived. They confirmed her identity and rushed her to Anne Arundel Medical Center. About twenty of us convened in the waiting room while they examined her.

"The doctor decided to keep her for observation. My mother refused to let her out of her sight. The rest of us hung around the waiting room till mid-morning just talking, eating, and dozing off. We took shifts sitting with Mom and Grandma. We discovered that our relief was as exhausting as our worry had been.

"When Grandma spoke to Mom, I was in the room. She kept saying she wanted to attend the Knitters Club (a group she and her friends had formed twenty or so years ago but hasn't met for four or five years now; they knitted, crocheted, caned chairs, assisted one another in creating quilts for family members, and brought bag lunches to one another's houses every Wednesday for years). But the two men who offered her a ride there took her to a nasty place. That frightened us more than anything. We could conjure up all sorts of horrors she'd been subjected to. We had to ask the hospital staff if she'd been examined for sexual abuse. We were told she had been, and there was no sign of abuse. That horrible possibility just stayed with me…what if…

"So, what was so 'nasty' about where they took her?" Patrick asked.

"To answer, we tried sifting through what she said, separating fantasy from reality. Finally, we learned the room was crowded and smelly. Nobody would talk to her or tell her where she was. There weren't any good chairs to sit on, just hard orange ones."

I gasped loudly, then nodded for her to continue.

"The food they handed out was dry and stale. The waitresses were dressed in obscene uniforms. They wouldn't write down orders, and there were no desserts except for those painted on the two ladies.

"I felt tears form in my eyes, and goosebumps rise on my arms as I recognized bits that Sarah had related. I didn't want to alarm my mother even more, so I kept my ideas to myself. Once I had a moment alone, I wrote down everything I remembered from Grandma Barb's account. Early that afternoon, Grandma was released. I finally returned here. I impatiently waited for Sarah to get home from work. I nearly accosted her as she walked through the front entry about four. I fixed mugs of tea and insisted she tell me again every detail she could remember about her experience.

"She looked at me strangely, but I didn't want to divulge my suspicions till I had again listened to her account. Sarah tried hard to recall every little detail. I took copious notes.

"She described the building as at least three stories, brick, but sooty looking. The outside steps were cement, but crumbling at the edges, and the door was heavy and made of dark wood, possibly painted black or dark gray."

I interrupted Joy. "Yes, that's as accurate a description as I could supply," I said, then lapsed into silence, allowing her to proceed.

"I asked Sarah about the women she called the cheerleaders. She described their outfits as very short, pleated skirts with skimpy tops with felt megaphones appliqued across their chests and pompoms dangling from their high-heeled shoes. She said they wore so much make up it looked painted on. She said they had actual cheers written down on their arms, like tattoos. On their foreheads were diagrams of pyramid stunts. One had her cheeks painted blue and gold to match her uniform colors. The other's cheeks were done in black and red to coordinate with her uniform. The blue and gold cheerleader had a mascot like an eagle or a falcon painted in gold over the blue area on one cheek and the reverse on the other. Her legs were done that way too—bare legs, just paint. So much paint! She told me the other woman, in red and black, had a horse or unicorn, painted on her cheeks and legs."

My mind raced back to the two merwomen. *They had to be the same women!*

"I thanked Sarah then related my grandma's ordeal. She wept. It was scary for her to know someone else, someone so vulnerable, had been through what she had. She knows my grandma isn't well and said it must have been worse for her, since she gets confused. I nodded but wasn't about to diminish Sarah's experience.

"I questioned Grandma the next day, December thirtieth. She said the two girls wore short tight skirts and tops open almost to their waists, and short aprons covering most of their skirts. She called them 'painted ladies.' I'd imagined that she'd meant prostitutes, but she said no, somebody had painted them, and the paint covered them up better than their outfits did. She described them as covered with desserts- up their arms: cupcakes, tarts, cookies, cakes. Their faces resembled decorated cakes. I asked her to describe that. She said there were ridges, like rows of sagging lines on a birthday cake which outlined their faces and went down their necks. One woman had pink paint, the other had yellow; on their chests were raised roses- the one with pink lines had yellow and orange icing-like roses, and the other had purple and pink roses, both with green leaves. Their faces were painted very white with little pieces of confetti painted in rainbow colors. Their eyelids were outlined in thick rainbows, their noses painted like cherries. They called themselves 'Delicious' and 'Tasty.'

"After that, Grandma faded out. Her eyes lost their clarity, glazed over. If I hadn't known Sarah's story, I wouldn't have understood that Grandma was accurately telling what she'd seen."

Patrick and I exchanged glances. We felt for all of them, especially Joy. Dealing with someone whose mind is confused must have been hard, so draining. Our hearts went out to Joy.

"That's when I resolved to do something pro-active. I didn't go to the police. Maybe I should have, but it didn't seem they had made the connection, and I didn't have proof—just the word of an eighty-four-year-old who I knew was of sound mind, and a seventy-six-year-old who I knew wasn't. The police had recorded Sarah's account of her capture and were skeptical.

"My next day off, since I'd taken time with Grandma, wasn't till the thirteenth of January. I recall the date because it was when reports started coming in about the earthquake in Haiti. I tried to visualize how traumatic life was there, so much worse than what I faced daily here. The complete chaos of life turned upside down and inside out for everyone was beyond comprehension. We organized a prayer vigil here in our chapel inviting people to sign up for times to reflect and pray for the victims. As you know, we Catholics have prayers for everything, so I copied a section from the *Book of Blessings* that people could read for a starter. Other staff members rearranged the chapel with extra candles set in a large tray of sand; the tea lights could be lit by individuals when they stopped by. To keep within our fire regulations, each candle had to be extinguished by the person who lit it before he or she left. Our group has no funds to donate, but we know how to pray.

"I went to Vintage Value and put together an 'outfit.' I stopped at my parents' house and rummaged through their storage closet. I borrowed my dad's old hunting jacket and spent the day near our neighborhood—the shelter's that is. Too many people recognized me, so I spent most of my time talking to locals. I learned there had been other incidents, but our neighborhood had closed ranks and sort of formed an unofficial watch group. I felt I'd not gained much information, but people did say that I blended in more, so I decided to keep wearing Dad's jacket. Besides, it had so many compartments—more pockets than anything I'd ever worn. One criticism I got was that my shoes were too nice, so I made sure I got out my worst scuffed-up loafers for my second foray.

"I had to wait for the following Monday, the eighteenth, to patrol the area in my get-up. I was out on the streets before noon and feeling more like I blended in. After two hours, I wandered over to K-Mart to pick up a sinus prescription. I felt awkward showing up like a street person. The pharmacist didn't recognize me and asked for my ID. Buying junk food and soda didn't make me look any classier—gum, candy, and a diet soda—my lunch and afternoon snack. The pharmacist viewed my ID, the clerk checked me out, and I went back on duty. I walked up and down streets, sat on benches, congregated with street people, but no one accosted me. At four-thirty, I was about to give up, when out of nowhere, I saw two men approach someone down the block from where I sat. The man reacted, apparently arguing with them. They backed off and left him. Then they systematically worked their way toward me, targeting anyone who looked disheveled or dirty. By the time they were within earshot, I was bent over pretending to pull up my socks—I couldn't pretend to be tying my shoes while wearing loafers. They had two other people with them—people who apparently hadn't passed their quiz. They started on me. I found myself paralyzed with fear. I couldn't get a coherent sentence to come out of my mouth. If I'd tried faking confusion, I'd have failed, but anxiety took over.

"They questioned why I was on the street. They challenged me to tell them why I wasn't at work or why I didn't go home. I babbled. Before I could calm down and become lucid, I had been forcibly put into the back passenger seat of a car with the other two. Next to me was an older man wearing a worn, dark colored wool overcoat; he was foreign, maybe eastern European. He spoke heavily accented English, but his grammar was better than that of the two in the front. He wore well-polished black shoes. I remember staring at them. To his left was a small guy, bald, with a runny nose he kept wiping on his jacket sleeve. He was snuffling so much I couldn't decide if he was crying, or sick. We rode around for a while. When I looked back on it, I realized they hadn't been trolling for more people (there wasn't any more room in the car) but were killing time till it was dark enough so we wouldn't be able to recall where we'd been taken.

"It was about five-thirty when we parked on a street, no name visible. I looked out. I did not see the building Sarah had described. This building was sculptured cement block, had two sets of garage doors on one end, and on the other end, a street-level door painted beige or some other light color. The only lighting was intermittent from passing vehicles' headlights.

"We got out. We were helped, not gently, and to my surprise, we didn't enter the building beside where we had parked. We were roughly dragged down the street past several structures.

"And there was the building Sarah had described. I felt relief in recognizing it as something familiar, but also had chills realizing what I'd finally accomplished. I knew I had no plan to get out of the mess. No TV or radio coverage or police report had been filed. Nobody knew I was gone.

"As we made our way down the street, I found myself pulling

off my gloves despite the chills. I wanted to get to things in my jacket. I jammed both gloves in an empty pocket and managed to remove my prescription to a jeans pocket. I remembered I was carrying jewelry. I took my locket and hid it in the collar zip compartment I had discovered when I'd snagged my wool scarf on the zipper. How I did this without their seeing, I don't know, except I was almost shaking anyway, and maybe my jerking movements fit in. I always wear the locket around my neck, but being on the street wasn't a place to wear jewelry, so I'd tucked it into a pouch and had placed it in a top pocket where some smokers carry their cigarettes. I just always had it with me. I had left my earrings on since they were invisible with my wool hat pushed down on my head. But I knew they'd be visible if I were ordered to remove it. I managed to get one out. The other two were still in when we got to the entry of the building. The best I could do was wad one in a tissue and jam it in the sleeve pocket. What cash I had and my work ID were already in my jeans pocket.

"Our escorts ushered us in separating us in the order they had collected us. They directed the first person, the sniffling gentleman, to approach the reception committee comprised of two different men. I couldn't hear the brief conversation. The second one's encounter was similar. The men who had brought us in stayed long enough to escort the first person down the hall and off to the right. Another set of men arrived before they left and took charge of the second person. I was left alone briefly with the reception committee, the inquisitors, and I wanted desperately to bolt out the door, though my brain couldn't convince my feet to move. I was paralyzed. No real opportunity materialized.

The original escorts and the second pair emerged from the room. The original two approached me and listened as my questioning began. The other two went farther down the hall and disappeared. I heard a door open and close, and sounds echoed like feet on metal stairs, but I wasn't sure that's what it was. A snarling, short, muscular, middle-aged man with a blond crew cut appeared.

"Then my interrogation began:

'Why were you loitering on the street?'

'I…wasn't loitering.'

'You were under observation for three hours. You did nothing productive. Didn't go anywhere, but up and down that street.'

"But I was just walking around. It's not a crime. Is it?"

"Loitering most definitely is and so's vagrancy."

"You're calling me homeless?"

"Yes."

"Do you have a permanent address?"

"Yes, of course, I do."

"Where do you live then?"

"At Brisson Shelter."

"Case closed. A shelter is not a permanent address."

"Before I could argue or explain, they jerked me toward the room down on the right. Just as they were shoving me toward a chair, the second duo returned with the dogs."

CHAPTER 34: FLASHBACK

At this I nodded in recognition. I felt myself shudder as I visualized that room—the dogs, the merwomen, the smells.

"Joy, I imagine they unnerved you as much as they did me."

"Probably. I went numb…fingers, toes. My eyelids twitched."

Then Joy continued her narrative.

"The dogs each seemed to pick one new arrival. The scruffy alien-looking dog stared at me. The first person ahead of me was paired with the jumpy little dog, a kind of terrier. My dog just sat motionless. I don't think it ever blinked. The second person was assigned to a mangy-looking mutt.

"I came to my senses and recognized we weren't the only people occupying the room. It was so eerie. So quiet. There were at least a dozen others there. All those orange plastic chairs were in use, and a few rusty metal ones were occupied too.

"When the first person, a young, maybe teenaged, blond guy was escorted out the other door, there was a ruckus. He alternately shouted and whined at the officers. Immediately after, another officer, a woman, entered the room. Wait. I know I keep using the word 'officer', but these people didn't have uniforms or anything. They were just in charge of us. They subdued the guy, but not before shoving him to his knees and kicking him. It was horrible. I remember crying out to them to stop, but they ignored me and pulled him back upright and half dragged him out through the doorway. I only called out once, because my dog made a move toward me. He raised his head and I swear he glared at me, baring his teeth, just daring me to challenge what was happening.

"As soon as the door closed, everybody in the room collectively exhaled. It seemed we had all been holding our breath during those last moments. We all gasped for air at the same time. It was like we'd been underwater and just got back to the surface.

"Then I heard a growling voice saying, 'Don't do that again!'

I looked around, and an old woman in layers of multi-colored sweaters glared at me. 'Don't do that again!' she repeated. Whether it was a warning or advice, I couldn't tell. It wasn't friendly, that was for sure!

"I replied, 'But, why? Shouldn't we help each other?'

And she replied, 'Who do you think's gonna win?'

'But we've got them by triples, numbers wise.'

'There's more a them just millin' aroun' in this buildin'.'

'Oh, so we do nothing?'

'Thas' right, Miss.'

'Where do they take us?'

'Don' know fer sure, since nobody's come back a 'gin'. I reckon they go to the real jail.'

'Then what's this?'

'Can' say fer sure. It might as well be a real jail, I guess.' Then she just lapsed back into silence.

"After what seemed like hours but might have been less than half an hour, someone got up and knocked on the entry door. I was surprised by the movement. Two officers arrived and the person requested to use the bathroom. They led him out, and he returned not long afterward. Two others then requested the same courtesy. After them the guards made it plain, they weren't obliging any additional requests any time soon.

"Then two females appeared after that. I knew they were the two waitresses Grandma had described, and Sarah's two cheerleaders. When I saw them, they were dressed differently. I had lots of time to observe them as they zeroed in first on one of my car companions, then the other. I can vividly see them now.

"They were outfitted like cowgirls with fake braids, cowgirl hats, short, short suede skirts, and matching colored knee-high leather boots with spurs on them. One woman's skirt and boots were a kind of caramel apple color. The other's were more like dark chocolate. They had embroidered leather vests. The caramel apple woman's vest was sandy-colored and decorated with cacti, skulls of cattle, and outlined with lasso ropes. The chocolate one's outfit was laced with red-orange trim and stitched with black and white horses with braided lasso rope wandering around them. They didn't seem to be wearing blouses under their vests. They had considerable makeup on. Very theatrical! They looked spray-tanned all over. Both had star-shaped deputy badges painted on their right cheeks. They had braided rope designs going around their faces and back toward their hair, almost like they were a continuation of their hair braids or their vest ropes. For each woman, the plaited ropes matched her hair color. On each of their left arms, was a painted cattle brand. One was a circle with lettering inside- an F connected to a P, which was connected to an S on the right. The other was an oval with what appeared to be a white trash bag inside. The bag seemed to have red flaps or strings hanging down from where it was drawn shut. There was a black line or bar running diagonally across the trash bag. On their opposite arms, each had a design in red, gold, and black diamonds, kind of variations of the Maryland flag. They had gold stars painted on their knees and upper legs.

"They finally approached me. They spooked me, so I gave the briefest responses I could. I hoped whatever I said didn't set off alarms and cause them to drag me out. They threatened that I would be put in jail for at least six months. That frightened me though it made no sense. I hadn't been arrested or tried. They got my name, but I only gave my first name—Barbara. I don't know why I did that. No one calls me that, but it's my name. They guessed my age as younger than it is, so I let them think I was only nineteen. On their own, they concluded I was a high school dropout and had been living on the streets for a few years.

"Unlike when my grandma and Sarah went missing, no one knew I was gone. My supervisor here at Brisson didn't expect me back till my shift late Tuesday. My family members weren't expecting me at all. They knew I had the day off, but I'd told them not to plan on seeing me because I had errands to run. I was beginning to see the foolishness of not sharing my plan. I knew everyone would have cautioned me against it. So, there I was.

"Abruptly, the cowgirls left. They just stopped questioning me, got up, and walked out. As weird as they were, I was more on edge after they left. It might have been because they had unsettled but fascinated me. Now I had time to stew over my predicament.

"Later, maybe hours after, I got up the nerve to request to use the bathroom. That was an experience. Here at Brisson, we don't boast, but we have clean bathrooms! Theirs smelled awful! The last one to use it hadn't flushed and it had aged. I gagged. My eyes watered. I breathed through my mouth to keep from vomiting."

We were getting to the note writing, and I couldn't wait to hear how she'd managed to conceal her message. But, just then, an alarm sounded on her desk. I jumped. Patrick looked up quickly. Joy apologized, saying it was five forty-five, time for her to join the residents for an evening greeting. Everyone had to be accounted for and checked in to be sure they were okay. It was a daily routine that must be followed and was also a venting time. It was Joy's job to facilitate it. She asked us to wait in her office.

We had no alternative. We wanted to hear her entire story, so we sat alone with our thoughts. After only five or six minutes, there was a knock on the door. A tentative older woman, comfortably dressed in cords and a flowing forest green gauzy tunic over a rich brown sweater, introduced herself as Sarah. Her hands were what I noticed first. Expressive, kind, gentle hands. An artist's hands. Sarah asked if we might care to join their evening gathering. She said they had discussed our presence at Brisson and had agreed we should join them if we were open to it. My heart skipped a beat. This was SARAH!

We thanked her for the invitation. By silent assent, we knew what the other was thinking about this gesture from the household. Patrick waved me ahead of him, then followed.

CHAPTER 35: DINNER INVITATION

She escorted us to a recreation room. Nearly everyone was seated on the sofas or extra chairs brought in from other rooms. There were several children on small chairs seated in a cluster and older ones seated sporadically around the room in twos and threes. The few standing adults leaned comfortably with hands or elbows resting on the backs of the sofas. There were two vacant wooden chairs with plaid throw pillows placed on them for cushions. They gestured to us to sit there. Patrick presented more of a graced sense of ease than I felt or probably showed. Momentarily, we were the center of everyone's attention. Joy told the residents they could introduce themselves to us, if they wished, once the gathering concluded.

She opened up the business of the evening with an announcement about scheduled neighborhood activities- GED classes beginning the next week at a YMCA branch. Then she mentioned a mandatory evacuation drill to be completed by the end of the month and that everyone should please review procedure charts displayed in every room. Health department workers would provide flu shots for any new resident since

December fifteenth, the date of the last round of shots, and everyone was expected to take advantage of this for the health benefit of all Brisson residents. She told them Sarah was starting a new series of art lessons on 'found things from nature'. She deferred to Sarah to expound on it.

Sarah spoke quietly, but compellingly, about the natural things she had in mind—pinecones, acorns, leaves, even mud, stones, weeds, grasses, bare branches. She said the greater the variety of items they acquired, the better the displays could represent their environment. She asked for creative donations to be gathered and brought to a large twig basket she would place in the alcove near the main entry. She then said there were to be no contributions of animals, living or deceased, which elicited a few chuckles, and one or two slight blushes. She knew her audience. Someone raised a hand and asked about bird feathers. She responded negatively to them because of the possibility of spreading disease. She also commented that she did know that most weeds and grasses were out-of-season items, but just because it was winter did not mean the landscape was desolate. They'd have to consciously search a bit harder.

She enjoined them to train their eyes to be on the lookout for pieces of nature. They should think about objects of interesting texture and shape, not just color. She announced that Vintage Value was donating any wooden crates they came across to be transformed into dioramas or shadow boxes. To encourage participation, Sarah promised no real skill was needed, just enthusiasm, imagination, and patience. There were several murmurs of approval. A couple of the children clapped excitedly about the project.

Finally, Joy asked for housekeeping comments. There were several. I was impressed with how would-be- complaints were phrased positively. 'Please remember to remove shoes in the entry to avoid wet floors and someone slipping.' 'Reminder to empty trash cans on Wednesday and Friday mornings so the city garbage pick-up can remove everything and Brisson Shelter isn't cited for excessive trash piled up in the alley.' 'Caution, don't run washers and dryers after ten pm, since some residents work early shifts.' Occasionally, I observed someone's hand go to his or her mouth in a reflexive 'Oops. I did that.'

A bell, I assumed the dinner summons, rang. No one moved. All faced a young dark-haired woman in her thirties.

Joy simply said, "I turn things over to you, DeeDee." The young woman rose. I noticed her frail frame, her slender arms lightly covered in a lavender crocheted shawl. DeeDee began a prayer, reminding all gathered they were always in the Lord's presence. She continued, after a brief pause, thanking God for everyone at Brisson, for the shelter provided, the improved circumstances of living there, the blessing of looking out for one another. She asked a blessing on the spaghetti and meatballs they were about to consume (clever way to inform them what was for dinner). She ended with, "May God be praised!" and everyone responded, "Amen."

Her closing sentence I had heard often. The Oblate priests used that statement to end their homilies at Mass. The Oblate Sisters at Mount Aviat Academy, my high school alma mater, used that phrase to end school assemblies. Patrick and I had years of experience listening to them while our granddaughters Sally and Maglie attended Mount Aviat from nursery through eighth grade. Our grandson, Francis, would be graduating from eighth grade in May. Considering their age differences, we had spent the last seventeen years hearing, 'May God be praised!' a lot. I felt included by that simple statement.

We conversed with a few people as they moved past us. Despite the rush for dinner, several stopped to greet us and give us their names. It was a very eclectic group. They all ritually stepped into a side room containing three sinks and washed their hands before proceeding to the dining room. Sarah invited us to dinner. At first, we declined, not wanting to take away from what was prepared for them. But Joy assured us there were always leftovers for late night snacks and for night shift workers. So, we joined the hand-washing line and accompanied the residents for dinner.

We walked into the dining room and stood uncertainly just inside the doorway. We noticed some smaller tables that seemed arranged for families with highchairs and booster seats located in a nearby alcove. We didn't want to take anyone's spot. Sarah noticed and beckoned us to her table. As we took our seats, Sarah introduced us to a guy named Gabe and a woman named Freddie to her left. Darius and Hook, both guys, were on her right. On our side, beginning at our far left across from Hook, were DeeDee and Amir, then Patrick and me, followed by Sam. At the left end, at right angles from Hook and DeeDee, was Heather. Jorge and Alexi faced her at the other end. There was one empty seat at each table. I mentioned this. Darius explained.

"That's for Elijah the prophet. Or St. Frank if he cares to join us. Or St. Jane, and one for St. John Bosco, one for St. Leonie Aviat, and one for Blessed Louis Brisson. If we have any guests, we honor them as if they were these holy people and let them occupy a saint's spot for dinner."

"We're not saints," joked Patrick, "so, it's good you kept those seats open in case a saint shows up."

"I'm surprised you call St. Francis de Sales 'Frank'," I blurted out. "We once had a retreat director who did that. Other than that priest and those of us who picked it up from him, I've never heard of anyone else refer to him like that. We like it. It feels like we know him," I added.

"We do," said Darius very seriously. Then he told us about Joy's evening meet and greet sessions introducing Salesian saints, reading from their works, telling of their lives, introducing their human and their 'saintly' sides. They did 'know' these saints.

The spaghetti and meatballs supper included a tossed salad served from a huge plastic bowl and divvied out by the acting head of the table. On a blue and green platter were large crusty loaves of bread from which each person tore off chunks. Olive oil and herb dipping sauce took the place of butter. They said a local Italian restaurant supplied their bread and dipping oil for spaghetti nights. It was delicious.

The main course was served family style—spaghetti in a huge pasta bowl and red gravy from a high-gloss ceramic tureen. The red spaghetti gravy was richly flavored with garlic and basil, my favorite herb. The meatballs contained a spicy blend of at least a bit of hot red pepper, garlic, oregano, onion, and basil. There was a delightful hint of heat left in my mouth after each bite. My compliments went out to the chef. To prepare dinner for such a huge crowd was impressive. To achieve something this delicious was really over the top. Oversized metal pitchers contained water and iced tea and pint-sized canning jars served as glasses. I'd seen this done in bars and restaurants. I converted jelly jars into juice glasses at home and appreciated the re-purposing. Dessert was a selection of citrus flavored sherbets.

Aluminum urns along one wall held hot drinks- coffee, tea, cocoa. The mugs were a grand collection of advertising promos for everything from travel destinations like Detroit and Los Angeles, to a local radio station and even a scrapple brand. They were as varied as my collection accrued over the years at cities hosting the annual American Pyrotechnics Association conventions in Washington D. C., Chicago, Seattle, Toronto, Boston, San Francisco, Orlando. I'd always sought the cheapest, most touristy mug available. They represented memories, experiences, relationships beyond price. I fixed Patrick's coffee in a Baltimore Charm City mug and poured my tea into a mustard-colored McCormick Spice Company mug.

We drank our coffee and tea listening to conversations familiar to any extended family gathering. As we finished our meal, each person at our table began revealing a few personal things.

CHAPTER 36: WHAT'S IN A NAME?

Hook went first.

"My name has nothing to do with the *Peter Pan* villain, Captain Hook. I love fishing, and when I was eight, I got a hook caught in my left big toe. To this day, thirty years later, I don't know how I managed to do that. I had an ambulance ride, the attention of the whole emergency room staff—they all had to look at what the idiot kid had done—and a surgeon attending me. I had the biggest bandage you could imagine on my foot. I couldn't walk on it for a couple of weeks, and don't you know, since it was summer, I didn't even get to brag to my classmates or miss a day of school. My real name's Jeffrey, but I haven't been called that since 1979."

"Me. I'm bi-racial," stated Darius matter-of-factly. "Guess you figured that out. But, really, I'm tri-racial. My pop's family were Piscataway Indians and African Americans. My mamma's family came from Ireland during the potato famine. Both sides of my family have been Catholic for generations. How I got a name like 'Darius'—it's always sounded Roman to me—I've not yet figured out. My middle name's Patrick. Mamma snuck that

Irish name in there. So, I guess I'm a thirty-five-year-old red-black Irishman. But I don't have that 'fey' gift of intuiting things like my mamma."

Patrick grinned at him. "I don't have the gift either. But I am, or was, a blond Irishman. With the gray my hair's closer to black now, but I still don't have the gift either."

"Uh, hi. I'll go next. I'm Heather Shamrock. I'm not Irish. When my great-grandfather came from Poland, the immigration official couldn't understand him, so they gave him a new last name We have been 'Shamrocks' ever since. I don't know our real Polish last name. I've lived here at Brisson for six months." No one else had offered this kind of information. "I have a two-year-old daughter I can't see, because I can't support her. I lost her to my parents, but at least she's with family. I'm not allowed to visit till I get my life together. Her father left when she was ten days old. He just left. My August will be three in August." She stopped. She couldn't continue, her voice choked with emotion.

"My grandfather was supposed to be named August," I lamely injected into the silence. "But he ended up Christian. I like August."

Sarah picked up the thread, commenting that the name August was one of the sisters in the novel, *The Secret Life of Bees*. She asked Heather if she had read the book.

"That's where the name came from. August was strong and caring and dependable, so I gave my August that name."

"I'm Sam, not short for Samuel. I spent twenty-six years working for a construction company. Now it's outta business because of the housing market, and the owner using low grade materials which are less costly than what he guaranteed he'd provide…and now he's gettin' sued for it. My twin brother, Eric, has a similar story, but he's got a home. My wife Emma's with me here, but tonight she's sitting with her friend who's had a bad day. At least Emma's with me and our kids are grown. I wish we could be supportive of them and not dependent on others. I work part-time at Lowe's installing flooring. Emma's a cashier there. By spring we hope to move out."

"That's what we all want," said Sarah dabbing her eyes. "Not that we don't enjoy your company. Sam, tell the origin of your name."

"Oh, yeah," grinned Sam. "My mother and dad met in high school. They were reading *Lord of the Flies*, and my dad told her that if she'd marry him, and one day have twin boys they would have to be named SamnEric. They did marry years later. Then along came twins. My mother'd forgotten about the ultimatum and was set to name us Gary and Larry for our grandfathers. But Dad came into her hospital room with a ratty copy of the novel and the page where my mother'd sworn to name us Sam and Eric. She got really upset 'cause she'd already told our grandparents her choices. So, I'm Sam Nelson and my brother's Norman Eric. We got our granddads' other names. We also got the 'N' in there.

"What a story!" Patrick murmured. "Does everybody here have a name connected to a book?"

"Not me! I'm Freddie. Real name, Lindsey. When I played sports in high school, there were two Lindseys, so since I was younger, I renamed myself. My dad had called me Freddie since I could talk. I thought it was my name. He wanted a boy, so he called me Freddie after his friend. Freddie suits me. Twenty-five years later, I'm still Freddie."

"Did you ever get a brother?" Sarah asked.

"Yeah, I did."

"And did he get real masculine name?"

"You be the judge. He's Shannon."

"I'm Alexi, Russian, born. I don't remember anything about life there. Twenty-eight years ago, I came to the United States with my grandmother. I was only four when she sent me to school, so I graduated from high school when I was sixteen. No one checked my birth certificate when I started school. I had arrived in June, just after my fourth birthday. By September I spoke good enough English that I fit in with the other first graders. My grandmother didn't realize I needed to be six. She saw the other families preparing their kids for school, so she got me ready. I was as big as the six-year-olds I had spent all summer with. When the counselor asked for my birth certificate, she gave them my immigration papers. Someone had smeared my birth year, so our counselor filled it in clearly, and I was enrolled in first grade."

"Four's young for all-day school, especially if you didn't go to kindergarten," Patrick observed.

"Yes, but I was an only child used to being around an older female. I learned early not to cross females in charge. That habit carried over to school. I still work from that principle."

"Smart man!" I concurred.

"I'm next. I'm Jorge. I don't have a story about my name. I worked for an auto repair shop in Annapolis till a year ago. My company got bought out. My job evaporated. I was offered a pay cut to work out of Delaware for the new company. I had to work for less pay and travel two hours to the job. They took away my health insurance and wanted to turn me into a delivery and pick-up person, not a mechanic.

"I couldn't afford the job, so I turned it down. Then didn't qualify for unemployment because I refused the offer. Now I deliver flowers for a local florist. I applied to be a mechanic and had an interview set up. But I missed the interview because of some guys who took me by force to a lock-up. They interrogated me and released me to the streets with a threat not to be out again. I was too nervous to return home, so I begged for Brisson to take me in temporarily. I haven't been here long. I worry about my friend who was picked up with me. This is the first time I have revealed my circumstances."

Patrick and I exchanged glances. It was so close to home. Our son-in-law, Scott, had been through a similar struggle. His unemployment had fortunately been short. But more than that, here I was staring at one of my fellow inmates. I had not recognized him till now.

Soft-spoken Gabe went next. I was sitting next to him and hardly heard him when he spoke.

"I'm Gabe, short for Gabriel. I'm the youngest of three boys. Yes, my brothers are Raphael and Michael. Boy did we get teased by kids who called us the Teenage Mutant Ninja Turtles. I hated that. It was so bad that my brothers, instead of going by Ralph or Mike today, use their middle names. I didn't get a middle name. It's not so bad now that we three aren't together. My parents named us after angels in the Bible. Of course that backfired. Kids teased us for being cartoon turtles. We defended ourselves and liked being aggressors. We were anything but angels by high school. I think a kid should develop before he gets stuck with a name that doesn't suit him."

"Some cultures do that; others predict what a child will be like by placing a name on him or her. We Catholics have Confirmation. When we're confirmed we choose a new name after a saint. It's a chance to research people from the past and claim something from them we would like to identify with." Patrick offered. "Our granddaughter, Magdalena is named for her great aunt's Confirmation name, St. Mary Magdalene.

"Excuse me. I can see you are all engrossed in conversation, but I want to finish meeting with Patrick and Norah, if they're agreeable." Joy had walked up behind us. We rose and thanked those at our table for sharing their meal with us. We felt like we were leaving old friends.

CHAPTER 37: CORROBORATING INFORMATION

As we followed Joy out of the room, we passed a clock and were shocked it was almost seven-thirty. We also glimpsed an adult supervising children who were engrossed in a Disney movie, playing games at a table and a few doing homework.

"Joy, since it's late, Norah and I should call a motel to set up lodging for tonight." Patrick suggested. "Then we can leave early tomorrow morning. Would you suggest one for us?"

"Yes, seven-thirty approaches. It's *Wheel of Fortune* time for many residents, an almost sacred half hour. Instead of a motel, I can offer you two rooms here. Sorry, no double-occupancy rooms are available. Are you comfortable spending the night in a shelter? There's a minimal charge in the form of a donation."

"We've stayed in separate quarters for retreats. Here would be less embarrassing than telling a hotel manager we have no luggage," Patrick looked at me. "What's your take, Wife of Mine?"

"Your wife is all for not having to find another place to spend the night. Besides, we may get another opportunity to get to know these people. But we must call Rose and Scott to take care of Maggie tonight and in the morning. The cats will be fine, though."

"We can lend you pajamas from our emergency stash," offered Joy graciously.

"That's great!" we said in unison. Our overnight accommodation was made. Patrick checked with Rose, who with Scott, agreed to handle pet coverage.

We settled in Joy's office. I stared at this confident young woman now dressed casually in striped green and beige comfortable slacks and a forest green pullover sweater which highlighted the subtle colors in her hair now braided and tucked in around her head in a crown, creating a soft aura about her. We prepared to hear her story to the end, or as far as she would take us.

"Let me see. Where did I leave off? Oh, yes. I was in the bathroom. By the way, we'll supply you with bathroom necessities tonight. You know, scratchy towels, harsh soap." She winked and I smiled. I really liked this feisty young woman.

"Back to my experience," Joy continued. "The bathroom was horrible, reeking of stale urine and unwashed-body odor. I closed my eyes and reached across to flush the toilet before using it. I worried about the foolishness of not letting anybody know what I was doing. In a panic, I scribbled my name and cell phone number on the bathroom wall. I envisioned someone seeing my note years later and wondering about it. I didn't have time for more because the guard started banging on the door for me to hurry up. I got out as fast as I could. I jammed the pencil back in my jacket pocket, flushed the toilet, and washed my hands in cold water. I knew they wouldn't wait for the water to heat up. They'd heard the toilet flush twice. On the way back upstairs, I found my gum and started chewing it to replace the bathroom smell.

"Once back in the room, I wished desperately for a book or

magazine—something to keep my mind occupied. One new person had joined the group. No one had left. The room got hotter and hotter. One by one, people began hanging up coats and jackets. I held out for ages, first using mine as a pillow. Then, I stuffed it behind my back for support. Finally, I walked across the room, hung up my jacket, looked around, and walked back to my chair. Then I realized the three dogs were gone. I wanted to ask somebody about that, but no one would make contact, so I let it go.

"Hours later, two police arrived and removed three people. I guess I'd been in a kind of trance. It was a moment before I understood what was happening. It was surreal. I was part of something yet detached. I was like a bit-part actor, superfluous to the drama, yet still there on stage. That's the best analogy I can come up with. The three people who were taken out looked like they were related with the same thick wavy dark brown hair, freckles, of the same general height. They seemed resigned to following the barked orders and the brandishing of batons. Almost as soon as the police brutality began, it was over. Everyone was still for a while. Later bathroom requests resumed. Different guards escorted the people.

"Then the unthinkable happened. One of the women with us started acting out oddly. I realized she might be having some sort of seizure. I shouted for someone to go to her to keep her from falling on the floor. Three people held on to her and I pounded on the door till the guards responded. By then people were scared for the woman and themselves. Panic took over. The guards tried to assess the problem without touching her. I and another had loosened her clothing. Two others were still holding her arms to keep her from harming herself. She began thrashing about, and it required more people to hold her feet. Everyone in the room was either helping her or freaking out in the pandemonium. I shouted for somebody to get water for her.

"That was when everyone realized the door was open. One guy ran out offering to get the water…and never returned. Someone else ran out to supposedly get more "help.". The guards both left the room while another guy and I kept our hold on the woman. In the chaos, others saw their chance for escape and scrambled out the door. The old woman was calming down. I looked at the guy holding her arms and legs and nodded toward the door. I told him to make a run for it. They all got out just in time. Moments later the guards returned with a stretcher and a first aid kit, only to discover just me and the woman.

"They took over from me and one of them pointed to the open door and said I shouldn't be the only one to remain. Since I was the only one who had stayed behind with the woman, I deserved some consideration. But the second officer told me if they found me again, they wouldn't hesitate to jail me for good.

"I ran as fast as I could. I heard the siren of an approaching ambulance. There were cars leaving the area. I saw the cowgirls get in a van driven by one of the men who had taken me to the bathroom. I kept in the shadows, away from streetlights, and wandered the rest of the night. I had no idea where I was. I had traveled down and across several streets before I thought to search for a street name. I was rattled. My common sense left me. Or I didn't want to know where I'd been, as if that might protect me.

"The sky lightened, and I started seeing morning traffic on the streets. People were picking up newspapers from their front steps and going out to their vehicles. Some were walking dogs. It was chilly. I could see my breath. It finally penetrated my mind that I'd left my jacket. It was no real loss, I thought, just Dad's old fishing jacket, but it had been warm. I couldn't go get it because I had no idea where I'd been. I also wouldn't have returned there voluntarily. I was so tired, dull-witted by that point. I walked down street after street, crossed an alley, and finally recognized the neighborhood. Uncle Cam's shop, with his overhead apartment, was not far. When I rang the bell, I prayed he could hear it with his slight hearing loss. Jewelry shops don't open at the crack of dawn, but I was worried he might have gotten up and gone out for breakfast.

"After three rings, I gave up and sat on the bottom step and cried. I was spent. That's how he found me. He was wonderful. He got me inside, made tea, shared his still-warm croissants smothered with honey. He wanted to call my parents, but I begged him not to. I needed to sort out what had happened. I was telling him a short version of the story, when I realized what I had left behind in the jacket—Grandma's locket. I sobbed. He thought it had to do with my experience. When I calmed down, I told him about the locket. He said it wasn't as important as my safety. He offered to replace the locket. He knew the design. I told him, no, it would have to be all right the way it was. Probably Grandma wouldn't notice I wasn't wearing it.

"After a while, I realized I was due back at Brisson, and he had a business to open. I cleaned up, trying to wipe the remnants of my tears from my face. He lent me cab fare, and I returned here to Brisson. By then, it was nearly ten. I slipped in without notice and got through my daily routine. We did an inventory of consumable, non-edible supplies in the afternoon, so I was absorbed with that. It helped calm me down. That was January nineteenth. Now it's February second. Besides Uncle Cam, you are the only ones I have spoken to about this. I gave him the abbreviated version. I've wanted to sit down with Sarah, but didn't know how to broach the subject, or if I should bring it up and have her relive her experience. I can't talk to Grandma without my parents learning what I did. So, for two weeks, I've kept it bottled up inside. I'm grateful to have you hear me out." She exhaled and shuddered with relief.

We nodded. It was a lot to take in. For someone so young,

she had undertaken a task daunting for anyone, much less someone not skilled at facing danger. I felt I had indeed discovered a kindred spirit. I was overwhelmed with emotion that she now had the locket.

"I'm so glad you got your locket back. That puts everything I endured in a different light."

"What are you talking about? I just told you how I lost it."

"Your Uncle Cam didn't tell you he had something for you?"

"I don't think so. He seemed keen on my coming to his shop to meet with you. I assumed he wanted to protect me."

"He probably does," said Patrick. "But he has other news."

"Like?"

"Why don't you call him, if it's not too late," I suggested.

"Oh, him? Uncle Cam watches the late news and switches back and forth between David Letterman and Jay Leno."

Joy brought out her phone, punched in a speed-dial number, and waited only seconds before her uncle picked up.

"Hi, Uncle Cam. It's Joy. You were right to advise me to meet with the people who were in your shop today. Yes. In fact, they're still here. They're going to spend the night and go home tomorrow. They wanted me to call you. They said you had some good news to tell me." She was silent, listening to him. Then we saw tears in her eyes which she wiped while holding the phone. She thanked him. After a few more words she hung up.

"Thank you." She beamed a smile at both of us. "Getting the locket back means so much. After hearing my story, you know how prized Grandma's locket is."

We assured her we did.

At this moment I reached into my pocket and handed Joy the earring I had found in the jacket.

"Oh! I forgot all about it. I know I mentioned it but, honestly, I didn't think I would see my jewelry again."

We told Joy we would see the jacket was returned when

everything was sorted out.

Between us we recounted as much of my experience as we could share. We left out Grace and alluded to UMCO without naming it. We stopped with my escape, not going into the Virginia trip or farm debriefing. One thing I wanted to ascertain but didn't know how to approach was if Joy had had a sense of being observed or followed. Patrick must have read my mind, because he introduced the idea, using my suspicious encounters as a segue. Then he bluntly asked Joy if she had experienced any impressions of being observed.

She was silent for a full moment before she replied. I wondered if she was analyzing some incidents from a fresh perspective. Finally, she shook her head and said there was nothing she could label suspicious. She had been paranoid for two weeks, rarely going anywhere, delegating others to run errands. She had cancelled a routine dental check-up and spent her days off at Brisson. She had not given anyone much opportunity to follow her around.

But she had wondered if Sarah had felt a presence. She reminded us she had not, even two weeks later, admitted to Sarah what she'd done. Joy suggested it was time Sarah joined the conversation. Hers was the first illegal capture. We agreed Sarah should be informed. We needed to know what she could add to the developing scenario.

CHAPTER 38: SARAH SPEAKS

Joy excused herself and went to see if Sarah was available. While we waited, Patrick reminded me to leave out UMCO during our discussion. I was offended that he felt it necessary to remind me and told him so. His grin revealed his real aim—seeing little sparks in my eyes. Why he enjoys stirring up fireworks in me I will never figure out. Unfortunately for him, the longer we've been married, the harder it has become for him to goad me into those little flashes, because I long ago caught on. But tonight, he caught me off guard. He was inordinately pleased with himself.

Joy returned with Sarah. We all got comfortable. She told Sarah of her jail experience, promising details later. We told our story, leaving out many details, but sharing enough to assure her we had been there. Sarah did not comment during our story. She pursed her lips, narrowed her eyes, but said nothing.

"Our oldest grandchild is Sarah Rebecca, named for Sarah. a special family friend, but she goes by Sally," I told her hoping to ease the tension.

I'm Sarah R. also, but my 'R' is for Rachael."

"Sarah Rachael, could you think back to your experience and

tell us if there is anything you remember, a detail or an incident, even a word, you didn't mention before, but you have thought of since you shared your ordeal?" Patrick asked.

There was a pause before Sarah found her voice. I began to suspect she didn't feel comfortable enough to speak up.

But then she did. "It was a conversation I didn't understand. It was just after I arrived, before I was questioned. I didn't recall it when the police and Joy talked to me. Then, when I did think of it, since it was puzzling to me anyway, I just let it go. The guards were talking between themselves and mentioned 'forn.' I thought they said 'porn.' Later they said something about 'Forn.' I guessed it was some other guard's name. The more I considered it, the less likely it seemed to be a nickname, or a given name, but I don't know what it could be. Maybe it's not important?"

"Sarah, it could be important. Details give us the best understanding. Do you remember anything else about Forn?" Patrick queried.

Sarah thought before answering. I expected her to tell us there was nothing else, but she had more to contribute.

"One said Forn would not be pleased about how much contact they had with the undesirables," she added. "Then the other one sort of snickered."

"That may be very helpful. There is something else we want to know. Have you noticed anyone following you, or anyone suspicious around here or where you work?" Patrick continued.

"I can't say I've seen anyone. But I've felt eyes on me. I know it sounds odd, so I haven't mentioned it. I can't point to a person and say he was following me, but I feel like I'm not alone. I guess I feel uneasy a lot of the time. I've tried to convince myself I'm paranoid after what I went through. Why do you ask?"

I responded because I had been the one to imagine or experience strangers about me.

"I was in a dry cleaner business near home and a man came

in. He was rude to the clerk, then stormed out. I felt like he just came in to get a good look at me. I was wearing Joy's jacket then. Yesterday a man was staring at me during Mass. It was snowy outside, so not many people were in church. He didn't know when to kneel, or sit or stand, or what to say when he went to communion. He wasn't with anybody. I know he wasn't there to worship. When we left to go to our truck, we saw him in the truck, the same truck from the dry cleaners, and the driver was the man from the dry cleaners. When we got home, there were recent footprints up to our back deck, and our dog had covered the glass slider on the inside with slobber by jumping against it. Also, there were two men in our town park who seemed very interested in us."

"Either you imagine things, or you stirred up unrest in someone's beehive," Sarah responded. "How about since you came down here? Have you noticed anyone suspicious?"

"I didn't consider it. I was so wound up about finding Joy and learning she was all right, I didn't think about it," I admitted.

"I was aware and didn't see anyone suspicious," Patrick added. "I regularly had an eye on the rearview mirror. I was cautious when we walked on the streets. I'm confident we were not observed down here," he assured. I was proud of his vigilance.

"So, what happens now?" questioned Joy.

"Yes, now what do we do?" echoed Sarah.

"We don't do anything ourselves," Patrick stated with emphasis on his last word. "We need to report everything. We must defer to the authorities who will connect the dots. They may need more proof than we as a group, including your grandmother Joy, can provide, but what we have collectively is more powerful than our individual stories. For the time being, promise us, Sarah, that you won't take chances. Do not walk the streets any more than necessary. Make sure you don't resemble a 'bag lady' or someone who could be singled out as an outcast. Perhaps you should not change your work uniform before you leave. Wearing the uniform shows you have a job. If the weather is warm enough, maybe you should even keep your coat unbuttoned to show the uniform," offered Patrick. His advice impressed me. and I nodded my assent. Sarah agreed to follow his directions.

"I'd like to add you should walk home with people you know," said Joy. "I can generate a list of residents who'd be glad to meet you at work and escort you home. Before you refuse, remember all your tutoring, babysitting, and homework help. Residents appreciate you. Let them show their appreciation. They'll want to help. It will be good for them to give back. You know it's true. We can start with your dinner table crew. I'll let them organize a 'Sarah Watch'. It's settled!" Joy exclaimed.

Sarah tearfully nodded her assent looking grateful and embarrassed. Her body language reflected her relief. We had removed one stressful burden from her shoulders.

At this juncture we were eager to end the day. Joy promised to speak to Sarah's dinner crew before she retired- one more task. Sarah volunteered to get us settled. Joy told her which rooms we were to occupy and asked her to fetch supplies. Sarah seemed pleased to have a purpose. We were grateful for her cheerful offer.

CHAPTER 39: SHELTERING IN A SHELTER

Sarah led us to the utility closet and filled our outstretched arms with towels, washcloths, pairs of generic striped cotton pajamas, soap, shampoo, toothbrushes, and toothpaste. She paused in the dining room retrieving two bottles of water. We climbed to the second floor. Here she turned left and showed Patrick his room, one door from the staircase, two doors from the bathroom. Patrick briefly kissed me goodnight and traced the sign of the cross on my forehead. I did the same to him, our private parting blessing. On the third floor, diagonally across from the staircase, Sarah opened the door to my room. She noted the bathroom was located above the one on the second floor. She wished me a good night. I thanked her for her kindness, and she went on her way.

I stood on the threshold of my room. Soothing soft gray walls enveloped me. They were accented by deep ocean blue woodwork. Across from me was a narrow twin bed covered in a blue and green quilt, with a gray wool blanket folded precisely at the foot. To the left of the cot was a low, scarred dark blue wooden dresser positioned directly under the room's only window. A three-drawer gray painted desk and matching, gray-painted wooden kitchen chair were along the wall to my right. The only item on the desk was a no-frills electric alarm clock. Between the bed and desk was a braided area rug in rich shades of blue and green with white seashells painted on it. There was no closet, but three hooks on the back of the door. I placed toiletries and pajamas on the dresser and hung my purse and coat on the hooks.

The room's only ornament was a framed print hung above the desk, I immediately recognized as the work of Brother Michael O'Neill McGrath, an Oblate of St. Francis de Sales. I moved closer to read the title, 'Star of the Sea'. I realized the entire room had been subtly planned around that iconic depiction of Mary, the mother of God. The only light Sarah had turned on for me was a frosted globe hanging from the aquamarine-colored ceiling.

All I wanted to do was flop on the bed and close my eyes. I stopped by the wall and hit the light switch. I groped my way to the bed. As if magically, stars twinkled from the ceiling. I repeated aloud, 'Star of the Sea'. It was a delightful sensation lying under the stars. So many memories kaleidoscoped through my mind- Evie and Rose surprising us with a similar display on our bedroom ceiling years ago…lying flat on our backs on lounge chairs on St. Croix 'oohing' and 'aahing' as meteor showers sprinted across the velvet blackness…walking our dog Maggie on moonlit nights surrounded by hundreds of lightning bugs in strobe mode…the foggy night in Annapolis we crept through streets ending up in front of an abandoned factory…the dusky evening we sprinted through other Annapolis streets escaping to our car. Not all the memories were welcome.

I reluctantly rose and turned on the light. Going to my purse I dug out my restless legs prescription, opened the bottle of water and swallowed the pill. Finally, I gathered my bathroom supplies. I felt awkward going down the hall passing closed doors decorated with names scrolled on card stock or bits of tissue paper forming collages. The utilitarian bathroom contained five faux gray marble toilet stalls, three showers with very white shower curtains, and five white porcelain sinks. My footsteps echoed on the black geometric patterned floor. Sarah had said each floor in this wing was either only men or only women, so there was only one bathroom. I trusted she was right. After showering and shampooing my hair, I dressed in my pajamas, brushed my teeth, and trudged back to my room towel drying my hair, feeling clean and soothed. I glanced at the clock and was shocked it was nearly midnight. No wonder I was alone in the bathroom.

I must have fallen asleep before I mentally formed more than a whisper of a prayer of wonder at all that had occurred in one day.

The early morning activity brought me to consciousness. Shuffling, muffled footfalls moved back and forth in the hall. Doors opened and closed, showers and sinks turned on and off. Toilets flushed.

Moments passed before I was fully aware of my location or what day it was. I sat up. It was quite dark outside. The only light was a rectangular halo around the door. I mused on things for a bit, drifting into half-sleep as soft voices droned in the background. I roused myself again and sat up. I might intrude on people's routines, if I barged into the bathroom, so I waited for a lull in the background noise. It wasn't long before it grew quiet. I rose, picked up my things, and headed down the hall.

I returned to my room and dressed for the day ahead and the trip home. I desperately wanted a very hot cup of tea but knew Patrick could not deliver it. I had to make my way downstairs if I wanted tea.

Of course, Patrick, the penultimate early riser, was already seated at a table in the dining room. He was in conversation with two of our dinner partners from last night. They greeted me but didn't wave me over. I found tea, oatmeal, fresh fruit, and juice. I sat at the table closest to the tea, so refills would be close by. One other person, a short inconspicuous woman with dark hair and thin eyebrows approached and asked if I minded her company. I assured her I was a passing guest in her house, and she was welcome to sit with me. She smiled and a couple of missing teeth caught my attention. She grinned even more broadly.

"I won. In the end I won."

"Pardon?" I asked.

"He knocked me around, knocked my teeth loose, but in the end, I won. I went to court. He won't hassle me again. So, I won."

"I didn't mean to be staring. I'm sorry."

"No need to be. Your stare isn't the first I ever got. I'm used to it. Soon my teeth'll be fixed. I had the others pulled. They couldn't save 'em. There's a good dental clinic nearby. I'm paying for the work- no free stuff. It's taking a while, but I'll have new teeth and be proud of my smile and my life again."

"I think you already have pride in yourself, new teeth or not."

"Yes, I suspect you're right."

"By the way, I'm Norah, but you probably know that."

"I'm Hattie. Nice to meet you." She sat across from me with black coffee and a lot of toast spread with a mound of peanut butter.

"You're eating one of my husband's favorite foods- peanut butter on anything," I confided.

"I can tell. It looks like he found the jar before I did. He has peanut butter on a bagel and an English muffin."

"Tell me did he leave enough for others?"

"Don't fret. We have econo-gigantic size jars. They last at least three days. The jar was just opened this morning. He's fine.

Everybody else is safe. Are you and your husband friends of Joy?"

I was taken by surprise. I wasn't prepared for the question. I dug in my mix of information to find something nearly true.

"We just met Joy, but we're friends with one of her relatives. We had wanted to meet her before, but she was away at college, so this time we made a point of getting in touch, and we just lost track of time." She seemed satisfied with my explanation.

I concentrated on my oatmeal, finding it comforting, like my grandma's had been. I never found out what made hers so creamy and delicious, while any other bowl of oatmeal had made me want to gag. I went for a tea refill and topped off Hattie's coffee. We talked for a bit more, and then she headed off to her job at a drycleaner's. She had to be at work at six-thirty. I was shocked. I'd been awake and functioning and it was barely six. After Hattie left, Patrick and his companions waved me over. They mumbled something about allowing a female at their table, even if it was against morning policy. What I guessed was that they felt slightly guilty about seeing me sit alone across the room, so they allowed me to join them. I accepted.

Their conversation bored me. I rued the move but couldn't find a reason to abandon such non-sparkling morning communication. The men soon scattered to their jobs leaving Patrick and me in companionable silence. He leaned over kissing me good morning. Now that was better. He asked how I had slept and was surprised to hear I'd slept solidly. I knew he had slept well. He could doze off anywhere within seconds of closing his eyes.

We were both thinking of the day ahead. Patrick broached the subject first.

"What Sarah recalled is puzzling, what she overheard about 'Forn' while she waited to be questioned. We must pursue that."

"I agree. How do we proceed?"

"We contact UMCO."

I groaned, but knew he was right.

CHAPTER 40: FORN

We located Joy asking if we might borrow a private place at the shelter to make a call. She offered her office. We sat in the chairs we'd occupied hours earlier, before meeting so many people and being welcomed into their community. I listened closely to Patrick's conversation, filling in what I guessed was coming from the other end.

"Yes, we are in Annapolis."

(What are you doing there?)

"Following up on a lead."

(What lead?)

"Norah grabbed a jacket on her way out from the holding cell."

(And? So?)

"She threw it into our car trunk and forgot about it till Saturday when she went to get something from the trunk."

(And you checked out the jacket?)

"Norah did and found several items. We traced one thing, a locket, to a jewelry store in Annapolis. We drove down here yesterday to…"

(Without checking in? You haven't mentioned UMCO?)

"Certainly, we kept it out of our conversations. We met the store owner, a Mr. Cameron, who led us to the locket's owner. It's the person who left the phone number on the bathroom wall in the prison- the one Norah reported about in her debriefing."

(I don't recall any phone number information.)

"Did you rely on a summary report or the transcript of Norah's debriefing?"

(I'll check into that. What else did you learn?)

"What else did we learn? This victim, Joy Flemming, was captured because she set out to be 'caught.' She was on a mission after two people—her grandmother and a resident at the shelter where she works were previously held captive. She connected details from their stories and took things into her own hands."

(Is she impetuous or what?)

"No, she's not impetuous, just frustrated and outraged because no one is visibly working to solve the problem."

(Where are you right now?)

"At Brisson Shelter, where Joy works as a resident counselor. We spent the night here. We interviewed her and the lady who lives here, who was also imprisoned."

(What about the grandmother?)

"Well, she has Alzheimer's. So far, we are relying on her granddaughter's recollections."

(We'll let that stand for now. But we won't rule out interviewing her later. Where does she live?)

"I'll inform Joy we may have to meet her grandmother. She's local. She lives here in Annapolis with her daughter and son-in-law."

(Are they agreeable to our meeting with her if we need to pursue this?)

"Ah, they might be agreeable to our meeting with her. I don't think they know about the connection. Joy hasn't confided in them about her experience. All they know is that their mother/mother-in-law was missing and somehow returned."

(Before we determine if we need to interview her grandmother, I suggest she come clean to her family.)

"Yes, that seems appropriate. We'll pass on to Joy the urgency of enlightening her family. I'm sure she now knows it's necessary. And furthermore, Norah has recognized a resident here who was imprisoned with her. He was the Hispanic young man who was taken forcibly from the room before I arrived to free them. No, we did not reveal ourselves. He did not seem to recognize Norah, so we said nothing."

(As for the two of you going off without official assignments…)

"Yes? Are we in trouble for showing initiative?"

(We'll take up that matter later. For now, maintain regular contact with us.)

"Yes, I speak for both of us. We will. But before we end, there is another reason we called."

(Yes?)

"We were given a word, maybe a proper name of a person or a place, 'Forn'—the shelter resident, Sarah, who was imprisoned heard it twice but didn't recall it when she gave her police report."

(So, you don't know the exact spelling?)

"No, we're just assuming for now that it's spelled F O R N."

(We'll update you on any information we uncover.)

"Thanks." Patrick ended the call.

"We will what?" I demanded.

"What?" Patrick seemed genuinely confused.

"You said we will do something before you told him or her about 'FORN'."

"Oh, we'll keep them in the loop, won't go off on our own, and follow protocol."

"That's it? They're not forbidding us to continue?"

"No, not yet."

"What's that mean?"

"Well, we developed the lead and should go where it takes us. If they discover we're off base, or they get another lead that converges with ours, they may have us hand off what we're doing to someone else. For now, we are on the case, both of us. Although, what more we can do I don't know."

"Patrick, there's always reviewing the evidence. We know more than when we first went over it. Also, we can start a computer search for 'Forn'."

"All right, Norah, but we can't keep Joy's office occupied. Maybe we could wait till we're in the truck."

"What if we get information that leads us to ask Joy or Sarah more questions?"

"At least we should ask Joy if she needs her office. Maybe she shares this space with the other counselors." We sought out Joy and secured the use of the room for the next half hour. That was long enough to Google 'Forn'.

We discovered a farming organization based in the Midwest. We also found a federation supporting retired nurses in the New England states. There were several others, but an obscure entry made us pause. FORN- Follow Observe Report Non-contact. What was that acronym all about?

"Patrick, I was followed and observed."

"Yes, and we met with no direct contact. I'm willing to bet we were reported on."

"How did they find us?"

"Well…perhaps they copied our tag number. No, the back tag light was off. It can't have been that."

"Patrick, is there video surveillance? You know, like street traffic cameras?"

"Let's ask the residents."

There were still a few residents eating breakfast. Most of them were children, but a few adults were there. DeeDee was one of them. She assured us that there were some police surveillance cameras in Annapolis, but not all over the city. She had no idea why we wanted the information and didn't ask. We were relieved. What could we have told her? Perhaps later she would put two and two together about our visit and Sarah's needing escorts.

We pondered how official police cameras might be accessed by outsiders, and if it were possible to find out if they had been previously viewed. We thought our son-in-law, Scott, might be able to answer our question, so we called his cell phone. We were sent to voice mail. Patrick left a cryptic message.

Almost immediately Scott called back. Now Patrick had to take someone else into his confidence. Telling him only as much as was necessary, he explained what we needed to know. Essentially, Scott said almost any system could be hacked, but an easier way would be for someone to feed information to an outside entity, probably for a price.

How could we be so naïve? It had been mentioned during the debriefing that some police officers didn't probe or ask too many questions of their "gift" arrest, those who'd been arrested and turned over to the real authorities. How much of a stretch would it be to have officers more directly cooperating with, even assisting, the vigilantes? Were any of the "officers" legitimate off-duty police officers? How complex was the web the vigilantes wove?

Patrick called his contact at UMCO. This time he mentioned my suspicions of being followed and the possibility of someone having reviewed traffic surveillance to locate us as we returned home before. His contact promised to check on our latest concern and advised us to return home before our car was spotted. Patrick assured him we weren't in our car. Then he told them about our home having had foot traffic across the lawn up to our back deck entry. There wasn't any evidence of anyone being in the driveway side of our property, but someone had been in our church when we were there, so someone must have been watching the house and knew about our truck. If we had been followed down here, had we now put the shelter in danger? Patrick's contact assured us he would immediately put protection in place for the shelter, contact Joy's director, and arrange for subtle, but effective safety measures, including in-house protection.

Our last charge was to bring Joy up to speed. We found her alone in the dining room. We gave her our donation, thanked her for the shelter's hospitality, then told her of the latest developments. We told her about Jorge and recommended she talk with him privately and warn him about the dangers and get his support. We also advised Joy to share her experience with her family in case it became necessary to question her grandmother. We suggested her uncle Cam might help. Shortly afterward, we were homeward bound. I offered to drive.

CHAPTER 41: PURSUIT

Our drive to Cecil County was uneventful. No one seemed to be watching or following us.

That is, until we were on Route 213 just south of Elkton.

Were we spotted crossing the Chesapeake City Bridge? I was driving and saw in the rearview mirror the red Chevy pickup truck was two vehicles back. Did they think we wouldn't recognize the truck after two encounters? Did they believe we hadn't noticed them at either the dry cleaners or outside Immaculate Conception Church?

Patrick got out his phone and called in the truck's license plate mentioning it was a "Treasure the Bay" Maryland tag. When I heard him rattle off the tag information, I interrupted him.

"Wait. That's not the tag I copied. The one I copied was a Maryland farm tag. Take the red notebook from my purse. I recorded the tag information Saturday at the dry cleaners. On Sunday I saw the same tag, even with snow on the truck."

Patrick asked his contact to hold on while he checked something. He fished out the notebook and found the page with the tag information. He relayed it to the person at the other end of the connection, who was excited. If the vehicle operator switched tags, that was clearly illegal. However, even though it was unrelated to the vigilante investigation, this tangential connection might be a way to officially question them. They directed us to bypass our house and enter the North East town limits where the town police would be on the lookout for a stolen truck. Our job was to lure it into their jurisdiction so they could investigate.

Since it was Tuesday, we drove down Main Street following it all the way to the edge of town to Paradise Grille. We drove by the restaurant, slowly, as if checking for parking in their lot. Just for good measure, we proceeded to the second intersection past the restaurant, turned around, and drove the one block past Rose and Scott's house, then turned back onto Main Street.

Before we turned, I glanced to the right, back up the street, and caught sight of a town police cruiser about three blocks away. This time, without using a turn signal, we pulled into the entry to Paradise Grille's parking area along the North East Creek.

The Chevy truck followed us all the way to the restaurant, managing to keep just one vehicle away. Our sudden turn into the parking lot caught him off guard. Not using the turn signal kept from tipping him off. His surprise was obvious, as he hesitated, slowed down, stopped, started slowly forward again, then stopped again. He then foolishly tried to pull into a compact car sized parking space opposite the restaurant.

From our car in the restaurant parking lot, we observed the bizarre slow-motion repercussions.

A Comcast van following directly behind the red truck swerved to the left toward Paradise Grille to avoid hitting it. A young couple, maybe in their thirties, had just exited the restaurant. They were holding hands, waiting for a break in the traffic, and had started to cross the street when they had to jump back away from the swerving van. They found themselves able to move only one step backward because of the wrought iron fence separating the outdoor seating area from the sidewalk. The van, driving slightly onto the pavement, barely missed them. The woman lost her grip on her take-out container. Its contents made a bloody looking splash on the slush of Main Street. She raised her arm to wipe off the strips of red sauce from her yellow ski jacket. Her male companion pulled her closer to him. I thought how chivalrous he was.

Suddenly the red truck began backing up recklessly into the parking space. He hit the curb with his right rear tire. An older, gray-bearded man heavily bundled in a black and red plaid hooded jacket walked his Siberian Husky on the sidewalk parallel to the red truck, oblivious of the truck's erratic movement. His dog, however, sensed the impending danger, reacted by violently tugging his leash, and pulled the now-startled man away from the danger of the colliding vehicles. The two of them, with the dog controlling the man, picked up speed. The man stumbled but was mercifully dragged away in time.

Realizing he could not fit into the parking space, the truck driver whipped back out onto Main Street without a glance. A driver in a shiny, very new-looking black Dodge Ram was cautiously attempting to navigate around him. The attempt failed. Side view mirrors became entangled. The Dodge Ram driver laid on his horn and lurched forward, removing the side view mirror from the red truck.

Simultaneously, just a few yards up the street from the dog and man, two stylishly attired women laden with bagged purchases emerged from a local gift shop, England's Colony on the Bay. The taller of the two conversed with her companion and hit the remote control opening the trunk of her car parked directly in front of the shop. As the trunk popped open the clash of metal and fiberglass filled the air. Then the truck horn blared. Reacting to the commotion, the shorter woman lost her grip on her purchases. Bags went flying, tires screeched. The woman shook her fist at the red truck's driver for causing the mayhem and at the black truck's driver for blowing his horn. She took a step toward them unmindful of Main Street traffic trying to come to a stop. Her companion grabbed her by the sleeve of her navy-blue pea coat just in time to keep her from becoming someone's hood ornament.

A teenaged boy lugging a bulging backpack and wearing khaki shorts and a royal blue North East High hoodie walked up our side of the street. He stopped and shook his head and stayed where he was, rooted to the sidewalk, taking pictures with his cell phone as cars dominoed into one another.

None of us noticed the silently approaching North East town police car until the officer turned on the siren as he maneuvered into the restaurant parking lot in the space beside us. He mouthed something to us from his vehicle as he reached to put on his hat.

"Hey, Patrick and Norah, did you witness this?"

"Yes." My husband tersely answered.

"Hang around inside till I'm done out here, please."

"Not a problem, Tom."

Quickly Officer Tom Daniels assessed the situation and directed the red Chevy truck into a full-sized parking spot farther down the street. The black truck was assigned a space just beyond it. He motioned for both drivers to remain in their vehicles.

Meanwhile, Patrick and I made our way across the slushy parking lot, around the back of the restaurant, and entered by the Creekside door. Once inside, we headed for a front-row seat to view the "silent movie" excitement.

Our host, Carol, joined us to witness the drama. Megan, our regular waitress, arrived with our usual drinks she had prepared as soon as she spied us entering the building. She paused to stare out at the continuing action. We gazed without interruption as Officer Daniels checked each bystander for injuries. He spoke into his radio. We wondered if he was ordering an ambulance but couldn't imagine why until the young woman who had dropped her to-go container turned around.

Patrick and I gasped. She was very, very pregnant. She was clutching her stomach which the ski jacket could not quite cover. Her companion, Officer Daniels, and the teen helped her around the fence and onto a wrought iron chair. The town fire siren blared. Carol hurried out the Main Street door to offer what assistance she could. She shouted instructions to Megan who rushed to the back of the restaurant and quickly returned with blankets and coats. She handed them over to Carol who wrapped them around the woman.

Officer Daniels had begun checking drivers of vehicles attached to one another. Efficiently he guided them onto Church Point Road along the stone wall bordering St. Mary Anne's Episcopal Church. All vehicles not involved he waved through. Backup assistance arrived in the person of Police Chief Darrell Hamilton, who took over traffic control.

This freed Officer Daniels to deal with the two truck drivers. He walked to the Chevy pickup and motioned for the driver to roll down his window. He complied and stuck his head out toward Officer Daniels who motioned him to turn off his engine, and we assumed he told him to produce his license and registration. The man nodded his seeming compliance.

Next Officer Daniels approached the Dodge Ram. He made the same 'turn off your engine' motion to the driver and began speaking.

Suddenly Officer Daniels whirled around. We hadn't heard what he heard—the Chevy truck engine started up. Tom stepped out into the street, arms flailing, shouting for the driver to turn off his truck. Instead, the man put the truck in drive and attempted to pull out of the parking space. Officer Daniels, in a fluid movement, shot out a front tire. He raised the gun level to the Chevy truck's windshield.

Chief Hamilton, abandoning traffic patrol, stomped to the truck and with gun pulled, yanked open the driver's door. The driver's hands were up above his head as he clambered out of the still-running truck. This was our opportunity to scrutinize the man who had been our shadow. It was the same man I'd first seen at the dry cleaners!

He was not young, but not old, maybe in his late forties or so, very thin and at least six feet tall. He sported a reddish-gray beard, knit brown cap pulled low, almost covering his ears, longish red hair curling out at the back onto the corduroy collar of his faded jeans jacket, stained, faded jeans, and scuffed brown work boots. He was the same man.

The teenager was rooted to the pavement, still taking pictures. I could imagine the frenzy he was creating on Facebook.

They cuffed the man. Officer Daniels jumped in the truck, backed it bumpily into the parking space, turned off the truck, and locked it. He handed over the keys to Chief Hamilton. They escorted the slump-shouldered driver to the chief's car.

A third officer arrived on the scene and directed backed-up traffic down Main Street. As the paramedic's vehicle and the ambulance's sirens screamed in the distance, he motioned traffic to move over to allow for them to get through. Both emergency vehicles arrived within seconds of each other. They parked side by side in the restaurant parking lot entrance. A stretcher was brought out while the woman's vitals were taken.

Chief Hamilton ensconced his man in the back seat of his patrol car and left the scene.

Officer Daniels finally went to the driver of the Dodge Ram. For anyone just now driving by, he may have appeared to be conducting a routine traffic stop. He accepted items from the driver and went back toward the parking lot to his patrol car.

We continued our observation as EMTs attended the pregnant woman and helped her onto a stretcher. We waited anxiously for Carol to report on her condition.

I glanced out at Main Street. Traffic was moving. A few people were on the sidewalk. Nothing remained of the recent drama except red sauce on slush and the abandoned red truck. Even the Dodge Ram had disappeared.

Megan materialized to take our order. We'd forgotten about food. Recalling it was still Burger Tuesday Patrick chose Tex-Mex, while I picked the Italian burger. He added an order of nachos to be brought out first. Waiting for our food, we speculated about what was occurring at North East Police Station. Then the nachos arrived and smelled incredible. We dug in.

Whoever had orchestrated the surveillance on us had not anticipated the ensuing near-catastrophic developments. What we knew, we could not share with those seated around us. We speculated what they had gleaned from the occurrences. I wondered if other diners glimpsed anything sinister in these events.

When Tom Daniels strode in, we had just begun enjoying our burgers. He headed right for us. We gestured for him to join us. He called Megan who immediately arrived with a soda. He waved off her offer of a meal. He couldn't stay long enough.

"It's only Tuesday afternoon in February. It's not Friday evening in the summer with everybody heading to Elk Neck State Park or the camps or boatyards. What's going on in this town?"

We looked at each other and with a nod mutually decided it was time to explain everything to the local police.

"Well, Tom, the guy Chief Hamilton took away from the scene had been following us," I started.

"What?"

"Yeah, since Route 213 near the shopping center where Redner's grocery store is located, just south of Elkton."

"How did you know he was following you?"

"We wanted to be sure, so we drove past Paradise Grille, circled back, then quickly pulled into the parking lot. He wasn't expecting the quick turn. That's when he caused all the commotion."

"This was the truck with stolen tags we were on the lookout for?"

"Yes," continued Patrick, "Norah saw the same Chevy truck Saturday when she was in Elkton. The guy acted weird at the dry cleaners; created quite a scene, so she copied his license tag. She didn't mention this to me till late Saturday evening."

They both gave me a clear look of disapproval for keeping possibly dangerous information to myself.

"Then, at Sunday Mass in Elkton there was a different guy staring at Norah. After church he pulled out of the parking lot in that same red truck with the first guy, the one from the dry cleaners, at the wheel. We saw them drive from Bow Street to Park Way but were not yet in our vehicle. By the time we got to Park Way and North Street, the truck was out of sight."

"Did you report this to the Elkton police?"

"No. What could we really accuse them of?"

"So, tell me why you think it's a stolen vehicle."

I answered this one.

"Because the tags on the truck aren't the same as they were on Saturday and Sunday. Switching tags is illegal too, right?"

Before Tom could answer, his radio came alive. Chief Hamilton was requesting his location. Tom replied that he was at Paradise Grille, finalizing witnesses' reports of the incident. Chief Hamilton asked that he wrap up ASAP. Tom took a last gulp of his soda, copied the original tag number from my notebook, and said he had to go.

"Would you like me to stop by your house when I get off duty? I may have answers, information, I can legally share with you."

"Please," I answered. "You know where we live. We're headed there as soon as we finish up here."

He nodded. With a wave in the direction of Carol behind the bar, he was gone.

We settled our bill with Megan and stopped to talk to Carol about the pregnant woman.

As we got into our truck, we noted other town police officers still attending to drivers of damaged vehicles on Church Point Road.

Patrick offered to drive, and I didn't discourage him.

CHAPTER 42: CLANDESTINE COMMUNICATIONS

I distracted myself the rest of the afternoon with a home project. Patrick contented himself with repotting four amaryllis plants on the kitchen table.

When the phone rang at seven-thirty I knew it was Tom. *Wrong.* Our oldest granddaughter Sally said she was checking on us. I felt old, like Grandmother Barbette, but was pleased to be checked up on despite it being the granddaughter who'd announced years ago she'd be the one choosing our nursing home in our golden years.

Sally, or Sar-eye, as her then toddler brother, Francis, had pronounced his sister's name, mentioned a novel she was reading for a college class. It was about two girls who met when they were five and had never got along. When they were twelve, one girl's mom and the other's dad began dating. A year later they were coping badly as stepsisters. She said she could see using it in upper elementary grades. Where had this career-focused adult hidden the teen that I remembered?

Then she asked if I'd heard about a novel centered around a giant oak tree in a park where teens hid secret notes because their families refused to let them call each other. I said it sounded like a cross between *To Kill a Mockingbird* and *Romeo and Juliet.* She said yes, but the story was about two boys, Tom and Daniel.

Hearing those two names, I listened more intensely.

"So, the kids weren't allowed to communicate, huh?"

"Yeah. Right. They were resourceful, though. For years they shared information."

"Did the adults ever find out?"

"No. The book's narrated by them as middle-aged guys in a flashback starting when they were in high school and covers four years, then jumps to when they joined the same military unit. They were both military police. One later became a private eye, the other a member of their hometown police force. The secret message practice had gotten them interested in solving mysteries."

"How intriguing. I might borrow it when you're done."

"I'll bring it tonight if you like. I've written my review of it."

"Come on over. I'm sure we have ice cream in the freezer."

I got off the phone and was tingling from my fingertips to my toes.

Still, I didn't like Sally being dragged into something sinister.

I relayed the conversation to Patrick. He counseled patience till we knew how Sally was involved. Half an hour later she hadn't arrived. Her apartment was ten minutes away. I stewed and grew more and more annoyed with Tom, assuming he had contacted and informed her about events. Another fifteen minutes passed before she arrived. Patrick almost physically held me back from rushing out the door. She sauntered in with her denim purse and a book.

"What took you so long?" Patrick demanded.

"I had a phone call just as I was going out the door."

"I guess we have some explaining to do?" Patrick offered.

"Um, yes. And is ice cream really on the agenda?"

"Definitely!" I responded heading to the freezer, taking out maple walnut ice cream for us, and cherry vanilla for her. We settled in the living room, since the kitchen was still inundated with displaced plants.

"You have a message for us?" Patrick asked.

"Yes, PopPop, from Officer Daniels. He said it was urgent, but it wasn't a good idea for him to phone or visit you. Your phone might be tapped, or your house watched."

"How did he contact you?"

"He called me. He was sure my cell phone was safe."

"Do you know Tom?"

"I do now. I've never met him, but I guess I know something about him after tonight. He got my number from Maglie."

"So, he has a message he couldn't deliver himself," I prompted, entering the conversation.

"Wait. You two owe me some explanation."

"Earlier today we witnessed an accident in North East," Patrick offered.

"That can't be everything."

"No, we had been followed by one of the vehicles involved," I added.

"Officer Daniels is investigating it, and he was supposed to stop by to update us," Patrick told her.

"He claimed he couldn't tell me what he knew. He said I'd be safe if I just delivered his message using the phone conversation he scripted and then carry a book to you once you picked up on the hints using his names and referencing the tree.

"So, we should act normally, pretending it's a regular visit," Patrick concluded.

"Yes. Now I must tell you about contacting him."

"He obviously referenced the town park. We're familiar with the hole in the tree," I volunteered.

"Officer Daniels said he would leave a message there early

tomorrow morning during his first round through town before the park opens. He said to tell you to stop there around noon, not midnight. Why did he say that?"

"Because I joked with him about it being a spot for lovers to leave messages to meet during the full moon at midnight," I explained.

"Why were you even talking about a hole in a tree?"

"He saw me taking photos there and asked what I found interesting." I responded.

"You took pictures of a hole in a tree?"

"Come on, Sally," Patrick said rolling his eyes. "You know the sort of pictures she takes—kneeling in the sand, looking through open spaces in driftwood instead of just capturing the waves."

Sally laughed. "True. So, are you going to the park at noon?"

"Absolutely!" we chorused.

"Will you let me know what's going on?"

"Not till we are sure there's no danger," said a decisive grandfather.

We finished our ice cream and Sally left shortly after with two books I knew she'd enjoy reading.

We watched from behind our drapes for any sign she was being followed but saw nothing. As prearranged, she called us when she got safely to her apartment.

CHAPTER 43: MESSAGE IN THE TREE

Waking up at six Wednesday morning with no possibility of returning to sleep created a view of endlessly slowly passing hours until noon. Patrick was already up with his coffee brewing. I admitted sleep was not returning, so I got dressed in brown cords and a cream-colored cotton blend turtleneck. When I rummaged in the craft room wardrobe for my favorite, much-worn oatmeal-colored Irish cable knit pullover, I tripped over my grandmother's old faded blue suitcase I had left on the floor. It was full of old family photos, especially ones from our two cross-country family trips. I had planned to separate the photos and distribute them to my siblings. I set the suitcase up on its side in front of the closet. If I put the suitcase back in the closet, I'd never finish the project.

I greeted Maggie, then set about making my Irish Breakfast tea. I noticed immediately a 'plant fairy' had restored order and cleanliness to the kitchen table. Hardly any dirt was left smudging the blue and white shell print placemats. Patrick offered to fix oatmeal, so I prepared bowls of fresh fruit—mango, bananas, and blueberries. Most of his fruit he would stir into his oatmeal. I didn't like the squishy blueberries in hot cereal. I segregated my fruit in a daffodil yellow petal-shaped bowl. Its spring color and flower shape reminded me gardening wasn't far in the future.

Our breakfast was over, and the kitchen cleaned up by seven-thirty. We watched the morning news and checked the Weather Channel for a local forecast. We could expect cold and clouds, but no new precipitation. By nine I was sated with news and interviews. I did two loads of laundry. I was restless, too energized to do the newspaper sudoku. I walked back to our bedroom glancing in the craft room. The blue suitcase almost shouted like Donkey to Shrek, "Pick me! Pick me!" I dragged the hard, battered suitcase to the dining room, and opened it. The sorting began. Somehow, Patrick and I both filled the morning hours. By eleven-thirty I urged him to get his jacket. I felt like we were in danger of being late for an important meeting.

"The hole in the tree will be there when we get there," my laid-back husband insisted. "It won't erode. I'm positive Tom tucked the note deep inside so it wouldn't blow away."

"But aren't you anxious to get it and see what it says?"

"Of course," he admitted, a hint of a smile in his eyes.

I grabbed my camera and binoculars. Patrick took bottles of water from the refrigerator. We looked like our usual walking-the-park-path selves.

"Wait a minute!" I called out.

"What else could you possibly need to walk in the park?"

"A dog! Let's take Maggie!"

"You're kidding. Really? Today? You are kidding." Seeing my crestfallen face, Patrick knew I was not kidding. I had been inspired by an idea he rashly judged foolish. I was hurt to have a suggestion so abruptly dismissed.

"Wait. I'm sorry. You took me completely by surprise. Maybe we should discuss this."

"This?"

"Your idea. Tell me why you want to take Maggie."

"When we veer off course, it will seem our pet is the reason."

"All right."

"All right, what?"

"Well, you've provided a reason. It makes good sense. I'll get her leash."

"Great!" My disappointment faded to anticipation.

When Maggie realized she was going too, she couldn't contain her ecstasy. Her entire body moved, wagged, jumped, and quivered. Total joy. It took us both to get her secured into her harness in the back seat.

I watched through the rearview mirror for signs of being followed. I saw nothing. The weather was as predicted: dreary, chilly, but dry.

Maggie's anxious whimper reminded us she was just like a child. Her mantra seemed to be 'Are we there yet?'.

I pulled into the first parking spot beyond the gray cement block building once used for storage by the town maintenance crew but now utilized for boat-building classes. We faced away from the park's walking path and toward the only road in and out of the park. There were very few vehicles around on such a dismal day. It was too wintry to eat at the picnic tables, even though they were under pavilions. The ever-present breeze off the Northeast River chilled us immediately. Maggie leaped out with uncontainable enthusiasm and looked toward the playground—no kids to call out to her. She stared at the picnic tables—nobody there. She pulled at her leash as if to say, 'What are we waiting for? Let's go!'

So, we went with Patrick in minimal control of our pet.

She was the perfect accompaniment tugging to the right to investigate mallards on the bank of the creek, then lurching ahead to catch up with noisy gulls at a picnic spot trash can, then lunging to the left to get close to the Canada geese patrolling the wintry grass. As we rounded the far curve of the path, we furtively glanced toward the point of land jutting out to where the creek waters join the river, and toward The Tree. By silent assent, we agreed to take one more lap before investigating.

We neared the playground to our left and saw two teenaged girls I surmised were skipping class. They seemed to be just killing time, hanging out on the bench nearest the swings. They were sitting side by side, each engrossed in her own cell phone chat, fingers texting away. Maggie wanted to greet them, but Patrick kept her back. The girls looked up nodding to our greeting. They called out to Maggie who enthusiastically wagged her tail acknowledging what she took as high praise.

We continued along the straight area bordering the parking lot. There were more vehicles there now. An older couple emerged from a dark green Saturn. The man stepped cautiously from the passenger side leaning heavily on a carved walking stick. The woman, getting out from behind the wheel, carried a large shoulder bag which pulled her off balance. She listed to the right as she closed her car door with her left hand. She approached the rear of the car and turned to accompany her companion. She attempted to take his hand, but her shoulder bag knocked into him. She switched sides again only to be summarily brushed off by her male counterpart apparently desperate to maintain his independence. So, they set out, him leaning on the walking stick in his left hand, she weighed down by the shoulder bag on her right shoulder, then her left, then her right. We three slowed down to appreciate the minor comedy. We'd soon have to maneuver around them or take a break. We opted to stop at the second picnic table. Maggie found a chickadee to annoy.

We let the older couple pass The Tree before we resumed walking. We allowed Maggie to steer us off course several times before approaching the point. We wandered out on the rocks to let her step into the cold river water. She had a glorious time. I picked around the driftwood for any curious shapes my imagination could turn into something else. I chose a snaky piece but left it behind for one resembling a face. With driftwood in hand, it took just a moment to lean against the Tree. To others I hoped it appeared as if I was examining my find. In reality I was reaching up into the hole and retrieving the note. As my fingers grasped the cold, crisp paper, I felt an electric thrill followed by chills. Were the teens and the older couple as ordinary as we had supposed? Was anyone watching? I couldn't scan the shoreline now without feeling I was acting suspiciously myself. I slipped the paper into my jacket pocket and went on admiring my driftwood.

Patrick called from the rocks that he and Maggie were ready to move on. I assured him it was a good idea. He hadn't directly seen me retrieve the note, but his peripheral vision was good. He knew I had it. We both wanted to race to the car to read the note but knew we shouldn't risk being observed rushing.

While securing Maggie in her backseat harness, I managed to pass the note to Patrick. I hoped he'd surreptitiously open it and read it while I drove.

CHAPTER 44: THE NOTE

The envelope contained a copy of an accident report with a narrative from interviews with those involved. We were not mentioned, though all street-side witnesses were listed with contact information. Another sheet contained information on Andy Ray Hummerfield, age 47, white male, 6'1," 188 lbs. of Bohemia Avenue, Chesapeake City, who had followed us. UMCO had already been investigating him for belonging to an organization known to foster hate crimes. His previous activities were fringe behaviors. This accident, resulting from his tailing us, had ramped up interest in him. His behavior at the police station hadn't endeared him to Chief Hamilton as detailed in his notes.

"Hummerfield acted erratically, first saying he had an urgent appointment. When that didn't speed up the process, he ranted about being a law-abiding citizen whose rights were being violated. He loudly threatened to sue the North East Police Department for unlawful imprisonment. He claimed his organization would provide him a lawyer, that real cops didn't treat their supporters with disrespect. He had important work to finish. He was being kept from completing his assignment. When asked what assignment and what organization, he fell silent. A primitive-looking business card in his wallet showed him to be a member of 'F.O.R.N.'"

Copies of that and the other membership items in his wallet were photocopied: Confederate Sons Rally Organization, Homeless Hypocrisy Headquarters, and Americans for Real Americans. We could imagine what prejudices each advocated.

The North East Police Department had issued Andy Ray Hummerfield a citation for erratic driving, indicating he was at fault in the accident, and had given his insurance information to the other driver. They charged him with driving on illegal tags (those on the vehicle he drove were not registered to it but to a black 2004 Toyota Corolla owned by him). The truck was not registered to him but hadn't been reported stolen. Hummerfield refused to name the owner. Vehicle theft charges were pending.

Meanwhile, Chesapeake Service towed the truck from Main Street to their mechanic shop where the owner, once notified, could claim it. The towing company would supply the truck's VIN number to the North East Police Department to track down the owner.

Chief Hamilton had also charged Hummerfield with disruptive behavior and inhibiting an ongoing investigation. A handwritten margin comment expressed doubt these two charges would stick but might cause an interesting ripple effect. Possible charges relating to the pregnant woman transferred by ambulance and those suffering damage to belongings and vehicles were pending.

The bottom line was that Hummerfield became an overnight guest of Cecil County Detention Center. Chief Hamilton's note suggested Hummerfield might be released before Thursday. Tom added he would communicate further information about the man's release to Patrick's cell phone since he had secured that number from Sally.

Now what?

Wait again, naturally.

No one followed us.

CHAPTER 45: FURTHER ASSESSMENTS

While I prepared a late lunch, Patrick and Maggie walked to the back garden depositing kitchen compost and returned reporting no fresh tracks or footprints. Our meal was quiet as we mused over developments. Later Patrick ensconced himself on his side of our double recliner and opened the latest issue of *Smithsonian Magazine*. I curled up on the couch with *A Prayer for Owen Meanie*. Still, we ruminated about the recent course of events and rehashed activities in which we'd become involved, trying to see things from different perspectives. Were events spiraling? Were we approaching a climax? Or was this network of evil—a long-lived active tornado picking up and discarding people and wreaking destruction on their lives—just beginning to gain momentum? We abandoned print material for ruled notebook paper to generate lists:

What did we know for sure?

- Targeted people in Annapolis were falsely imprisoned.
- Some escaped.
- Others were still missing (as far as we knew).

- FORN exists.
- Its membership extended north to Cecil County.
- The North East Police Department and UMCO were cooperating.
- FORN had identified us.

What did we need to know?

- Enough information to dismantle FORN.
- The locations of missing people, especially the ones I met in 'prison.'
- How FORN identified us.

What could we do?

- Review everything we had learned.
- Keep a low profile to avoid helping FORN.

Suddenly a thought broke through when I re-read the last bullet point suggesting we do the opposite. Why not be obvious? Let them follow us. Lead FORN astray.

Patrick's cell phone rang. I glanced at the clock—ten after five. I listened, trying to piece together the conversation from his remarks but couldn't follow. He seemed deliberately cryptic. He hung up. Then he said nothing. I couldn't outwait him.

"Tell me what is going on!"

"Why? Are you interested?" My withering glance warned him to stop tormenting me.

"Well, our stalker was released. This came from Tom. Everyone was curious to find who would arrange for his release. They now have a name—Carl Amberson, from Rock Hall in Kent County. He's a realtor and insurance agent. He's been on UMCO's radar for several months. Incidentally, Amberson's only connection to Hummerfield seems to be as his insurance agent. Odd for an insurance agent to bail you out of jail. Must be some policy! UMCO is now closely observing Hummerfield.

"One other nugget Tom was asked to pass on is that UMCO

has identified the person responsible for sharing our vehicle tag number with FORN. That Annapolis police officer, along with three others, has been given a temporary assignment supposedly to liaison with other police departments around the state. They hope this will stop the leak without alerting FORN prematurely."

"So, now we know how they found out about us, "I ruminated aloud. "Since Hummerfield is being watched, we should feel free to investigate. We'll have instant backup—those following the one following us."

"No. If FORN has any intelligence at all, they will call off our recent tracker. He's received too much notoriety. He's a liability."

"It was a thought," I added.

"We might want to look out for the man we saw in church."

"Oh! I'd forgotten about him. He needs to be added to our list: 'Identify man seen in church'.

"Now I'm going to inquire about the farm tag license plates we called in," Patrick said. "Following up on that was sidetracked by our other drama. Maybe the tags belong to that man we saw on Sunday."

"Yes. If so, we can check him out. Before you say 'no' to me, all I mean is I just want to find out about him—where he works, where he lives- stuff like that. No contact!"

"Maybe." Patrick made his call. I watched as he scribbled on a note pad. Even I couldn't decipher his handwriting this time. He deliberately made it more obscure than usual to bait me into asking what had been said. My need to know was stronger than my willingness to pretend I wasn't interested, so I asked.

"Well? What else do you know?"

"The farm plates belong on the red truck. The owner is Nestor Calvin Creighton, age 59, white male, 6'2", 205 lbs., driving restriction for wearing glasses. He lives at 5494 Walter Boulden Street, Elkton. That describes our stranger in church last Sunday."

"So, if Hummerfield headed directly to Creighton's house after leaving Immaculate Conception parking lot, he would have turned right onto North Street from Park Way. That jives with our not spotting him when we turned left. We knew we had a 50/50 chance. It just didn't go our way. Why was Hummerfield the one driving the truck all three times I saw it? Why switch tags two days later? Why not just drive his own vehicle?"

"Suppose Hummerfield's vehicle is not operational." Patrick stroked his chin in thought. "Maybe he was in a wreck or had mechanical trouble? That might explain why he borrowed the truck," he surmised. "But doesn't explain why he switched tags."

"We must find out. But how? Or better yet, who do we know who could do a couple of drive by's in Elkton and Chesapeake City using different vehicles for each one?"

"Sean, from Chesapeake Service!" Patrick exclaimed. "He already has the truck in his possession!"

"Oh! I'm impressed. He could easily take another vehicle out for a test run after working on it. His shop's not that far from either address. We need to get him involved without telling him why. Any thoughts on this, Husband?"

"We won't need to tell him about our connection to the accident. He'll do it for a gift card to Pier 1 or Paradise Grille, or to our fireworks outlet."

"Yes! Let him choose."

"Before I call him, I want to touch base with Tom about the farm tags."

While that call was placed, I began preparing a pasta dinner. While the sauce simmered and the pork and chicken browned, I made a huge spinach salad. The three cats and Maggie came to the kitchen to appreciate the cooking aromas. I found treats for them all and went about setting the table. It was nearly six before Patrick came into the kitchen.

This time he gave me an instant report. "Tom said Chief Hamilton had received the truck owner's information an hour before. Neither he nor Tom knew the man. They weren't surprised that he was likely the person we'd seen in church. That indicated the truck wasn't stolen, unless the two men had had a disagreement, but didn't solve the switched tags mystery. The owner would have to present the legal tags and explain why he removed them from his vehicle. The truck might or might not be released to him. It was possible he was liable for damage caused by his vehicle during the accident even though he wasn't the driver. Chief Hamilton would contact the other driver in the accident providing the truck owner's name and insurance information. And the insurance agent was the one who had bailed out Andy Ray Hummerfield. Imagine that!"

Patrick had Sean on speed dial, but since it was after closing, it seemed prudent to wait until Thursday. In the morning Patrick was scheduled to work a funeral. I would have to wait until he returned home for an update.

CHAPTER 46: NEIGHBORHOOD WATCH

I awoke to February eleventh early enough to enjoy my tea while Patrick had his coffee. He departed before eight with a promise to call me when he finished work. He would be busy during the viewing, but the deceased was to be cremated, so interment would be later. I was determined to successfully make a paint selection. Before I left, I washed dishes, straightened up clutter in the kitchen, then cleared off the side table in the dining room—Patrick's drop space for keys, gloves, notes, anything. On top of a pile of junk mail lay a newsletter from American Home and Hardware. Idly I picked it up and glanced at it. Inside was a coupon for five dollars off a gallon of paint. That's what I'd do. Use a different paint store. Off I went, coupon in hand, on a mission to return with paint for the bedroom ceiling.

I returned with a gallon of paint for the kitchen. I had made a decision and taken advantage of the coupon. I spent the rest of the morning transferring items from the kitchen to the dining room table. I relocated chairs, tea cart, and Patrick's wooden childhood highchair around the dining room table. The corner cupboard contents I emptied onto the library coffee table, recently the location of the jacket contents investigation. Had that only been last Saturday? I maneuvered the corner cupboard into the hall, blocking access to the library.

The upheaval confused Maggie and the cats. Wilbur pawed open the cellar door disappearing into his man/cat cave. Susie showed her disdain by going to sleep in our bed. W.C. demanded release into the wilds of the backyard. To continue, I had to retrieve the ladder, so Maggie accompanied me to our garden shed. While lugging the ladder across the frozen yard, I noticed our neighbor outside walking his dog. We waved and called out greetings. Maggie left me to visit with his collie her friend, Daisy. I headed on without her, knowing she would only be a minute. Before I had taken two steps, I heard my name. Hank, from his yard, called out he had something he'd like to ask me about. I set down the ladder. We both tread carefully on the icy surface, separating us.

"Last Sunday, did you have an emergency or something?"

"What? Why do you ask?"

"I got up late and saw footprints up and down my drive and going across to your house."

"We saw them too when we got back from church."

"So, you didn't make them?"

"No. Not us."

"You know, I was in the driveway smoking Saturday and there was a dark colored car idling in Wawa's parking lot. Later, I walked over there to get Betty butter pecan ice cream and saw the store employees chase the car out of there. It wasn't a customer. They said it had been there a couple of times lately, but no one got out to go in the store or pump gas. I bet that car came back on Sunday. The store lot wasn't plowed till late afternoon."

I thanked Hank and asked him to tell us if he saw anything suspicious. I alluded to the possibility of break-ins in the neighborhood. That seemed a reasonable ploy to encourage him and Betty to be vigilant. It couldn't hurt.

Finally, I got the ladder inside and removed the wall, window and woodwork decorations, realizing I had to start paring down all the knickknacks in my house. I peeled off the row of miniature churches, including Evie's milk carton creation from Vacation Bible School. I had hot glued them on; it was a challenge getting them off.

I took down the fox painted-slate, and the winter fox photo taken locally—the poor fox looked so cold and mangy. I paused. *Mangy.* Had either Barbette or Sarah experienced the 'dogs'? Was it important? What would happen to them once their handlers were apprehended?

I decided to phone Joy. She answered but couldn't say if Sarah or her grandmother had mentioned the dogs. She recalled them. Their descriptions of the painted ladies had been vivid, but nothing came to mind about the dogs. She'd check with Sarah and try to find out from her grandmother.

At twelve-thirty Patrick called saying he'd be finished in time to meet me for our Thursday taco bowl lunch date at Paradise Grille to tell me the latest news. He said he'd fill me in then. Exasperating man! I surveyed the dismantled kitchen with a sense of satisfaction and cleaned up my appearance before leaving for lunch.

CHAPTER 47: PARADISE GRILLE

Megan had our drinks on the table and our food order to the kitchen before we sat. Our Thursday order never varied. The only wintry concession was indoor eating. We looked longingly at our favorite outside table along the frozen Northeast Creek.

Our beef taco bowls appeared momentarily, and we savored the flavors. The only meal Patrick ever consumed faster than I did was this one. I don't know how he did it. I could barely get to the end of the meal, and often couldn't finish. Every week he stared at his empty plate, watching me struggle to the delicious end.

Patrick jumped right in with his news. He had negotiated the deal with his friend, the garage owner, Sean. There were four vehicles to be road tested before the close of business today. Sean would drive by Nestor Creighton's residence on Walter Boulden Street in Elkton and Ray Hummerfield's home on Bohemia Avenue in nearby Chesapeake City checking for activity, people or vehicles. All he cared to know was that we had personal reasons to find out about these two addresses and didn't want to do it ourselves. He had chosen the Pier 1 gift certificate option for his services. Patrick expected Sean to report by seven.

I considered telling Patrick about the switch in paint plans, but he'd see it soon. I wanted to get him up to date about our neighbor Hank's information. I related our conversation. We agreed Hank's observations were connected to us. Then I added my inquiry about the dogs. He wondered why I cared. And I replied I had no sympathy with humans who deliberately broke the law, but animals had no choice but to obey their masters. Then he understood my looking forward to opening our arms to new furry creatures.

The only drama of the afternoon was Carol's report following lunch on the pregnant woman from Tuesday, which seemed a lifetime ago. The woman had been kept overnight at Union Hospital. She had exhibited symptoms of labor pains, but they had subsided. She was sent home for two days of bed rest. Carol had offered free dinners for them Wednesday through Friday if the husband would pick them up. He had taken her up on the idea and planned to return. It was good customer relations, and a way to keep tabs on the woman's progress. We decided to contribute to Carol's expenses and left fifty dollars toward Thursday's meals. We were the catalyst for the sequence of events culminating in the woman's near accident.

After lunch, we ran errands and didn't meet till five. Our light dinner was a spinach salad with red salmon, splashed with Greek salad dressing and garnished with rosemary olive oil Triscuits. Patrick mentioned the kitchen. Painting time was close. Dinner was over by seven-thirty. We hadn't heard from Sean.

The phone rang. Joy informed us that Sarah and her grandmother Barbette had both seen the dogs but were so traumatized they had erased them from their memories until she questioned them.

It rang again. Rose told us news she and Scott had tried a new restaurant but wouldn't recommend going there until they got their staffing kinks worked out. Maybe in a few weeks the food would be hot and edible. Patrick thanked her for the heads up, and said we'd steer clear of it.

He hadn't been off the phone for ten seconds when it rang again. From his change in demeanor, I surmised it was Sean. Patrick grabbed a tablet and scribbled down a lot of information he'd gleaned from more than a couple of drive-by sweeps. Had Sean been a detective in a previous life? Yes, he had, Patrick relayed to me. In the military.

The pertinent information surprised us. At the Walter Boulden Street address everything seemed shut down, closed up tight. Since Sean knew someone who lived on that street, he used that as an excuse to stop and drop off a sales brochure he knew the guy wanted. They had talked about how quiet the neighborhood was. His pal had told him just recently, on Tuesday, one neighbor had had numerous cars and trucks dropped off in his drive at all hours. He had seen them out there and had thought they might be running a kind of repossession business or vehicle theft ring. Then it stopped. No visitors. Even the guy's girlfriend was gone. The lights hadn't come on for two evenings, and he hoped they were on vacation or gone for good.

It seemed Nestor Creighton, the sidekick from the red truck, had dropped out of sight the day Hummerfield had borrowed his truck to tail us, damaging it in the collision on Main Street and becoming incapacitated after his altercation with the North East Police Department. It certainly was not a coincidence.

Meanwhile, the Chesapeake City address of Andy Ray Hummerfield was a beehive of activity. Sean discreetly took photos of comings and goings. He had been test driving a heater-repair van, so he parked down the street, approached a house to ask about a fictitious name for that address, then went back to the van and acted like he was checking in with his main office while taking more pictures. What he saw in seven minutes convinced him we were in trouble. It was mid evening, just dusk, and he shot pictures of four cars leaving, two arriving, and two others idling on the street. It looked like drug trafficking. Then it seemed more like people handing in reports and picking up assignments. There were gestures of good luck with the distribution of papers and congratulations on some of those turned in. He left before drawing attention to himself.

He emailed Patrick the photos and offered to do follow ups or check other addresses. Patrick promised we'd call if the need arose. He thanked Sean and told him he'd deliver the gift certificate in the morning.

Patrick immediately downloaded the photos as I watched over his shoulder. Then he called UMCO.

CHAPTER 48: ANOTHER CLOSE ENCOUNTER

I listened in as he presented his update to UMCO. Then he listened to new information.

"There's a postcard or two coming. We are to check our mail," Patrick informed me.

"Is it good news?" I asked.

"They wouldn't say, but there's more than one postcard."

"Oh!" I turned to Patrick. "Did you check the mail today? I didn't." Patrick shook his head to say he hadn't. I grabbed my jacket from the hook by the back door and took off. Halfway down the lane I knew I wasn't alone. What should I do? Act like I didn't know someone was there? Their code was for 'No Contact.' Was it 'them'? I slowed down then heard the back door slide open and closed.

Patrick called loudly that someone wanted to accompany me. I turned and was greeted by Maggie. But she bypassed me as she rounded the corner of the house and I saw she'd transformed into a menacing savage beast. I had only heard her growl once before. This was guttural, deep, and serious. She approached in an attack mode. I stood still until she reached me. Together we advanced toward the mailbox. I heard rustling in the trees to the west, then outright footsteps, as someone frantically tried to escape our presence. Maggie barked in her low voice. I reached the rear door of the mailbox and pulled out the mail, then turned back and was just starting up the driveway when Patrick called out from our front entry. I headed toward him with Maggie on my heels.

"Now we know they're still watching us," he said as he looked at my face and our dog's stiff body language, the hairs on her neck standing straight up.

"Good girl, Maggie!" Patrick stroked her fur, calming her. You're some special breed of watch dog. Thanks for protecting your mother tonight."

I had to agree wholeheartedly. Maggie wagged her tail.

"Now, Norah, sit down and I'll tell you the rest of the news."

"There's more?"

"Yes, but you ran out so fast for the postcards I didn't have time to tell you."

"I'm going to sit right here and listen. I won't even look at the postcards till you finish."

I gave him my undivided attention. UMCO had closed down the Annapolis operation of FORN headquartered where I had been kept prisoner. They had used the testimony of my fellow escapees to build the case and raided the building today. It might make the late-night news. We should listen carefully to the broadcasts. Fifteen people were taken into custody. Eleven inmates went by ambulance for observation. The "crew" on duty was arrested first, including the two women parading as Betty and Wilma from *The Flintstones.* Then as teams of pseudo-officers arrived with additional "prisoners," they were arrested. There had had been one female officer at the reception desk, two male officers in the prison holding room, two in the interrogation room, and two on break downstairs. Paperwork, as scant as it was, and all electronic devices were confiscated. The papers were especially valuable because they contained FORN membership information. At least one part of the organization had been rooted out. Of course, I asked about the dogs. Patrick acknowledged the dogs had been apprehended and taken to a temporary shelter.

Our next assignment was to be invisibly involved in interrogations. We were to be prepared to report wherever and whenever we received notice. At that revelation we set out clothing and prepared small travel bags of necessities, in case we were called to travel and stay overnight. We put Rose and Scott on alert without explaining.

Within the hour we had another call. Chief Hamilton, Officer Daniels, Maryland State Police, and the Cecil County Sheriff's Department had brought the Elkton and Chesapeake City Police Departments into the case, and using unprecedented interagency cooperation, were currently raiding the Chesapeake City and Elkton addresses we knew about. They told us they would be visiting additional addresses in Cecil County as the FORN membership list became available. They would pursue all leads. Also, the Kent County Sheriff's Department was currently visiting the insurance broker who probably was very high up in the organization.

We were informed we would be sitting in on many interrogations, but not so anyone would know, to protect our identity for future assignments. Our testimony, evidence, or observations would never be used in cases against these people.

"So, whoever was outside here tonight isn't going to be picked up by the authorities?"

"Depends on how fast he or she scrambles back to report being detected here. Imagine the humiliation of being ferreted out by a dog, then going to report your failure, only to find your network collapsing."

"I'd say that adds up to a pretty bad night."

We waited until after the late news, listening intently to the broadcast information. Once more, a lot was said, yet very little was revealed. The police activity was alluded to as a bust on a possible car theft ring with possible drug sales connections. No names of those apprehended were yet available. It seemed a recent arrest for an unrelated charge had spurred the investigation. There were no more communications. Finally, off to bed.

A dreary, gray morning broke and we found we couldn't sleep past five-thirty. We dressed, made coffee, hot tea, and cinnamon toast and ate in front of the TV while we awaited a summons. The Baltimore TV news was vague, but the Chesapeake City address and one in Rock Hall had been added to the others as sites of police raids. Since the Rock Hall address was a place of business, the broker's name was bandied about as a possible suspect, but for what crime reporters could only surmise. It was linked to the Cecil County raids, but that was as much as authorities would divulge.

CHAPTER 49: INTERROGATIONS

At six-thirty we were given twenty minutes to arrive at the state police barrack in North East. There we were to wait in the parking lot for an escort. We grabbed our bags and left. We hadn't considered interviews would be handled by Maryland State police.

When we arrived, we were directed to a rear entrance and shepherded into an area without observing anyone. From our vantage point we witnessed person after person being questioned. We made notes, passing on information using laptops they provided. Almost simultaneously, some point one of us raised was uttered by one of the interrogators. We realized UMCO agents, not state police officers, were conducting the interviews.

In total, eleven people were interrogated. The process went on for hours. Packaged sandwiches were served. They were no comparison to the Pier 1 turkey Rueben I was yearning for. We had no breaks, but the interrogators switched after every two or three interviews. We surmised the changes were determined by the length of questioning sessions. Time moved heavily. The monotonous repetition of opening questions, establishing identities, and gaining pertinent information dragged on. In a lineup we recognized the truck driver Andy Ray Hummerfield (number two) from Chesapeake City and Nestor Creighton the truck owner from Elkton (number five) as the men we had encountered, but the others were unfamiliar, although with familiar stories.

They all seemed to have been brainwashed into thinking they were recruits in the Great American Clean-Out Project. We were mentioned, not by name, but by our home location, as two undesirables whom they had been charged to observe but not encounter. They could not say what our crimes were, only that we were objects of extreme interest. Listening to them, we realized that FORN was a mirror image of UMCO.

That made my skin crawl. Had they been approached as we were with an appeal to their sense of duty? Responsibility? How far had they acted outside the law? We listened to recruitment stories, with insistence they and police forces were on the same side. Yes, they had trespassed on private property and looked through windows and doors like peeping Toms. What had they expected would happen to us based on their reports? They thought we'd be arrested. For what? Didn't know. Not their business. Stalking us was? Just an assignment, like for a private detective. Were they licensed? No, but they'd had basic training.

Basic training?

The basic training information came out during the third suspect's questioning. Right away we were sending questions for follow-up: Where was training conducted? How involved was the training? How many were trained? Who trained them? It seemed all the suspects were trained in Annapolis, at the holding cell building. How official! How convincing and clever. Invite recruits to the state capital, tour past official government buildings and deliver them to the unofficial headquarters for training. What a multi-purpose site.

These men were convinced they and the interrogation team were ultimately on the same side and supplied names and dates to verify their good work. It seemed their handlers had been too thorough in convincing them of the righteousness of their missions.

Now, if the names weren't aliases, UMCO could proceed.

Midafternoon we received a message that Kent County interrogations had ended. A synopsis of proceedings was provided, along with formal charges against Carl Amberson for conspiracy against the government and hate crimes connected to his involvement with FORN. He had been much less forthcoming than the lower echelon members but seemed to become aware that his involvement was leading to dire consequences. He did not share names or any helpful information at first, but his mute stance gradually wore off, and he asked for his lawyer. This request had temporarily halted the interrogation, but the report said he was visibly distressed, almost aging before their eyes.

Person number seven, Vincent Waggoner, was a braggart. His bravado subsided however when he was given proof of Carl Amberson the Kent County real estate insurance man's arrest and charges he faced dealing with authorizing and coordinating criminal activity. Number seven immediately became a changed man. He provided more detailed information than the first six, adding eight new names of FORN members with addresses in Cecil County and Harford County to the west. He admitted to trespassing on our property the night before. That information was a good faith offering as he became nervous. Now we could put a face to the stalker.

After listening to all eleven, we expected officers to have rounded up additional suspects and add them to our day's work, but we were released as soon as we could be safely guarded from those who had been questioned. We'd felt since we'd been followed and tracked, we were well known, but we were categorized as undesirables, not agents. Our cover wasn't compromised. They knew I had been in their custody from information gathered by the merwomen, but my escape was accounted for as part of the general breakout. Interest in Patrick was because of me. The dry cleaners and church had been about me.

But on the way home from Annapolis, when we were spotted on Route 213 in the truck, how had they known we would be there? That made us uneasy.

CHAPTER 50: HATTIE

We drove directly home, let out Maggie, locked the doors, and rued we had never installed an alarm system. The unfinished, haphazard kitchen greeted us, a testimony to the crazy mess our lives had become of late, affecting not only our lives but those of our family, plus our dog, and even our home. I audibly sighed. Where was the normal life we had been living for so many years? Tomorrow I would paint. Maybe.

A late call from UMCO reassured us of our safety. They shared Harford County investigation information. A network of bottom-of-the-chain-of-command FORN operatives had routinely surveilled major traffic locations crossing bodies of water including the Susquehanna River bridges on Route 40 and Interstate-95, the Chesapeake City Bridge on Route 213, the Francis Scott Key Bridge, the Baltimore Harbor and Fort McHenry Tunnels, the Bay Bridge, even the Conowingo Dam. UMCO had been supplied with license plate information cross-referenced to escaped detainees the FORN informant had accessed before his transfer.

Joy probably had been followed without being aware. Since Sarah didn't drive, her being shadowed must have been from saying she lived at Brisson Shelter which may have been under close watch. Infiltrated? Might he or she still be there? We pondered before phoning Joy.

There were eight recently established residents. A married

couple, four single men including Jorge, and two single women. The couple had been referred by a former resident. Joy was comfortable there was nothing duplicitous about them. The single men all had day jobs and showed no signs of being unduly curious about Sarah's traumatic experience. One female was elderly, unable to get around outside the shelter.

Now that potential infiltration had been brought to Joy's attention, another female became extremely suspicious. Joy told us she gave her an uneasy feeling but wasn't sure why. She'd arrived just after Christmas under mysterious circumstances, claiming physical abuse from her male companion, but had refused medical attention and abuse counseling. She had attached herself to Sarah and insisted she should be one of Sarah's walking companions, even though it was a task already cheerfully accepted by Sarah's table mates. She seemed to be the first one up in the morning, and the last to retire at night.

"Her name is Hattie," Joy said.

I gasped as an alarm went off in my head. *Hattie!* The resident who sought me out at breakfast. She'd told me vaguely about her abuse. I'd totally believed her. Were her injuries real? Her teeth were a mess. Could that have been from a car or other kind of accident? Joy assured us evidence of her injuries, other than her teeth, had faded quickly, and bruising coloration hadn't followed the normal sequence. Her injuries had more or less been erased. Her refusal of treatment might have been to disguise fake wounds.

"I met her when I was there! I exclaimed, recalling the small darkhaired woman who had shared breakfast with me.

Joy further explained how she'd seen her coming from her office one day. Hattie insisted she had not gone in but was looking for Joy and had just stuck her head in the open door. Joy knew she had closed the door because on her desk was a letter and form containing personal information about a former resident. It had just arrived, and she hadn't wanted it seen or shared till she had had time to review it. House rules were, if the door was closed, one knocked. If no one responded, no one was there, so there was no reason to enter. If someone was in the room, he or she would respond since it was possible there was an emergency.

Hattie had no excuse for entering, and when asked by Joy what had been so urgent, had just said 'never mind, it could wait,' leaving Joy convinced there had been no reason.

I asked if Hattie was still at Brisson.

Joy answered yes. She had been in all day, which was odd. Even on weekends she left for most of the day. I asked her to observe Hattie. We would contact her with more information.

Patrick contacted UMCO. He relayed the latest development, then phoned Joy. Within five minutes, she'd receive information of a new client, Grace, who'd arrive ten minutes later. Grace would handle Hattie and secure Brisson from further intrusions. We assured Joy we knew Grace and she'd endured our common imprisonment. Joy hung up to prepare for Grace's arrival.

Speaking to Joy about Grace jogged my memory of those others who had been held against their will with me.

Then it struck me that I'd completely forgotten about checking the mail, to see if there were any postcards. Finding the pile on the living room coffee table, I tore through it.

There were three postcards. One depicted the main campus of the University of Maryland. Scrawled across it were the words, "Greetings from College Park! I took in a Terps basketball game and got a new Terps sweatshirt. Tony." He'd been the only inmate who had conversed with me, protected me even. I felt enormous relief he was accounted for.

The second card showed a view of the Potomac River and inscribed on the back was, "Hey Baby doll! The cherry blossoms aren't out yet! So disappointing! Cathi and Rita." The teens were on the safe list. I breathed a sigh of relief even though Maglie had unwittingly informed me of their safety.

The last had a photo of the Conowingo Dam. On the reverse was written, "Did a motorcycle tour of Harford County. Now I've crossed the dam into Cecil County to begin my new job working for a Chesapeake repair shop." Since Jorge had been removed before our breakout and was currently at Brisson Shelter, I knew this represented the other mechanic in the "holding" room. I had a flashback to the Chesapeake Service truck assisting the teens in the snowstorm. I had noticed Sean had a new employee who had looked vaguely familiar. I hadn't recognized him as one of my fellow inmates but now memories flooded back. We truly lived in a small world!

The mysterious person, I already knew, had been taken to a safe place to recover. Obviously, none of these messages referred to her.

I prayed a silent prayer of thanks that all seven in the room with me had been accounted for. Then I passed each postcard to Patrick who made no comments. We turned to each other and embraced for a long moment.

We commented how cleverly the postcards had been scripted reflecting my debriefing recollections. The University of Maryland postcard was impressive. We tried to guess which of our debriefers had written them, or was it someone who had read the transcript? We simultaneously had the same idea. "Grace!"

We knew where she would spend the night. We both said a silent prayer for the success of her mission and the safety of Brisson's residents.

CHAPTER 51: GRACE UNDER PRESSURE

Grace updated us by phone the next day in a detailed report....

She'd entered Brisson Shelter dressed similarly to what she had worn during her Annapolis incarceration. She registered formally with Joy as prearranged. They privately exchanged concerns about Hattie. Joy provided a detailed description of her. Grace matriculated into the community with kind Sarah running interference introducing her and settling her into her new accommodations. Grace lugged her shabby tan suitcase, three totes overflowing with clothing, and a few knickknacks in a sack over her shoulder up to her third-floor room. Sarah supplied her with bathing necessities and left her to settle in. Grace had set out personal items on the dresser and sat down on the one chair, just inside the doorway, and assumed the persona of one overwhelmed with new circumstances. Then she waited.

Soon the flow of curious, well-meaning, and sincere residents began. Sarah did not reappear, having made it clear she was available when wanted, where her room was, and where she might be found if she weren't there. Heather poked her head in saying her room was nearby and she would be welcome to join

Grace for a late evening cup of coffee downstairs. Grace thanked her but said she didn't have the energy to move. Heather smiled sympathetically and went to her room. Freddie dropped by with her version of a house-warming gift—a three-day-old newspaper. Grace thanked her and tried to project weak gratitude but showed no interest in conversation. Freddie invited her to join her table for meals. That invitation was welcome, but Grace told her Sarah had already asked her to join her. Freddie smiled and told her it was the same table. She'd be pleased to share dinner with her the following night.

Grace knew there'd be no males stopping by, not because they were unconcerned, but because she was on a female-only floor.

She was marveling at a print of St. Mary Magdalene on the wall because it projected such an aura of serenity when she heard approaching footsteps along the corridor. She angled herself to see a reflection from the glass on the print without seeming to be aware of anyone. The footsteps neared, then stopped as a small darkhaired woman came into distorted view. She spoke in a friendly enough fashion.

It was none other than Hattie at her door. "Who's your saint?" the bold woman had asked. "Mine's St. Cecilia, patron saint of music. It fits me since I play guitar and sing. Funny how that works out—the saint matching the person living in the room.

"Mine is St. Mary Magdalene," Grace had responded softly as she turned to greet the woman.

"I meant no harm saying the saint fits the occupant. I'm sure you aren't a prostitute like Mary Magdalene." Hattie shrugged.

"Was she a prostitute? I heard that was wrong. She was more like a faithful female follower, an unofficial apostle," Grace had replied smoothly. Her visitor stammered something indistinguishable. "In any case, I am Grace. And you are?"

"Oh! I'm Hattie. Welcome to your new home. See you at

breakfast?"

"I'm not sure when I'll be down for breakfast, but I'll be around at suppertime," Grace had informed her.

"Well, I will say good night then," answered Hattie who had hesitated as she backed out of the room. Grace knew what that was all about. She had caught Hattie's movement just before she announced her presence. Her hand had gone to Grace's sweater hanging over the chair. She had smoothly run one hand across it. As soon as the coast was clear, Grace checked for the tracking device. Her impulse to destroy it was great but controlled by professional patience. She knew results would be forthcoming. Hattie had quickly revealed herself.

Grace had wondered who else had been tracked. Sarah? Definitely. But Sarah only knew to be cautious, and not to go out unaccompanied. Grace considered whether Hattie had been placed in the shelter by FORN, or if she'd been recruited after her arrival. She glanced at her book on the desk. Inside it was a bookmark containing information about Hattie. It was all Joy had been able to assemble under short notice, but it was a place to start. More involved digging was taking place by UMCO personnel and would be communicated.

Grace had settled on the bed with her door ajar enough to be inviting, but not outright welcoming. She had the book in hand and began reading about Hattie. There was information indicating spousal abuse had brought her to the shelter, a description of her initial injuries, including bruising and missing teeth and a note she had availed herself of reduced-cost dental reconstruction, and that she currently worked the counter at Quick Release Dry Cleaners in Annapolis. She had been there since last July. She was thirty-three. Grace gasped. She would have put Hattie in her fifties. Had life dealt this woman such a rough time she had aged prematurely? Could it be carefully applied make-up? No, no amount of makeup could cover up that face. She must be a recent recruit. Perhaps FORN was helping finance her dental work. Grace couldn't blame her for getting assistance, but what did she think she was involved in? A righteous crusade?

From the interrogation reports, it was evident people had been recruited under the guise of patriotism. FORN! Grace felt for Hattie, and hoped her consequences would be far below those of the organizers of FORN, but she knew how often instigators cleverly passed on legal culpability to the less informed. They insulated themselves from the consequences of their evil plotting and planning. Now she had to concentrate on watching Hattie, while Hattie observed her in return.

Grace spent Saturday wandering around the shelter, conversing with those who didn't work weekends, or worked odd shifts or were unemployed. Without being overtly curious, she managed to gain a lot of information. She discovered Hattie had been hinting about extracurricular activities without divulging much. She'd repaid a fifteen-dollar loan and offered to lend out small sums. She had given the impression she'd soon be out on her own in a new place all because of extra funds she was accumulating.

No one could figure out when she did extra shifts at the dry cleaners or worked elsewhere. She seemed to be at the shelter more than usual. Grace learned Hattie had originally been very well liked, but several Brisson residents had cooled off toward her recently. Her offer to accompany Sarah to and from work would have been received gratefully, but her overbearing insistence about being involved bordered on commandeering the entire undertaking. She'd been so brazen they'd closed ranks on her, refusing her help.

By the end of the day, Grace had ascertained Sarah's room and the lavatory in that wing were bugged. She reported to Joy, and they conspired to call an 'exterminator' for emergency services. The entire floor was swept for bugs, which were exterminated. Grace's tracking device, attached to her sweater, remained on her chair till evening when she donned it before dinner.

The before-dinner announcements dwelt on news from those who had ventured out. One offered an update on a local deli that had been robbed two days before. It seemed the robbers took only Tastykakes and Reeses' Peanut Butter Cups. Speculation pointed the finger at local teens known for brazen behavior or someone attempting to imitate a certain Jimmy Buffett song. Joy announced a future Sunday afternoon program for adults wanting to hone music skills beginning in March at a nearby church hall. She introduced Grace as a temporary resident. Grace took some good-natured ribbing from some who said everyone came in under that guise. She accepted their comments with a smile.

At dinner she was led to Sarah's table where Hattie tried to invite herself. She was gently rebuffed and sent to her regular table. She became more vehement, so Grace offered to sit elsewhere so as not to disrupt everyone's routine. She was reassured she wasn't the interruption. Grace turned and walked to another table. Hattie, thinking she'd changed her mind, gave up her request to sit at Sarah's table, and headed speedily in Grace's direction, passing her and claiming one of two empty seats there.

Grace stopped to say hello to someone, then turned back to Sarah's table. Hattie's expression, when she realized she'd been outmaneuvered, was the first topic of conversation. Interest in her eventually dwindled and Grace was politely asked about her background as each of those dining with her offered personal histories. Grace didn't veer far from her true story of immigration with her parents from mainland China when she was a child, their life on Maryland's lower Eastern Shore, her challenge to learn English, and familiarizing herself with American foods and customs while valuing her Chinese heritage.

After dessert, clusters of residents gathered around the TV and game tables. Some sat at computer terminals. Voices drifted across the sounds from the TV, the rolling of dice and movement of game pieces. It was like a large extended family settling in for the evening.

Grace took time to watch them. She ensconced herself in an overstuffed upholstered chair and draped a knitted rainbow afghan around her. She felt quite content to observe. She knew her assignment at Brisson would be short-lived since UMCO was closing in on FORN from several directions. Follow-up investigations would proceed from new names provided. Additional Annapolis arrests were also taking place. She did not doubt that other Maryland counties would soon be involved. The number of FORN members might reach the hundreds. She knew many of them would not be prosecuted for lack of concrete evidence to connect minions' work all the way up the chain of command, but if enough people were disillusioned when they realized FORN's insidious intent, perhaps something would be accomplished. Progress.

Hattie finally approached Grace who appeared to be dozing. She hovered over her to make sure she was at least a little awake. When Grace responded, Hattie took it as her cue to settle in for a chat. At first her questions were innocently vague but took a sharp turn when she impertinently asked why Grace had really come to Brisson. Grace bit off the retort she wanted to give. It would be so satisfying to declare she was assigned to the shelter to spy on Hattie. What a reaction that would cause. Instead, she stared at Hattie for a full thirty seconds, sighed, and asked Hattie about *her* true reason for coming to this shelter. For a vacation? Because she was tired of paying rent? Because Brisson offered better accommodations than a motel?

When Hattie didn't immediately respond, Grace continued, "Maybe my reasons are personal. Not everyone has physical marks to show why they need protection. I can't talk about personal things. Not yet."

Hattie became hesitant, looking as if she might cry.

"You didn't even leave this place today. You must really need protection," said Hattie.

"I just arrived. I have nowhere else to be," answered Grace. "Why would I leave?"

"Because you'll go stir crazy staying in your room or just dragging yourself around this tomb."

"This place is a haven, not a tomb."

"Okay. Not a tomb. More like a prison," Hattie countered.

"How can you breathe out those words when you came here because the outside was so bad? You can leave whenever you want and not return. Can't you?" Grace expressed her frustration more strongly than she felt, hoping to elicit a response from Hattie.

"It's bad out there, but there are so many rules here," said Hattie. She stared at Grace to ascertain if she was wearing her sweater. Grace slipped off her sweater, walked to the far end of the room, and deposited it in a chair. Once satisfied the bug was far enough away, Hattie whispered, "Plus, I can't leave."

Grace scanned her face. Hattie was scared. Was she ready to turn on FORN? Slowly, Grace proceeded to bond with what she now perceived was a frightened woman who didn't know where to turn.

"I know what it's like to be locked up for committing no crime," said Grace. "I don't want to be on the streets and vulnerable like that again."

"So, do I. I mean I'm afraid of…" Hattie's voice trailed off to nothing.

"Are you shaking?" Grace asked in the quietest, concerned

tone she could produce.

"Yes."

"But why? I'm not threatening you. You are safe here."

"But you aren't!" Hattie whispered emphatically.

"Me? How would you know I'm not safe?"

"Because…"

"Go on. Tell me."

"You are not safe because…It's my fault!" Hattie's voice cracked. A solitary tear trailed down her right cheek. She let it fall.

"What do you mean? What did you do?"

"I made a bargain with devils. I came here to spy so I could be free, but now I'm not free, and I can't get out of trouble or stop them either. I bugged your room like I did Sarah's and tried to do the same to Joy's office. They both have been kind to me. I'm just a common traitor. But I can't stop." Hattie cried softly, her face in the crook of her right arm.

"How much, how badly, do you want to get out of your predicament?"

"It's not possible."

"Yes, it is. Are you brave enough?"

"What do you mean?"

"Are you brave enough to trust someone besides those 'devils'?"

"They're powerful with many connections. They can hurt me, make me disappear. Who would look for me? Nobody cares."

"Are you brave enough?" Grace asked again

"Don't you get it? Being brave won't help!"

"Yes, it will! But you must commit yourself to work to fix things. You must turn against the devils by exposing them. Before you say it's not possible, let me tell you that several of the devils have already been rounded up and are in real police custody."

"What? How do you know? Who are you?"

"I'm the one sent here to protect Sarah and Joy from you. I can protect you too. Do you want protection? It comes at the price of helping provide evidence to convict certain devils."

After three deep breaths, and closed eyes opening wide, Hattie nodded.

"Okay. We will make you safe. Are you the only person living here I should be worried about?"

"Yes. It's just me."

"Would you like to live in a different safe place?"

Yes…no, I mean, first let me help undo what I've caused."

"I'd like to get information from you. You're positive your room and Joy's office are not bugged?"

"Yeah. Just the tracking device on your sweater, and one on Sarah, and her room is bugged, but what a waste. She doesn't talk to herself, and other than sleep there, she's occupied helping people somewhere in this house."

"Good to know for Sarah's sake. Now, be aware. Once I confide in Joy, she has the authority to insist you leave. It would be reasonable for her to demand it. I'll attempt to convince her you can be an asset. In any event, I won't let you leave Brisson without an escort to take you somewhere safe."

"Okay. Okay to everything."

"I want you to stay here in this room with the others around while I speak with Joy and ah, the 'angels'."

Hattie smiled feebly through renewed tears. Grace took off the rainbow afghan and put it around Hattie. Her smile broadened.

"The rainbow was God's promise to Noah. Now it's yours to me and mine to you," Hattie whispered.

Grace thought that line of reasoning might appeal to Joy's sensibilities. She left to seek her and report to UMCO.

CHAPTER 52: UNDER ATTACK

My sleep moved into consciousness of a dim gray, dreary, and snowy Sunday morning with the aroma of Patrick's salted caramel coffee permeating the house. He arrived with a mug of tea for me. I sniffed to find out what he'd chosen. I smelled Earl Grey and smiled as I sipped the steaming liquid. Patrick sat on the bed beside me and turned on the TV for a weather update. The local temperature hovered at thirty degrees. The radar showed the familiar pattern of storms following the I-95 corridor. Only counties bordering the highway were getting snow. We were dodging the heavy stuff.

"We might as well get ready for Mass. This is going to be close to a non-event," Patrick declared.

I threw back the covers with more enthusiasm than I felt, and my feet hit the floor. After showering, I dressed. I made another cup of tea and prepared our church envelope and the Valentine's card while I waited for Patrick, who had walked in the snow with Maggie. I shook my head at the marks their six soggy feet made across the kitchen.

At St. Jude's the hillside driveway was slick, but navigable.

The usual Sunday crowd was slightly diminished. Patrick and I were scheduled as extraordinary ministers for Holy Communion so we arrived early. Our daughter Rose was scheduled to proclaim and arrived just in time.

The heat inside St. Jude's was below comfort zone, so few removed their coats. Some even kept their gloves on. Our opening song, "God Has Chosen Me," was lively enough to bring warmth to the congregation. Father Joe greeted everyone wishing them a 'Happy Valentine's Day.' Patrick audibly gasped. I smiled innocently and asked if he he'd forgotten something.

"I'm just glad I made those Pier 1 reservations last month. This month has been chaos." I took his hand in mine.

Soon we were seated listening to Rose proclaiming a reading from Jeremiah cursing those who trust only humans, but praising those who trust in the Lord, for they are like a tree planted beside the waters. I elbowed Patrick and whispered this referred to our tree in the park. He grinned and whispered back that I had a wild imagination. When Father Joe read the gospel from Luke, Patrick turned to me and said the words described living at Brisson, those that Joy and others running the shelter served every day. I nodded.

"…Blessed are you who are poor, for the kingdom of God is yours. Blessed are you who are hungry, for you will be satisfied. Blessed are you who are now weeping, for you will laugh. Blessed are you when people hate you, And when they exclude and insult you, and denounce your name as evil On account of the Son of Man. Rejoice and leap for joy on that day! Behold, your reward will be great in heaven…"

We sat for the homily. Father Joe started by asking, "Now, who here wants to be poor? Who would like to be hungry? Does anybody want to weep? Who can't wait to be hated or excluded? Or insulted? No one wants to be those things so they can be blessed? Or have you already been those things and gotten all the rewards our Lord promised? I see heads shaking side to side. I guess you have not all been rewarded yet…" He continued segueing to a reference that Ash Wednesday was in three days. We should consider ourselves the hands of God capable of turning the poor, the hungry, the weeping, the hated, the excluded, the insulted, into blessed people. That was our Lenten challenge—how were we going to respond?

By communion time the chill had somewhat dissipated. I couldn't imagine being up on the altar, in the sanctuary, wearing my coat. Off it went. The gospel had said nothing about those who are cold becoming warm.

As ever, the act of placing the host in peoples' outstretched hands while looking them in the eye and saying, "The Body of Christ," was overwhelmingly humbling.

Following Mass I phoned Stella at Pier 1 to tell her how many family members were joining us. We gathered there as a family for breakfast.

After ordering, we caught up on family news. Our thirteen-year-old grandson Francis, the last one attending Mount Aviat Academy, talked of an upcoming basketball game. Our son-in-law Scott, his dad and coach, added the game would be against a nearby school so Patrick and I might want to make the trek. Of course, we did. Francis, our only male and youngest grandchild, promised a victory from their superior team. We looked to Scott to verify the validity of his statement. He nodded in the affirmative. This was a team they might beat by a considerable margin.

Our younger daughter Rose was unusually quiet during breakfast. Finally, I drew her into the conversation. Her grocery chain company was being sold again. She was not yet positive she'd have a job beyond the next six weeks. We listened and reminded her of all the evaluations she had passed with excellent results.

Eventually the conversation turned to us. What had we been up to? *Nothing much.* Hadn't we recently been in Annapolis? *Oh, yes.* Hadn't we been there overnight? *We did stay over.* Where had we stayed? *At a shelter.* That was a conversation stopper. The three of them stared at us, wanting to laugh at our attempt at humor, but couldn't get us to reveal where we had stayed. *Caught!* Patrick could handle this. He'd be more cautious; he was more experienced.

"So?" prompted Rose.

"We were returning a lost item we ended up with the evening we went for Lobby Night. The person worked at a shelter. We got there late. We were invited to dinner, then asked to spend the night." Patrick supplied some of the truth.

"Wait, you were in Annapolis twice?" asked Rose.

"And the rest of the story? The part you aren't sharing?" asked Scott. "Knowing you two, there's a story." He grinned.

I looked around the restaurant. We were seated in the "cubby," an alcove providing three walls of privacy, but there were occupied tables within sight. Scott noticed my body language and lowered his voice.

Should we talk about this later?" Scott asked. Patrick and I nodded our grateful 'yes.' Patrick started up a new conversation about the Orioles' spring training about to begin in Florida. Pitchers and catchers were to report within days. We projected our hopes for a strong season, conjectured who'd be out with injuries, who would be our best heavy hitter, who would carry our team to new heights. When our food arrived, we drifted off to other short topics, but with an undercurrent of unsatisfied curiosity.

We left Pier 1 and were walking to our separate vehicles, noticing the snowfall had diminished to uninspired flurries. While walking across Cecil Avenue, Patrick mentioned we knew we owed them some news, and soon we should be able to talk about it.

We rounded the corner, entering the access to the town parking lot. We had walked maybe ten feet when a dented, rusty gray pickup truck came careering around the corner heading straight for us, veering away, then jerking forward in a direct line toward us. We were trapped, unable to move very far either to our left where there was a chain-linked fence or to the right, the side of Bella's Pizza. Patrick and I ended up pressed against Bella's stucco wall, while Scott, Rose and Francis rushed to the fence and climbed over. *Another truck intent on harming or even killing us!* Luckily, we were unharmed as the truck driver, seeing our family members running toward us, suddenly turned away from us and raced down the road.

"I got their license plate and the driver's face on my phone!" Francis shouted from the other side of the fence. "I didn't quite get the woman in the passenger seat, but I can provide an accurate, detailed description of her," he added importantly.

Patrick was on his phone.

I watched the truck speed east, running the red traffic light at the intersection with Main Street, and nearly sideswiping a car that had begun to exercise its right-of-way to turn left from the opposite direction. The truck swerved to the right to get through the intersection before the car, and almost hit a man about to cross Main Street.

I sprinted onto Cecil Avenue to follow the truck's progress. At the next intersection it ran another red light, leaving two vehicles traveling north to turn into one another to avoid colliding with the truck. Brakes screeched. Metal crunched. Horns blared. After that, the truck had a turn signal on indicating a left turn at the next intersection up the road, but it barely slowed, and instead, drove a few yards farther, and made a wild right turn disappearing onto Cemetery Road.

When I returned to the parking lot, Patrick was speaking to

Chief Hamilton. I detailed the direction of the truck and the accident it had caused. Francis had supplied the tag information and sent the driver's and tag photos to the town police. Officer Tom Daniels was heading up the search. The direction the truck had gone was almost a dead-end choice, unless the driver knew to turn onto a side road to the east. Surely, he wouldn't try to double back and face the bottleneck crash he had caused. His other choice was to head south on Turkey Point Rd. out of town toward Elk Neck State Park and Turkey Point Lighthouse which overlooked cliffs where the Northeast River met the Chesapeake Bay, a dead end into the waters. Eastbound back roads were the only escape routes.

Cecil County's sheriff's department vehicles were traveling west to cut off access by those routes. A state trooper was enroute along Old Elk Neck Road to block access to it from McKinneytown Road. The farther south the truck went, the closer it would get to the Turkey Point dead end. If the truck would circle back in our direction, a town police car driven by Officer Alex Bristow, the rookie member of the town police force, would seal off the roads. Officer Daniels was stationed at Thomas Avenue, where it emptied south onto Main Street. Chief Hamilton had notified North East Fire Department and county EMTs in case other casualties occurred in the wake of the truck. This happened in under three minutes.

Tracy and Stella emerged from Pier 1calling us back inside—an excellent idea. We waited in the back dining room.

Francis wanted to text the world about the excitement. Scott took possession of the phone before he could broadcast. Tracy brought us fresh drinks. Scott downed his Mt. Dew in seconds. Under the table, Patrick sought my hand. He continued holding his cell phone to his ear, staying connected with Chief Hamilton, drinking his coffee, and holding my hand. Rose sipped her coffee and studied the white placemat and toyed with the Valentine's

Day flower arrangement. I alternately held my breath and gasped for air. I found myself uttering prayers, thanking God for our safety and hoping no one would be seriously hurt.

Several minutes later we got a report of a truck sighting. From the description of the vehicle, the rusty gray truck had veered off-road through the North East United Methodist Church Cemetery, coming in contact with granite and cement. By the time it returned to Cemetery Road it was dented, at least one wheel was wobbling badly, and the hood was unhinged and had lifted almost high enough to obscure the driver's view. The driver was steering the truck with his head out the window.

He attempted to cross the blocked intersection by ramming into the town police car, but swerved sharply to the right just before impact, barreling over the snow-covered field belonging to the North East Fire Company. He traveled a short distance and went over the sidewalk and curb onto Mauldin Avenue. The exhaust pipe scraped the snowy road surface as the truck traveled south on the northbound-only street. Officer Bristow swung his vehicle around and entered the roadway behind the truck.

Officer Daniels, witnessing the wrong way driving, drove down Main Street, passed the crossover strip and noted the truck was still heading south. The truck wove around to avoid oncoming traffic, causing one car to turn sharply off the road into the parking area in front of Day Basket Factory. Losing traction on the snowy roadway, the pickup sideswiped a Verizon work van which skidded from the impact and headed into the median, driving over the stubble of ornamental grasses coming to a stop just inches from the North East town entrance sign.

Officer Daniels sped up to head off the crazy driver and the truck skidded to a stop. Directly in front of him was Tom Daniels glaring at him from his police car. To his right was the irate driver in the disabled van hugging the town sign. To the left was the visibly livid driver of the car he had run off the road. The truck driver realized he was blocked both ways. He threw up his hands.

The officers approached the vehicle and opened the door for the man to exit with his hands up. Officer Bristow turned off the motor. Officer Daniels cuffed him.

Hearing this news from the restaurant staff keeping tabs, we cheered. We clinked glasses and mugs toasting the North East Police Department.

"We were almost run down in broad daylight!" Francis shouted. We all nodded as reality penetrated our consciousness. Suddenly, I was uncontrollably shivering. Our family had been targeted. Patrick wrapped his arms around me in a tight embrace. Slowly his warmth conquered my chills. I noticed Scott and Rose were huddled close together with Francis. We had mistakenly allowed ourselves to think everything was winding down. We thought UMCO had matters well in hand with the multi-faceted sweeps around the state and subsequent interrogations.

"Yes, we were," Patrick belatedly answered our grandson.

We received word from Chief Hamilton that he wanted to see us face to face and would pick us up. He would arrive in two minutes. We rose from the table, putting on coats and gloves. Patrick went to pay for the drinks, only to be told they were on the house. We thanked Stella who said she and Tracy expected a full report later. We promised information. Tracy also told us she had alerted our daughter Evie about our circumstances. I groaned inwardly, imagining another family conclave explaining our misadventures. I braced myself for the inevitable call, then surreptitiously turned off my phone, postponing the explanation.

Patrick did the same with his personal cell phone, leaving his UMCO phone on.

CHAPTER 53: ANOTHER DEBRIEFING

Chief Hamilton strode in and herded us outside to two awaiting double parked police cars. They drove us to North East Town Hall on Main Street. We had anticipated going to the police station just down the street from the restaurant. We arrived at Town Hall where North East police officers and Cecil County Sheriff's deputies escorted us across the parking lot forming a protective column shielding us. Francis remarked this treatment only occurred on fake TV cop shows.

They took us to an inner office. Chief Hamilton sat at the mayor's desk. Officers carried in extra chairs for us. I collapsed into one of the original chairs. Patrick waved Rose over to the other. The males took the new chairs.

"What is going on this time?" Chief Hamilton opened the discussion, his eyes bulging at us.

Patrick and I made eye contact with our family members sitting adjacent to us, then faced the chief.

"Really, Darrell?" Patrick attempted to sound offended. Do you think we'd be mixed up in something? You know our family. We're ordinary law-abiding citizens," Patrick offered, but Chief wouldn't back off.

"I think the time for discretion has passed. Your family is involved now. You don't like it. I don't like it. They don't like it. They aren't even sure what it is."

"He's right," Scott interjected quietly. "We need to know."

I wrung my hands in my lap. Patrick exhaled deeply.

"Where do we begin? And do NOT tell me 'At the beginning'. That would take about two weeks. Norah doesn't even know the beginning. How about I tell you a story about a woman who was taken off the street in Annapolis, driven to a building, and kept there against her will?"

"Was that you?" a teary-eyed Rose asked me.

"No, listen to me," her father cut her off. "I'm telling the story. Now, was that woman Norah? Yes. But not her alone—this has also happened many times over the last several months to both men and women. There is a vigilante hate group operating out of Annapolis."

He paused, and before he could begin again, Francis commented.

"But G-Mom isn't somebody you just hate. Why pick on her?"

"Ah…it was a set-up. We needed to acquire more information about the operation, and someone was already on the inside, so Norah went in undercover," he explained.

All eyes shifted to me. I felt my cheeks flush warm. "Patrick!"

"All right, Norah. When she was apprehended, she didn't know the plan, didn't know she was undercover. For her own safety I couldn't warn her. Besides, I rescued her and set other people free at the same time, including someone we had on the inside."

"Wow! I bet the make-up sex was sizzling!" exclaimed Rose. Then she blushed a deep red.

Chief Hamilton cleared his throat reminding us of his

presence.

Reflecting on that night, I wondered if I had missed out on a great opportunity. Oh, well. Tomorrow or tomorrow.

"Rose!" Scott was embarrassed in front of Francis.

"We've been tracking down and interviewing victims," my husband continued. "That led us back to Annapolis. Three people we identified had been snatched off the street because they were targeted as homeless. One was an elderly woman with Alzheimer's, one was someone who resides at a shelter, and one was a recent college graduate using herself as a decoy, trying to get caught while seeking justice for her grandmother, the Alzheimer's lady."

"Tell me this—was Evie involved too?" Rose asked accusingly.

"No, Evie doesn't know. She only knows about the jacket," I explained.

"What jacket?" asked both Rose and Scott.

"The one I grabbed on my way out of the prison," I explained. "Later, I found items in the pockets which led us to the woman who had decoyed herself."

"Oh!" they chorused as though it made sense.

Chief Hamilton jumped in. "Anyway, these two," he motioned toward me and Patrick, "were spotted by one of the vigilantes and followed into my jurisdiction where they managed to get the man following them arrested for causing an accident, resisting arrest, and I don't know what else. But, back to today. Why were you targeted again?" he asked.

"I don't know," answered Patrick flatly.

The Chief shook his head in disapproval. He turned his attention to me.

"I didn't see anyone acting out of the ordinary until the truck came around the corner and headed toward us like a bowling ball trying to mow down all the pins." I fidgeted in my seat, feeling uncomfortable to say the least.

"Hey, G-Mom, that was a fantastic simile!" praised Francis. "But with only five of us, would that have been a strike, or a spare, or just a split. We scattered."

"None of the above because we weren't struck," I clarified.

The chief was not impressed, nor amused. Fortunately, before he could chastise us further, there was a knock on the door. Tom Daniels entered. He was not smiling.

"Do you want news now, or to wait for a private briefing, Chief?"

"Just go ahead. We seem to be getting close to being on the same page. Let's continue to the next chapter." He glanced at Francis who mouthed 'metaphor' and gave him a thumbs up. Chief Hamilton groaned.

"Okay. The truck is registered to a business but driven by an ex-con with no license. The female passenger bailed out somewhere inside of the cemetery." He drew in a breath and continued. "The company is a Baltimore County construction outfit. The company logo on metallic plates had been removed from the doors but stuffed behind the driver's seat. The driver was from Baltimore City, and as I said, an ex-con out on parole. The female, a minor from Rising Sun, is, or probably by now was, his girlfriend. The construction company is Bestest's Builders, owned by Jenson Besseter. The truck wasn't reported stolen. The driver is Jenson Besseter, Jr., age twenty. The female minor's name I can't reveal to anyone, but you, Chief. Any connection to FORN is being verified, but it seems the construction company regularly hires illegal aliens, so we're confused about that contradiction."

"Everybody's a hypocrite. Thank you, Tom. Quick work. I gather the female has been apprehended."

"Yes, Chief, and awaiting Juvenile Services." Tom paused to either be dismissed or assigned further duties.

"Stick around in the outer office. We must decide what to do with these five."

"What's a forn?" asked Francis as Tom turned to go.

The chief explained. "Son, FORN is an organization bent on making law officers go crazy and tear out their hair, if they have any. They claim to be doing good, but by carrying out their objectives, they cause a great deal of trouble by breaking laws and hurting innocent people."

"So. That is the name of the vigilante group?" asked Scott.

"Yes. It's an acronym for Follow Observe Report Non-Contact. The last part is being disregarded at an escalating rate. It describes the mission of the minions sent out to spy on unsuspecting people. These low levels are just supposed to watch and report, but their system is breaking down. Control is rapidly disintegrating. I anticipate we'll soon discover those at the top have cut bait with the bottom layers, and those bottom layers are thrashing about like fish on hooks, flailing about at anyone they sense has disrupted their lives or threatened their freedom. And, yes, that was a simile, son."

Francis grinned, nodding approval. I could see he was gleaning new facets of the law enforcement profession and perhaps imagining courtroom dramas to be enacted in the future. He was trying to decide if their puzzle solving and applying the law were akin to his nature. And here I had thought he would become a priest.

"So, where are we?" I asked.

"Don't have an answer, Norah, but it's not a good place. None of you should return to your homes," answered Chief Hamilton.

"We can't just shut down our lives," spoke up Rose. "I must go to work, and Scott too. Francis has school tomorrow."

"I can take off a day or two; it's only book report time in English and a test in Advanced Math," said Francis in a failed effort to convince us.

"Patrick, it's time UMCO voiced its opinion," Chief stated.

"Yes, I've reluctantly reached that conclusion. They got us into this. They should be involved in reaching a solution to our dilemma. I'll call now."

"Do you want privacy?" asked Chief.

"Too late for that. I'll call from here," he answered.

Patrick made his call. Three curious sets of eyes from family members searched my face. Three mouths silently formed the word 'umco' with questioning wrinkled brows I held up my hand to fend off questions, postpone explanations, and to hear every word Patrick uttered.

"Yes. Just now, within the last half hour," answered my husband… "No, all five of us are fine. Yes, we have three more people from our family who are now semi-initiated into the alternative lifestyle afforded by joining clandestine organizations… Yes, they need to know. They've met the bad guys and deserve to know there are good guys dedicated to opposing them…No more than necessary, but we need a protection detail or temporary relocation site… Are you sure?... Well, okay then."

"Well?" I asked before anyone else could draw breath to speak.

"We are going to Childs," Patrick informed us.

"We're going to my school?" asked a perplexed Francis.

"No. Mount Aviat Academy is not the only place in Childs," his grandfather apprised him.

"There's the old paper mill factory that has been re-purposed," Scott suggested.

"No, we're not going there," Patrick said.

"Oh, my!" I exclaimed, suddenly intuiting the plan. "We're going to make an all-male establishment co-ed."

"Yes," said Patrick.

"What?" asked Darrell Hamilton.

"The Oblate Fathers of St. Francis de Sales have their retirement home in Childs," Patrick was quick to supply. "And there is room for all of us. It seems it's been used previously for this purpose. It's like we are seeking sanctuary, isn't it?" he offered.

"Something useful I learned about in history class this year," Francis replied.

"You're accurate," Patrick answered. "Now, how do we get clothes together for a brief stay?"

"You don't," said Chief Hamilton. "It's foolish to show up at any of your residences. We had better get Evie, Gerry and Maglie up there too. And your granddaughter living in Elkton who was in contact with Officer Daniels needs to be taken there."

"A family campout without camping!" Francis said gleefully. His expression dimmed though, as he realized he'd be the only juvenile male with a female sibling and a female cousin.

"For our safety, we'll be followed, and driven in multiple vehicles," Patrick stood and continued. "Our vehicles will be driven to our houses after dark. Someone will stay at each of our homes. Chief's right. This must include four locations. Norah, call Evie and have the three of them ready to travel within the hour. There will be someone to drive them. She can bring extra clothes to share. Something she and Maglie have should fit you other females, at least pajamas," he added hopefully. "Rose, call Sally with the same information. Have her bring extra clothes too. You can mix and match. We guys are none of us the same size, so we'll rough it."

I called Evie and promised to explain. Rose talked to Sally. Soon they whisked us away in what looked like private vehicles operated by ordinary citizens. We took different routes and left at staggered times but ended up at the same location.

Reassurances were made that pets, teachers, and bosses would be taken care of during our absence.

CHAPTER 54: SANCTUARY

Midafternoon found us in the dining area of the Oblate Fathers retirement center. We gratefully accepted their hospitality. Our rooms were ready when we wished to retire to them. We would not be interacting with outside staff. The priests we knew had stopped by to welcome us. One of them was the usual presider at school Masses so our grandchildren had met him many times, but not seen him in civilian clothes. Three others Patrick and I knew from previous gatherings and retreats. We settled down in a parlor for the afternoon. Around dusk, Patrick remembered it was still Valentine's Day. He canceled our Pier 1 reservation.

Our family established a new tradition of communal Valentine's Day dining. The Oblates were gracious, serving baked chicken and stuffing, and for dessert, cherry pie, red velvet cookies, and raspberry tarts. We spent the evening joining in board and card games. Our grandchildren were surprised to see how ordained men could be so competitive over Yahtzee and Uno. They were almost a match for their grandfather's competitiveness.

By late evening we had shared what information we could

with our children and grandchildren. They weren't happy about the situation but couldn't change it. We were shown our rooms, and after Patrick and I said good night to the others, we stole down to the chapel. There, in the dim light of the sanctuary lamp, we prayed and plotted. We expected to sit in on further interrogations. We were worried our family would go stir crazy being cooped up together and out of sight of employees arriving on Monday. Patrick contacted UMCO one last time and relayed to me further information he was not authorized to share with the others.

First, Patrick and I, holding hands, settled ourselves on a pew in the cozy chapel lit only by wall sconces and the sanctuary lamp and offered our individual silent prayers, sat back and commiserated in God's presence.

Then Patrick whispered, "The head of FORN is under twenty-four-hour surveillance and won't be permitted to leave Maryland. He's an Annapolis resident, a life-long Marylander, and wealthy real estate broker with a vast network of real estate agents, some of whom are involved in FORN. UMCO's awaiting a federal judge to issue an arrest warrant. These are Homeland Security crimes. There's no assurance a local judge isn't involved or silently sympathetic to FORN's tactics. The leader's the son of deceased immigrants who risked their lives to get here from an eastern European country. I can't believe they'd be proud of their son's targeting people as vulnerable as they once were."

"How old is this guy?"

"UMCO says he is in his early fifties."

"What makes people turn out like that?"

"I don't know. I'd expect a first-generation person to be proud to be a citizen of the country his parents adopted, not a bully toward the next generation of immigrants, minorities, or marginal citizens."

"Maybe he can explain when he has his day in court."

"Not to my satisfaction," sighed Patrick. "There's no legitimate excuse for what he has spearheaded."

"Not to mine, either," I agreed wholeheartedly.

We left the solace of the silent chapel and went to the room we were sharing. The only décor was a crucifix on one wall, and an icon of St. Francis de Sales on another. We quietly slid the twin beds together and fell asleep holding hands. Soon Patrick was kicking and flailing his arms. I knew my brave Irish warrior was waging battle with some enemy. I rubbed his arms and legs till he woke mumbling about robed figures with swords. I soothed him back to sleep and found I was wide awake.

I lay there for a long time, turning over recent events. It seemed we were caught in a dream living out others' lives. I finally drifted off to sleep and dreamt of robed figures who were benign, carrying baskets of freshly picked vegetables. I smelled the earthy scent of the just-dug carrots. Patrick was speaking to me through a haze of warm sunshine. I felt his touch, opened my eyes, and found him grinning at me, a mug of strong tea in his hand. I took in the plain cream walls, stained wood windowsills, and trim. The rough brown tweed curtains were tied back by leather sashes. The daylight view was amazing. The sun did its best to enliven the stark February fifteenth world, awakening my spirits.

Our whole crew breakfasted in a small dining area away from staff who obviously knew there was extra food prepared even if they caught no glimpse of us. We are not fashion icons on a good day. Our mix and match shared wardrobe accentuated this, but we were okay, safe. I anticipated oatmeal, orange juice, coffee, tea, and perhaps fruit. I was partly correct. There were also scrambled eggs, bacon, scrapple, toast, and English muffins. Our assorted family members found nothing disappointing in such variety and abundance. Francis wanted to compliment the cook, but we persuaded him anonymity was more prudent.

After breakfast, Patrick shared news about the surveillance, which offered hope of release for us. Then he reported to UMCO while we listened intently to his side of the conversation awaiting further news. After a pause, Patrick downloaded an unofficial, preliminary report. There was little to share 'officially'. Sunday's reckless truck driver had been arrested. He was in violation of parole, driving without a license, and charged with attempted murder. That was us! I locked eyes with all my family as we simultaneously processed the statement. The judge had refused him bail. We were safe at least from him.

Jenson Besseter, Sr., owner of the business the truck was registered to, at first claimed he didn't know his son, Jenson Besseter, Jr.'s, driver's license had been suspended, but records reflected he had been present at the suspension hearing. He said he didn't know his son had been driving the truck, but witnesses put him and his son together daily on job sites from which he sent his son on errands to pick up and deliver materials. Finally, he admitted his son was out of his control. He didn't know how to remedy the situation and had for all practical purposes given up trying to make demands on him or ask questions. He paid him, but rarely got a day's work from him, and no longer inquired about how he spent his time away from the job. Jenson Besseter, Sr. seemed guilty of ineffectual parenting, but not of connection to FORN. He had over twenty foreign employees, mostly from Panama or Nicaragua. He supplied them with health insurance and decent, no-frills housing at minimal cost.

When questioned, most employees respected their boss but disparaged his son. Many said Junior never earned his wages. A couple condemned the 'lazy', 'useless', 'waste of space', 'lying', 'piece of garbage' son. Patrick quoted from the report on his phone. Agents had deleted most of the slurs, delivered in Spanish.

We were told to stay where we were. Once the attempted

murder charge had registered, we were emotionally rattled. I saw Rose gaze down at her shaking hands, willing the tremors to stop. Attempting to alter the atmosphere, Evie spoke to everyone and no one, proclaiming her family not as intelligent as Sheldon or Leonard on *The Big Bang Theory*, but a heck of a lot smarter at handling unexpected events. Her husband Gerry nodded in agreement. We all joined in trying to project how the science nerds would behave in our situation.

We laughed when Sally suggested, "If someone tried to run down Sheldon, it would be for unbearable annoyance."

Then Maglie added, "Or Sheldon would be hunted down by one of his friends like Leonard, who snapped because he couldn't follow that ridiculous roommate agreement anymore."

"No, come on all of you! It would be Penny," said Francis. He did not explain but waited for us to guess what he meant, then left the room, closed the door, and began Sheldon's alternating routine of knocking on the door and calling Penny's name till we begged him to stop. We admitted it was hilarious beyond bearing.

Our day unwound slowly. Outside it snowed fitfully, not adding any real accumulation. Bird feeders, attached to outside posts and to some windows, were the locations of the liveliest activity of the day. Our grandchildren had electronic devices which we allowed them to use if they remained on games with no posting on social media. They were sufficiently sobered by their situation and willingly complied.

Three different priest acquaintances dropped by separately to spend time with us. This broke up the monotony of doing very little in a strange place. We were invited to attend the noon Mass. We were assured we would not be in the way or recognized by outsiders. Patrick and I eagerly accepted. The others, except Rose and Scott, declined. We were glad they felt comfortable enough to make their own choices.

The chapel was a good place to be. I felt a sense of serenity infiltrate me. Patrick looked at me and whispered, "Clonmacnoise." I nodded in appreciation. The ruins in Ireland by that name were holy ground, one of the thin places. This chapel emanated a similar sense of the sacred. I looked at him and quoted a phrase from Julian of Norwich. He nodded in agreement. Yes, 'All will be well'. The Mass proceeded. An Oblate brother we knew from his ministering occasionally at St. Jude's played the organ. The familiar music wrapped around us. The homily was short, but something we could take away to mull over, a reprieve from our anxieties.

Lunch was hot and filling. There were soup choices: turkey vegetable or Italian wedding soup, and sandwich options: ham and cheese, peanut butter and jelly, or tuna salad. There was even a platter of cookies that Patrick and the kids eyed during the meal. They tried to be polite, not grabbing the cookies, but their longing for sweets was almost a scent in the air.

We wandered around the rooms where we were allowed. Patrick, Sally, Rose, and I ransacked the library for reading material. Evie and Gerry flipped through various TV channels before finding something acceptable. Francis and Maglie disappeared for a considerable time. We discovered them entertaining two elderly Oblates they knew from their having presided at Masses at Mount Aviat. They were reminiscing about songs they had had to learn, the yearly school drama presentations, classroom mishaps, and of course the annual Christmas bazaar, cream puff sales, and Grandparents' Day. We left them to enjoy one another's company.

"I'm surprised they are talking away at ease," I said to Patrick.

"Really? Francis has never been shy. And Maglie—remember the year her softball team won states and her team was honored at the Aberdeen Ironbirds stadium and she stood in the infield with a minor league player and carried on a long conversation? She was only ten, but she was talking shop with a professional baseball player." I smiled at the memory.

News arrived late that afternoon. All our residences had been secured for nearly twenty-four hours without incident. The connection between Besseter, Jr. and FORN had been established. His girlfriend's stepbrother was Ray Hummerfield. The not-so-innocent teen had convinced her boyfriend her brother was a crusader for a better life for real Marylanders, that he had been unjustly targeted, set up by people who caused his accident in North East. She persuaded Jenson he was unfairly treated by his father. Those aliens from across the border who worked on the construction projects were better off than he was. He could correct a wrong against society. He could put bad people on notice.

Besseter claimed he had not intended to hurt anyone, just scare them. When the truck swerved toward people, he had been arguing with his girlfriend, who had grabbed the wheel. He continued to argue with her through two red traffic signals, and finally shouted at her to get out of the truck after she caused him to swerve into a tombstone.

"It was the woman's fault," Patrick mouthed to me. I swatted my hand across the back of his head. He was expecting that.

Patrick proceeded to tell me that because Besseter had not been involved directly with FORN, we were free to return to our homes. We would be transported to our residences. Our vehicles had been returned. We would be home by nighttime.

We ate a farewell meal with those Oblates healthy enough to leave their rooms. We were surprised at how much these men knew about events connected to us. They had cleverly put two and two together and arrived at insightful conclusions. We shared what we could and let some threads remain a bit unraveled.

Our escorts transported us in unremarkable unmarked cars.

We understood the Oblates' involvement must be kept secret and knew we and the Oblates would be protected until UMCO dismantled FORN. We expected it to be a short-term protection detail.

CHAPTER 55: CONFERENCE TIME

We were home at last. Maggie was ecstatic to see us. All three cats showed their individual feline disdain. It would take time and treats for them to forget such blatant neglect. Our bed felt heavenly. It was a blissful dreamless night for me.

I answered the phone glancing at the kitchen clock: 7:36 am. UMCO calling. Patrick was in the shower, so I answered his phone on the kitchen table while I fixed coffee and tea. I was the first to receive the news. Grace had acquired the cooperation of a FORN member at Brisson Shelter. Good news. Everyone was presently safe. Extra agents were assigned to protect the shelter. The FORN member was currently providing all information gained pertaining to other agents, operations, locations and vehicles used.

"I hope that includes other possible victims, too," I commented.

"Indeed. It does."

What do we do next?" I queried, hoping it would be something other than listening to suspects' interrogations.

"Change of priorities. You and Patrick will report to North

East Police Headquarters by nine-thirty this morning. You are expected. There will be a small team assembled with others on a conference call beginning precisely at ten.

"We will be there."

"This is a strategy session and debriefing. It is time to gather all input and make final decisions."

"What about other interrogations we were to sit in on?"

"They'll be conducted this afternoon. This morning's conference will determine your next assignment. Your comments and questions from the first interrogations were forwarded to today's interviewers to incorporate into their format. Information gleaned will be acted upon ASAP. Any questions?"

"Has the head of FORN been arrested yet? If he is about to be in custody or already is, do we need a strategy session?"

"There's a complication," was the cryptic response. Then silence.

"We will be there at nine-thirty." I answered and hung up. Almost immediately, a dripping, towel-wrapped Patrick presented himself in the kitchen. He continued towel drying his hair as I updated him. He nodded and gratefully accepted his mug of Texas pecan brew. He left the room to put on his robe and returned in moments. I was at the table cradling a mug of Constant Comment tea, a Christmas gift from Sally. There was a pile of marble rye toast, unsalted butter, peanut butter, and lime curd to slather on the slices. Blueberries, banana and mango slices were in dishes. We ate quickly, dressed, avoided speculation, finished morning routines with pets and left the house.

"What do you think we'll learn?" I mused as Patrick drove.

"Maybe there will be some significant progress to report. Maybe evidence of an end to FORN…or not."

"Light at the end of the tunnel we've been crawling through

would be welcome, but after the hope we were given yesterday afternoon, and the avoidance of answering my question this morning, I'm concerned." I felt heart palpitations and tried to calm my breathing.

"Whatever it is, it has gotten more complicated if we are required to meet with the team and be in on a conference call."

"Like the governor's office? Or members of the Maryland General Assembly?"

"Perhaps. Don't forget Grace and others working like us."

"How many people can be in on one conference call?"

"Norah, it's not something I ever needed to know. Why ask?" I excused his exasperation. I felt it too.

"Well, there are twenty-three counties and Baltimore City. If only one person from each of those were on the phone with this committee that would be some gathering. I think it would be too many people providing input and hearing what others contribute."

"Like a meeting of the United Nations? Congress?"

"Exactly. We're almost there, so we will know soon."

Patrick drove on past Pier 1 and pulled into the North East Police Department parking lot. There were no empty spaces in front of the building or in the back lot. Patrick swung over to the Cecil County Library branch adjacent to the police department lot. There were three empty spaces. Before we exited our vehicle two more cars headed for them.

"We're almost twenty minutes early. Anyone else is going to have to walk a distance to join us," Patrick noted.

CHAPTER 56: CONFERENCE CALL

The station, not designed for large gatherings, was crowded. As we made our way into the anteroom, Officer Daniels escorted us through the sea of people to Chief Hamilton's office.

"This is a bureaucratic disaster!" Darrell grumbled, his arms folded across his stomach.

"What's wrong, Chief?" Patrick asked.

"Someone failed or forgot to inform me of this meeting. No one here received a heads up till eight o'clock THIS MORNING!"

I jumped in. "How can we help? How can we make this work? Tell us what needs to be done."

"We contacted UMCO and thanked them for arranging the meeting, and not so politely suggested they might have seen fit to inform us, because if they had, we would have told them there is no large conference room in this building. The most we can accommodate is a dozen people. After that, we are in violation of building capacity according to the fire code. We could arrest people in other venues for the size of the crowd we have sandwiched in here now. Our only quick solution is to move to the town library, but they have a book discussion scheduled."

"Could they move the book discussion to Pier 1?" I asked. "How many people are involved?"

"They claim to have fifteen or sixteen people set to arrive shortly."

"There is nowhere for them to park," Officer Daniels noted.

"We noticed," Patrick said.

"So, Chief. How about if I call Pier 1?" I persisted.

"Why should they have to pay for someone's incompetence?"

"Because they are accommodating when they can be and are curious as hell about what's been going on," offered Patrick.

Chief Hamilton nodded. I pulled out my phone and called before he could object. No answer. It was Tuesday. They were closed.

"Next idea?" I asked aloud.

"The book discussion will have to be rescheduled," said Chief.

"Why not invite them here?" asked Patrick. "There's enough room and it is sort of an emergency situation."

"Done!" the Chief barked. "Officer Daniels, you explain things to the head librarian, and get Officer Bristow to corral this mob through their back door in ten minutes. Send someone out to direct book discussion participants to park at the town lot by Bella's Pizza."

With the decision made, things fell into place. Chief Hamilton gave us the number of participants he knew of. We three abandoned the police station and accessed the main library conference room. Tom dealt with library personnel, then we rearranged tables and chairs, added more seating from storage, arranged pitchers and cups brought from the station, and took seats where we could advantageously observe and participate.

The group assembled amid grumbling and good-natured comments. We easily measured temperaments from this minor inconvenience. There were uniformed male and female state police troopers, sheriff's deputies, town officers from Perryville, Rising Sun, Elkton, Chesapeake City, Charlestown, Port Deposit, and Earlville. There were members of the Maryland National Guard, and military officers from both Aberdeen Proving Ground and Edgewood Arsenal in Harford County. Civilians were harder to identify till they donned stick-on tags providing names and positions held. County government was well represented. Patrick and I remained untagged. We got curious looks from some, but no one questioned us.

At three minutes after ten, we were connected on speaker phone. Until we heard the governor's voice, we had no idea who else would be participating. Governor O'Malley welcomed representatives from every county and Baltimore City. He then requested each location take time to become aware of fellow attendees, introduce themselves, and reveal their connection to the topic of the meeting. It was effectively the opposite of requesting a moment of silence.

After about four minutes he called all the groups to attention and continued. He provided a basic sketch of recent events, culminating in his even sketchier sketch about the mysterious entity known as UMCO. He introduced the head of UMCO, not giving his name, and briefly detailed its mission. Then UMCO ran the meeting.

"Some of you have been involved with our operations over the past two years." A deep voice resonated from the air waves. "Others are being brought on board today because of recent events. Our policy is to operate alone in the preliminary stages of an investigation assigned by the governor's office, then involve other police agencies necessary to complete the job. If you haven't worked with us previously, that's good. It means your area has not dealt with certain issues. Nothing we were checking out or tracking down affected your jurisdiction.

"Now we all need to bring a concerted effort to apprehend

one man who is our state's just-declared public enemy number one. He is Theodor Carlson, age- fifty-four, an Annapolis resident. Despite his house being under twenty-four-hour surveillance, he was not at home early this morning when our people presented his wife with his arrest warrant. A search of the property yielded a short basement tunnel connecting his house with the nearest neighbor's. It appears that, without his wife's knowledge, he and the neighbor, a widowed woman in her forties, had an ongoing dating arrangement. The tunnel dates from pre-Civil War days, and may have been part of the underground railroad, an irony that does not escape this office.

"This man is wanted for hate crimes against the indigent, the homeless, and racial and ethnic minorities. His own parents came from eastern Europe to escape a harsh political regime. He changed his birth surname when he turned twenty-one. He has education, wealth, a family, yet has jeopardized it all to finance and micromanage an organization known only by the code letters governing lower echelon members. FORN- which stands for Follow, Observe, Report, Non-contact. Their members have been breaking that last rule, drawing them to our attention. Through these rule-breakers we have traced membership upward during the last few weeks. We have placed operatives in their midst and learned of their association with legitimate police officers throughout the state. If you are in on this conference call, it is because we know you are uninvolved with FORN. Let me emphasize this does not mean you are to immediately suspect fellow law enforcement members by their absence.

"An APB has been issued for Theodor Carlson. We interrogated his wife, placed her and their children in protective custody, and are questioning the next-door neighbor and others who may be involved. Officers are canvassing the neighborhood. Airports, train stations, waterfront departure areas are on alert.

"Our next series of interviews with known FORN operatives is happening now in several counties and Baltimore City. As teams glean more information, we will process it and continue building a case against Carlson and all members of FORN. Our immediate objective is to shut down this hate-inspired group, bring to justice those responsible for terrorizing the vulnerable among us, and move on to tackle whatever new evil surfaces.

"Others among you will have to step up to try to make amends to those who have undeservedly been subjected to vigilante justice. These are our neighbors and fellow citizens.

"I am not taking many questions at this time, but first I want to apologize to Chief Hamilton, who I understand, learned of this meeting when participants began arriving early this morning. Thank you, whoever you are, for getting there ahead of the scheduled time. It allowed Chief Hamilton to effectively invent Plan B." Patrick and I smiled and winked at each other.

"Now, what clarifications are necessary?"

"Sir, this is Jay Barrows, St. Mary's County sheriff's department. I would like to know who you are. You haven't identified yourself. And the governor failed to introduce you. *Who are you?*"

"That is a matter of need-to-know. Even my operatives, and there are at least two UMCO members at each of today's meeting locations, do not know my identity. Clandestine operations require a level of anonymity. If ever I need to go public for the safety of the citizens of Maryland, I will do so, but will immediately resign from this position. Please address me as 'Joe'."

"Chief Hamilton from North East in Cecil County speaking. Joe is the real deal. Don't hesitate to be involved with him. His people are highly trained and effective." Darrell refused to look toward us. "His organization has been easy to network with."

"Well, that says a lot," conceded Barrows.

"This is Susan Kerenski, Howard County. How do we initiate contact with your group for assistance or information?"

"Contact procedures and information will be sent electronically to your departments. Look for a message from JOE, all caps. Is there anything else?"

No one spoke. Joe continued, "You will receive updates on our progress and requests for assistance we need. We will not hesitate to bring you on board if the situation warrants."

"Kendrick Rodriguez, Harford County government," another voice piped up. "Joe means what he says. We worked with his group in the last few days. He accurately described his operation in connection with local agencies. I'll feel confident asking for assistance or offering our county's services to UMCO in the future."

"Thank you, Ken," responded Joe. "Please check communications immediately. There is breaking news as I sign off. Thank you, fellow crusaders for justice."

Then there was the sound of silence as people checked their electronic devices. Patrick checked his phone. I read over his shoulder.

"Theodor Carlson's neighbor, Ruthann Finnigar, admits helping him leave the neighborhood last night around eight. She drove him in her car and left him near the waterfront. She claims he needed to get away from family responsibilities. His wife is apparently clueless about FORN or her husband's biases. She says he is paranoid about losing their social status or their neighborhood losing its prestige if certain people were to move in, but he is not prejudiced. Officers are scouring the Annapolis waterfront."

The group broke up. Patrick and I lingered just long enough to help return the library conference room back to its original configuration. We spoke no further to either Chief Hamilton or Tom Daniels about the situation.

CHAPTER 57: RETURN TRIP

Later at home and unwinding, we updated our family using Patrick's UMCO phone. We dined on grilled cheese and pear sandwiches and looked longingly out at the winter landscape for a hint of spring. After lunch Maggie and I wandered the backyard and picked dead looking forsythia branches. My grandfather's handed-down custom would gladden our hearts when the branches, set in water, opened inside, providing cheer in the lingering winter season. I tromped back to the house with Maggie at my heels. She wasn't quite ready to return, and I considered letting her roam, but was cut short by Patrick's shrill whistle. Maggie and I climbed the deck stairs in tandem. Patrick was in his jacket and waving for me to get a move on.

"Now, what?" I asked in a shrill voice.

"We've got to go. NOW!" I could hear the desperation in my husband's tone.

"Okay. I'll get my purse and be ready in a few minutes."

"No. Now." He spoke in a low, more urgent tone. "Rose

and Sally are on pet patrol. We're going to Brisson."

"Wait. What's happened? Is Joy okay?"

"I'm not sure."

"Isn't Grace there with her and the others?"

"Yes."

"Then what's the problem?"

"Remember the Poe story of hiding things in plain sight?"

"Yes. 'The Purloined Letter'. Why?"

"Grace suspects Carlson has taken up residence at Brisson."

"That's brilliant! I mean, clever, but wouldn't he be tortured just being in the same place with the people he designated his worst enemies?"

"That is what made Grace suspicious. Joy too."

"So, we are going back to…what exactly?"

"We'll know more by the time we arrive. Now get in the car and buckle up."

"But we need clothes, snacks, water at least."

"They're in the car."

"Am I allowed to go to the bathroom before we leave?"

"Yes, but hurry."

Five minutes later we were heading for Annapolis again.

"I left the forsythia on the kitchen counter."

"I put it in water in the empty iced tea pitcher in the sink."

"Thanks."

"This is what's happening." Patrick shared his latest update. When Grace had interviewed her, Hattie had provided names of additional FORN members. And an overheard conversation Hattie recounted to Grace led to establishing the real estate connection and identifying Carlson. Hattie had been recruited by FORN to switch her focus from Sarah to Grace, because Grace had been identified as an escapee who had resurfaced. That FORN could access new information from Brisson's roster was disconcerting, something that must be traced. FORN's interest in Sarah had been a simple follow-up. With Joy there was resentment she had tried to infiltrate their system. Now Hattie's information to UMCO was going a long way toward righting wrongs she had done

As we traveled, we learned over speakerphone that UMCO and Grace were in constant communication. Joy had sent Sarah with an escort to Vintage Value Thrift Store to help sort a new shipment of clothing, and from there, Sarah had been taken into protective custody till the shelter was determined to be a safe haven again. One family had moved out a day early under the pretense that their new lodgings had become available earlier than expected.

A little later, we learned that the man suspected to be Carlson had arrived late Monday night. Joy had been off-duty and at her parents' home. The overnight manager had not suspected anything amiss. He had enlisted the help of two male shelter residents to assist the newcomer, introducing him as Taylor Church. Grace, just another resident to him, had met the new guy soon after his knock on the door. His knee-jerk reaction of disdain to her ethnicity was the first inkling he wasn't the person he claimed to be. She later observed his increased bristling at being matched with Amir and Darius as escorts to his room and his introduction to the facility.

In the morning, when news of Carlson's escape reached her, Grace was more wary of the new arrival. She used Joy's office, with Joy present, to make the call. This transpired during our meeting at the North East Library. News was not passed immediately to us until it was determined Carlson and Church were the same person. We were selected to assist at the shelter.

The theory was our familiar presence would be calming, reassuring to the residents. Since they knew us, they would not suspect anything was wrong. Joy would prepare them for our visit, saying we had business in the area and would stop by.

Grace would play the part of a new resident who had not yet met us.

Unfortunately, Hattie had not yet been relocated to a safe house before the Carlson/Church arrival, so she was temporarily confined to her room with a rumor that she might have a contagious illness. One of her tracking devices had been placed in Church's room. So far, it had elicited little information beyond his ungracious then reluctant apologetic treatment of anyone who approached him. He had already showered and dressed this morning before Grace had received the official missing person/fugitive alert. He did not have a tracking device on his person.

Joy had requested that Church meet with her midmorning to gather more complete information about this new resident to flesh out the required intake report. However, she gleaned very little new information because he came across borderline surly, even to her. She suggested he try another shelter if Brisson was not to his satisfaction. After that, he curbed his tongue and adopted a more cooperative attitude. No, he admitted, he really had nowhere else to go. He claimed he was between jobs (but did not say what his occupation or skills were). His family had moved in with his in-laws who weren't welcoming of him. He expected a new job to be available soon. He just needed a place to stay for a short while till he landed his new job. Joy told him his story was familiar. She added that many shelter residents were employed, but still couldn't financially manage to move out because down payments for apartments and houses were so high. She caught a flicker of a reaction in his face in response to that information but did not push him further.

"Hey" he interjected, "You mean people here have full time jobs and still cannot live on their own? How's this possible?"

Joy told him of low-paying jobs, lack of health insurance, the necessity for security deposits to landlords, the lack of funds to afford childcare, and lack of public transportation. He appeared stunned.

Grace had used the registration form Church had filled in to remove fingerprints and sent them to UMCO. Headquarters confirmed the man was indeed not Taylor Church, but Theodor Carlson. His prints were on file because of an arrest for harassment of a young woman when he was in his early twenties.

So, we were going in with a positive identification.

CHAPTER 58: FACE TO FACE

Our arrival at Brisson coincided with the evening announcements. We waited for a break in the session before joining them. It was like a homecoming with many familiar faces. Sarah's tablemates invited us to eat with them. We noticed her absence and were told she had called saying she'd be back late. The thrift store owner was treating her to dinner and a movie.

The meal was delicious. We enjoyed tossed salad, meatloaf in a seasoned tomato gravy, garlic-flavored mashed potatoes, crisp steamed cauliflower and cornbread, almost as good as mine. There were scoops of vanilla or chocolate ice cream to top off slices of almond pound cake. As previously, the meal was filling, and the conversation was fulfilling.

We felt very much at home and would have enjoyed it more if we were not surreptitiously observing 'Taylor Church' at a nearby table. He seemed ungracious one moment, then apologetic the next. His body language reflected a conflicted spirit. Perhaps an earlier infiltration into this world would have produced a different man who would have made positive contributions to society instead of choosing to worsen the lot of the downtrodden.

We had to neutralize the situation and get this man away from the unsuspecting residents. I would follow Patrick's and Grace's lead. Amir noticed me looking at Church and mentioned he was their newest resident. Amir said it in such a way I had to inquire about him.

"So, you already don't care for him?"

"True. Hasn't been here a whole day, and he's shown his true colors."

"Oh," was my noncommittal answer. I let it go at that.

Amir took it for criticism of his rush to judgment.

"He doesn't like to be too close to anyone of a different color or nationality. I suspect he's afraid of catching something from us."

"If he were to catch anything from any of you, it would improve him," Patrick said.

"Thanks," answered Amir. I could feel his appreciation not only in his words, but a subtle change in the atmosphere.

"Amir's right, though. There's something about him. It's not just that he's a bigot, but something deeper. I just don't know if it's anger or what," added Darius.

"Well, maybe after dinner you can introduce us to this model citizen," Patrick suggested.

"You don't want to get introduced to him by the likes of me. You two are white. He's likely to bond with you. I guarantee you'll be sorry you made his acquaintance though," commented Darius.

We finished our meal and wandered to various tables to reconnect with others before everyone broke up and left the dining room. As we approached 'Church's' table, he glanced up.

We introduced ourselves, sat down in two vacant chairs without being invited, and began conversing with him. Joy joined us.

The room gradually emptied of diners except for the three of us and Joy. Grace and Jorge were discretely herding residents, including the children, into a communal room that could be secured, but also had outside access if that were needed. She and Jorge left Hattie, newly recovered from the mysterious illness, in charge of the residents.

Once every resident was safely secured in the room with Hattie, Grace and Jorge approached the main entrance of Brisson Shelter. She unlocked the front door and he signaled to five UMCO operatives waiting hidden in the darkness. The three women and two men approached from their five separate locations, entered the building, and followed Joy into the dining room while Jorge secured the door and stood guard.

When 'Church' saw the new faces entering the room, he did not appear surprised. He seemed resigned. He acknowledged them with a nod and made no move to avoid them. The look registered on his face seemed one of relief or a sense of 'let's just get this over with'. He rose unsteadily from his seat. One of the UMCO team members held out her hand to assist him.

He hesitantly approached Joy. He paused, looked down, and then away. He then raised his head, his hazel eyes looking directly into hers. He paused again. His words were spoken too low for me to discern. But I observed him reach out, take her hand and seemingly offer an apology, or maybe even confess his errors. He shook her hand. He handed her something.

He left quietly with the five UMCO team members.

Joy immediately followed them out and Jorge opened the door and closed it after them. She and Grace notified Hattie all was well. Before the residents left the room, Joy addressed them. She simply said Mr. Church had departed and would not return. They dispersed to their usual evening routines but with quizzical looks on their faces.

Joy convened a private meeting in her office with us and Grace. We sat in chairs in a room that had become familiar. We waited expectantly to hear what had transpired during their brief conversation. Joy did not waste time filling us in.

"Theodor Carlson admitted his identity and vowed he would financially support Brisson in the future because he had witnessed our staff and residents providing hope for others. He admitted this brief stay had opened his eyes to an alternate way of dealing with problems. He acknowledged he might be donating from prison, but he would support Brisson residents."

Was he a convert? A man trying to make amends? A man trying to gain sympathy and lessen his culpability? Who were we to judge?

"What did he hand you?" I asked.

"His lawyer's business card," Joy responded. "I am to meet with him to set up a fund to support Brisson."

We shook our heads, slowly rose from our chairs, said our farewells to Joy and Grace and put on our coats for the trip home. We stepped out into a night that was crisp, cold, clear and star blessed. The fog had lifted.

ABOUT THE AUTHOR

Cheryl Shivery Nickle, a native of Cecil County, Maryland, lives on the outskirts of North East (just west of Elkton) with her husband and soulmate John, dog Tucker, and cats Raven and Taffy. Between them they are blessed with two daughters, three grandchildren, and two great-grandchildren.

She has a bachelor's degree in English Education from the University of Delaware and a master's in Religious Studies, with a concentration in liturgy from La Salle University. Cheryl taught English at North East High and served as youth minister for Immaculate Conception/St. Jude Parish.

She is active in LAOH (Ladies Ancient Order of Hibernians) and its book club. She belongs to the Bookies, a book club of former colleagues and friends, participates in their parish book study and finds time to read other selections on her own. She spends warm weather creating literary displays in their gardens, getting her hands in the dirt, and rooting for the Baltimore Orioles. She enjoys cooking, baking, crafting, and repurposing items found in local thrift shops. She and John love to travel. St. Croix, USVI is their favorite destination.

A former English teacher, Catholic youth minister and Cecil County, Maryland native with a love of all three, Cheryl has been writing poetry and short stories since high school but has always loved reading a good mystery. With her debut novel, *Piercing the Fog,* she combines her love of her community, her Catholic faith and a good mystery into a chilling suspense that will keep you on the edge of your seat.

Made in the USA
Columbia, SC
07 August 2025

7bbc2465-5c00-4408-bc5f-1f3adb6fd45aR01